CHRISTOPH

Safe Haven: No Hope in Hell

Christopher Artinian

CHRISTOPHER ARTINIAN

ISBN: 9798396275799

CHRISTOPHER ARTINIAN

DEDICATION

To Raja. Sweet, loyal, and loving 'til the end.

ACKNOWLEDGEMENTS

To Tina. I will never be able to thank you enough for everything you do. Without you, none of these books would exist.

Thank you to the wonderful group over in the fan club. I will never take your support for granted.

Thanks to my mate, Christian Bentulan, for another fantastic cover. Also, many thanks to my editor, Ken – a brilliant editor and a lovely chap too.

And finally, a huge thank you to you for buying this book.

PROLOGUE

Mike stared out of the window as the scurrying bodies below continued to load the truck. The Skye Outward Bounds Centre had not been their home for long, and it was debatable whether it was ever a suitable location for them, but if nothing else, it was something they could call their own. It was not spoken for; they didn't have to integrate; they were the commanders of their own destiny within its grounds.

Granted, recent events had suggested that destiny would be one where they all died of starvation, but nobody ever truly knew what the future held.

"Are you okay?"

He almost jumped as he was snapped from his thoughts by his older sister, Emma. He turned to look at her, and for a moment, he could barely recognise the woman who stared back at him. All that time ago when they had left Leeds, she had been a shrinking violet. Now she was not just a relentless fighter but the leader of their people. In Shaw's absence, she had taken the reins and even though Shaw had returned, it had been decided that he was to concentrate purely on the security aspects of their survival from here on in, while Emma coordinated and managed everything else. It was a mammoth task, but one she was more than capable of.

Mike smiled. "I'm fine."

She walked up to join him at the window. "What were you thinking?"

"I was thinking I hope this works out. If we get everybody down there and it turns to crap, there's nowhere left for us to go."

"Why don't you think it will work out?"

"I'm not saying it won't. I'm just saying, if it doesn't."

"In which case we need to make it work, don't we?"

"Sometimes, that's easier said than done."

"I thought you said this Griz guy was okay."

Mike shrugged. "He is. He's better than okay, but, y'know.... I don't have a crystal ball."

Emma slipped her arm around her brother and the pair both watched the proceedings below for a moment before she spoke again. "We'll make it work, Bruv. We'll make it work long enough for us to catch our breath and regroup."

"Regroup? There aren't exactly a lot of us left to regroup, are there?"

It was true. There were just over seventy survivors remaining from the several hundred who had lived in Safe Haven. And out of those there were a number of older and infirm people who would struggle to walk let alone fight if push came to shove. "You know what I mean," Emma replied. "Hopefully, we'll have long enough for us to get our heads together and figure out what's next."

"What's next?" Mike turned to look at Emma and pulled back from her a little. "I thought we were both on the same page as far as what's next."

Their eyes locked for a few seconds before Emma

looked back down to the worker ants below. "We are. But no matter how much we wish for it, pulling Olsen's still beating heart out and showing it to her before she dies isn't something we're in a position to do right now. That's what I mean about regrouping. We just need a breath. I just need a breath."

Mike exhaled deeply. It was true. Vengeance boiled within him like a simmering pot whose lid kept rattling. But at the same time, he knew there was nothing they could do in their current state. "She's going to pay for what she's done, Em."

"I know. And when she does, you and I will be standing side by side."

"I thought I fuckin' saw the pair o' yous. I'm down there sweating my tits off, helping load the lorry, and you're up here lollygagging and watching us."

Smiles broke on the two siblings' faces as they turned to the door to see Jules in the entrance. "We weren't lollygagging," Mike replied. "We were strategising."

"Strategising. I'll give you fuckin' strategising you lazy arsed bastard. There's still work to do before we can set off y'know." Jules walked up to the pair of them and looked down as the others continued to load the truck. They didn't have that many possessions left, but as most of the remaining survivors would be travelling down to Glasgow in the back of it, it was essential that everything was secure to avoid injury or accidents.

George suddenly came into view below. He handed a bundle of garden tools they'd liberated from the shed up to one of the loaders in the back of the truck. "Have you spoken to him since you came back?" Emma asked.

"No," Mike replied. Before his trip down to Glasgow, George had made his feelings known about Mike's cavalier attitude towards the welfare of his granddaughters, and things had not gone well.

The caustic humour was gone when Jules spoke again. Instead, she placed a sisterly hand on Mike's back. "I love George like he was my own grandad. But what he said to you was bang out of order. Wren, Robyn and Mila are women. They're not little girls. And all things considered they were the only people you could have taken down there with you. You were right; he was wrong. It's as simple as that. But I think you're going to have to be the bigger man. I think you're the one who's going to have to make the first move. Otherwise, this fuckin' sulk of his is just going to deepen, and people need the pair of yous. They don't want to see you at each other's throats."

"That's a lot of thinking, for you, Jules. Are you sure you're feeling okay?"

She immediately removed her hand and punched Mike in the arm with it. "Fuck you, y' wee shite," she said, laughing. Emma joined in as did Mike.

"You're right. I was going to see him before we set off."

"Well, there's no time like the present."

"True enough." Mike turned and left the two friends at the window as he made his way down the grand staircase and through the foyer.

"Michael, darling. You've finally come down to help. How sweet of you," Jenny said, smiling.

He crouched down and made a fuss of Meg whose tail wagged enthusiastically. "I bet she wonders what the hell's going on," he said, kissing her on the nose before climbing to his feet.

"She's not the only one."

"I get that."

"We should be ready in the next half hour or so," Kat said, walking up to join the pair of them. It wasn't even seven thirty, but few people had slept given the news that they would be moving once again.

"Everything going okay?" Mike asked.

"Oh good grief, yes," Ephraim said, coming up behind Kat. "People are having a blast. The sense of optimism in the place is overwhelming. I think we might have to find an extra trailer just so we can fit in all their hopes and dreams for their new lives down in Glasgow."

Jenny let out a long sigh. "I've had to deal with this all morning."

"Well, look on the bright side," Ephraim replied. "We might all die horribly on the one-hundred-and-fifty-mile journey through a zombie-filled wasteland to the friendliest city in Scotland, so, after today you might never have to suffer me again."

"We can live in hope, I suppose."

"That's the spirit," Mike said, nodding and leaving the three of them standing there. He stepped out into the cool morning air and looked around. He was only there for a couple of seconds before Wolf made a beeline for him. He crouched down and made a fuss of him too before climbing to his feet.

"Morning," Wren said.

"Hi. I was looking for your grandad."

Wren pointed in the direction of the shed, which had become his workshop for the short time they'd been at the centre. "Are you going to try to make peace?"

"Try being the operative word."

"I'll tell Liz to be on standby."

"You have no faith in my diplomatic skills, I take it?"

"Err. On the advice of counsel, I refuse to answer that question for fear of incriminating myself."

"You are going to talk to George?"

"Jesus Christ," Mike said, spinning around and throwing his hand up to his chest. "Creep up behind me like that again, Mila, and it will be a moot point."

"Everyone always accuses me of creeping. I creep nowhere. I just walk deliberately, not like some drunken elephant."

"Okay. If you walk up deliberately behind me like that again, it will be a moot point. But to answer your question, yes, I'm going to see George."

"Would you like me to come?"

"Why the hell would I want you to come?"

Mila looked a little hurt. "I could act as a mediator, yes? In case things get out of hand, I could calm them down."

"Oh yeah. That'd just make my fucking day," Mike said more to himself than anyone else.

"What?"

Mike raised his hands placatingly. "There are some things that a man has to do by himself."

"Ah. Yes, you are probably right."

Mike nodded. "I'll see you in a couple of minutes."

"Good luck," Wren called after him as he headed in the direction of the workshop.

"I'm going to need it," he mumbled in reply. Mike walked around the corner and nearly straight into Robyn as she carried a box of garden tools in her hands.

"Grandad's in an arsey mood, this morning," she said, stopping for a moment.

"Great. I was going to go see him."

"Your funeral."

"Thanks for the encouragement."

"If you want me to be positive, let me sleep in until ten and wake me up slowly with coffee and Pop-Tarts."

"Don't take this the wrong way, but the last time I woke you up, you didn't seem that pleased to see me."

Robyn giggled as she thought back to the Christmas prank orchestrated by her family to teach her not to drink too much. "I'd forgotten about that. I'm telling you, though. You bring me coffee and Pop-Tarts, and I'll be a lot more welcoming," she replied with a wink.

"I hate to break it to you, but the chances of us ever having real coffee or Pop-Tarts again are pretty minimal."

Robyn looked forlorn for a moment but then perked up a little. "But, I mean, Glasgow's the biggest city in Scotland, isn't it? If we're going to find Pop-Tarts anywhere, it's going to be there, right?"

"Let me get this straight. We've been uprooted from our homes. We came here, risked death Christ knows how many times to make this work, only to be moving on again. And your primary concern is whether there's an undiscovered cache of Pop-Tarts in Glasgow?"

Robyn shrugged. "And what's your point?"

Mike thought about it for a second then shook his head. "In fairness, it's as good a reason as any."

"See. Bobbi logic strikes again." She glanced back to the workshop. "I think we're nearly done in there if you're wanting a quiet word with him."

Mike looked over to the open door. "Yeah. I suppose I can't put this off any longer."

"Oh. So talking to me was just putting it off was it?"

"Not at all. It's always enlightening talking to you, Robyn."

"Just so y'know, this box is really heavy, but in my head, I'm sticking my middle finger up at you right now."

They both smiled. "I'll see you in a bit."

"Good luck."

"Your sister said that."

"Yeah. With good cause."

"Thanks," Mike replied, walking away. His eyes focused on the small workshop to see George appear in the entrance momentarily, only to head back into the dim interior once he saw the younger man approach.

When Mike finally arrived at the door, George had his back to him. His hands gripped the workbench and he stared out of the rear window. "I thought you'd be coming to see me before we set off."

"You thought right."

"Well, say what you've got to say."

"I know you're pissed off with me, George. I know you weren't happy that I took Wren, Robyn and Mila down to Glasgow, but the truth is I'm glad I did it. Because if it wasn't for them, none of us would have returned. I know they're your family, but there aren't three people I would rather have by my side in a situation like that. If it wasn't for them, we wouldn't have made it off the boat, never mind into the city. We wouldn't have found Griz. If it wasn't for them, everyone here would be left to die slowly. That being said, there's a part of me that's sorry I had to take them too."

George finally relinquished his grip on the workbench and turned around. "What do you mean?"

"I'm sorry I had to take them because I love them. They're family, and the last thing I want to do is put them in harm's way. But at the same time, they fight better than anyone I've met. Their skills are second to none, and I knew that taking them down there would give us the best chance of finding a way out for everyone. I'd die before I let anything happen to any of them. But I was out of options, George. If they didn't come with us down to Glasgow, that would have been it for everyone. You have every right to hate me for what I did, but there's not a part of me that believes I didn't do the right thing."

George continued to stare for several seconds before he moved his eyes to the floor. "Those girls are my world. If anything happened to them, that would be it for me."

"I get that, George. But if we didn't go down to Glasgow, how long do you think we'd have lasted up here? How long would it have been before people slowly starved to death? Would you want that for them? Would you want them to know their last days on this earth were ones filled with misery and heartache and hopelessness?"

George's eyes moved back to Mike's. "You know as well as I do that wouldn't happen. They could—"

"They could escape from here whenever they wanted? They could survive out there better than anyone?"

George's eyes flared with anger for a moment; then he looked down to the floor once more. "Yes," he replied weakly.

"Yeah. They could. They could survive out there

easily because they've done it before. But they're three of the best people I've ever met, George. And I'm pretty certain that they'd rather die than run out on their friends and family. Just like you'd rather die too. It's not an accident that they're the way they are. They're good people. They're amazing people. This place would be lost without them just like you'd be lost without them. I took them down to Glasgow because they were the only people I'd trust to give my family a chance, to give us all a chance. I took them down there because they'd want to be a part of it. You can go on hating me if you like, but you know I'm telling the truth." Mike continued to stare at the old man even though his gaze was not returned. "Well, I've said what I came to say. I'll let you get back to packing." The floorboards creaked as they shifted slightly beneath his feet. Mike was almost out of the door when George spoke again.

"I remember when they came to stop with me one time."

Mike turned around. "I bet they were great kids."

"Ha. Not so much." He chuckled to himself. "Don't get me wrong. I loved them more than anything, and yes, they were great in some ways, but when they were together, they fought like rats in a sack."

"I can't imagine it. They're so close."

George lifted his eyes towards Mike once more. "They're close now. Back then it was a different story. I must have aged twenty years in the few days they were with me." He shook his head. "I'd never known anything like it. But since I found them both again, since we've all been back together, it's been … joy."

"I can't tell if you're being sarcastic or not."

George looked at him distantly for a moment then smiled and shook his head. "No. I'm not being sarcastic, and yes, it's a strange choice of word to use. We're in the middle of an apocalypse and I'm talking about joy. But it's the truth. It's been a joy for me to wake up every morning and see who my little girls have become. And yes, like you said, they are these amazing people who we all depend on, but at the same time, they'll always, always be my little girls. They're the same little girls who used to climb over the back garden fence and beg old Missus Williams for jam tarts. They're the same little girls who found the tin of pink paint I'd done their room in and decided to decorate my shed the same colour. They're the same little girls who I sprayed with a hose when I couldn't stop them fighting."

Mike laughed. "I can't imagine them like that."

George shrugged. "Children will be children."

Mike flashed back through the flip book of horrors that was his own childhood. "I suppose."

George let out a long breath. "I just wanted you to understand. They're everything to me, Mike. They're everything."

"I get that, George. And if they had turned out another way, we probably wouldn't be having this conversation now. But they turned out the way they did, and it's not just you who depends on them anymore. We all depend on them. Without them, we don't stand a chance."

George nodded sadly and thought for a moment. "I'm sorry. I'm sorry for the things I said to you."

"You don't need to apologise. You just need to understand that they're at the top of my call list when I need help."

The older man thought for a moment. "Well, let's hope once we get down to Glasgow, you're not going to need help for a long time, shall we?"

"Yeah. Let's hope." The two men smiled at each other and Mike started walking away when he stopped suddenly. "Oh, I nearly forgot. I found something in the administration section of the shelter in Glasgow."

"Oh?"

Mike reached into his inside pocket and walked back towards George. When his hand came back out, there were two packets strapped together with an elastic band. "I didn't tell Robyn or Wren 'cause I'm pretty sure they wouldn't approve."

George looked confused for a moment until his eyes focused on the objects he'd been given. The writing was Polish and he had no idea what it said, but as he looked inside the first packet, a broad smile lit his face. "You found me some tobacco?"

"Hopefully, I'll be able to find you a lot more down in Glasgow."

"Thank you, Mike."

"You're welcome, George."

"I was getting ready with the garden hose to separate you, but it looks like you're talking at least," Wren said from the doorway.

"Mike got me some tobacco," George replied, still beaming and looking towards his granddaughter.

"What?" Wren glared at Mike. "How? We barely left each other's side. Why didn't you say anything?"

"I'm sorry, I didn't realise I had to account for all my movements."

"Mike found Grandad some tobacco," Wren blurted as Robyn joined them.

"What? How? When? I thought I was never going to have to breathe in that shitty smell ever again. It gets in your clothes, in your hair, even on your skin. It's like you take a bath in it." She turned to look at Mike. "Thanks for nothing, dick face. Now I'm going to smell like a coal miner's arsehole for the next two months." She turned and marched off once again.

"Yeah. Thanks, Mike," Wren said, turning to follow her sister.

The two men looked towards the door for a few more seconds before Mike spoke again. "Yeah. Two lovely girls you've got there, George."

"Don't I know it."

1

It was a perfect day for sailing, and despite all the apprehension that hung in the air about their move to Glasgow, there was a broad smile on Raj's face as he stood on deck next to Shaw. They both remained in quiet reverence with their eyes cast out over the sea as Humphrey sat between them. His tail occasionally slapped against the deck, but for once, he seemed to be in a state of quiet contemplation too.

"It is good to have you back, my friend," Raj said, eventually breaking the silence.

"It's good to be back. I don't know what came over me."

"Pressure can do strange things to a person. If ever things become too much for you again, you know I am always here."

"Yeah. I do, Raj. Thank you." They both fell into a comfortable silence for a few moments before Shaw broke it again. "How do you think this thing's going to work down in Glasgow?"

Raj thought before replying. "It's going to be a big change for everyone, and it will take some adjustment. But I have faith that Mike would not lead us anywhere that jeopardised our well-being. He would not risk his family."

"No. I suppose not."

"What are you two talking about?" Trish asked, appearing behind them.

"Just pondering what this next chapter's going to be like," Shaw replied.

"Ah, yes. We're trying to do everything but down there. Andy and Doug are regaling everyone with stories about some of the Downing Street parties."

"Sounds fun. I'll have to go listen in."

"Not just yet," Trish replied, casting a fleeting glance at Raj.

"Err … we will go see how Talikha is getting on," Raj said, patting his thigh. Humphrey immediately stood and followed him as Trish and Shaw watched.

Trish reached into her bag and retrieved two bottles of tablets and a flask. "Put your hand out."

"Look. I really don't need—"

"Excuse me. Who's the doctor here?"

"You are," he admitted, throwing the tablets in his mouth and swallowing them with some lukewarm camomile tea.

"How are you feeling this morning?"

"I could have done with more sleep."

"Tell me about it, but you know I'm not talking about that. How are you feeling?"

"Good. The tablets must be working."

"Yeah. The tablets are going to take a while to get into your system, so it's not that."

"Oh. Okay. If you say so." He shrugged.

"I think it's more likely to be the fact that you've had this huge weight lifted from your shoulders, don't you?"

Shaw turned back towards the ocean waves. He

didn't answer for a while, but when he did, his voice trembled a little. "I've let everybody down."

Shaw's head drooped, and Trish placed a comforting arm around him as a single tear dropped to the deck. For someone who had come from such a privileged position, she was very down-to-earth and compassionate. She squeezed him a little tighter. "From everything I heard, it was you who kept Safe Haven going as long as it did. It was you who saved them countless times. It was you who kept everybody fed, clothed and warm. Not that you had any debt, but you paid these people a thousand times over and more. You gave them everything."

"And look where it left them."

"Listen to me because I know what I'm talking about. You can do everything right, but things can still go wrong. Andy did everything right. But there were people working against him, and things went to hell because of them, not because of anything he did. You can be the hardest working, most decent and honourable man in the world, but none of that matters if you've got the devil out to get you."

"The devil?"

"I'm speaking figuratively. You can't be responsible for the actions of others. You can plan, you can put up your absolute best defence, but when you're vastly outnumbered and outgunned, it's only going to be a matter of time. That's what happened to us with...." She broke off. "Look. Anyway, that doesn't matter. The point is that you didn't let anyone down. You gave these people everything, and now it's time for you to look after yourself a little and let them take the reins." She released her grip on him, and Shaw wiped fresh tears from his face.

"Thank you, Trish."

"You don't need to thank me for anything. You took us in. You looked after us. You made us part of this community. This is what we do. We look after each other. It's time that we looked after you for a while until you start feeling a bit better." A roar of laughter suddenly erupted from below as Darren emerged onto the deck.

"The PM's looking for you, Missus Beck," he said.

"Let me guess, one of his shoelaces has come undone and he doesn't know how to tie it because he's had everything done for him like the Sultan of Brunei these past few years."

Darren chuckled. "No, ma'am. I think he wanted help recalling the events that took place on the last state visit from the Brazilian president."

"Seriously? He's sent you up here to find me for that?"

"Err … yes, ma'am."

"Well, if it's a full-blown emergency, I'd better get back down there, hadn't I?" She looped her arm through Shaw's. "Come on. You can find out how we organised two separate apartments for his wife and mistress without them finding out about each other."

"Can't wait," Shaw replied, smiling.

"Of course, I use the term mistress loosely. I'm not quite sure what the politically correct terminology is for a secret girlfriend who's got an Adam's apple bigger than your average Granny Smith."

Shaw laughed out loud. "Well, now I've got to hear this story."

*

On the journey from Glasgow, they had run into concentrations of RAMs every time they ventured onto the main roads, so they'd made the decision to take as many back routes as possible on the way down. Raj and Talikha had set sail with most of the old and infirm. The journey would be more comfortable if longer. But it would mean that the others would have time to get to their new home and prepare for their arrival.

The conditions in the back of the lorry were far from ideal, but they were not unbearable. Several dynamo lanterns were positioned throughout the trailer providing enough light for people to read or play cards. Tommy sat in one corner with Ruby. They had found a pile of old newspapers at the Skye Outward Bounds Centre, which he was now working his way through. Jenny and Meg perched next to Emma, Sammy, Jules and Jon. Across from them sat Ephraim, Kat, Jack and James. The others were spread out through the rest of the cargo area, huddled in their own little groups, contemplating what lay ahead.

"It can't be too much longer I wouldn't have thought," Emma said as they went over another large pothole causing their bones to rattle.

"Thank fuck," Jules replied. "I swear I'm going to be five inches shorter by the time this journey's over."

"Yeah. I can't say this is the smoothest ride I've ever had."

"Look on the bright side, darling," Jenny replied. "At least we're not walking."

"I suppose there's—WAAAHHH!"

Suddenly, every occupant of the trailer was catapulted forward as the sound of multiple pops and bangs preceded the deafening screech of the truck's brakes.

"AAAGGGHHH!"

"MUUUM!"

"HELP!"

Cries erupted all around as some became airborne while others skidded over the floor of the lorry like curling stones.

*

George tried his hardest to bring the vehicle back under control, but it was impossible. Andy and Rob, his two passengers in the cab, both gripped their seats and tried not to scream like the passengers in the back, but it required a lot of self-control. Despite his ankle, driving hadn't been a problem up until this moment for George, but now a pained cry left his mouth as the brakes continued to squeal and the steering wheel shook.

"Hold on. HOLD ON!" he shouted as the lorry veered towards one of the giant pines lining the roadside.

There was part of him that wanted to hoick the wheel in the other direction, but he knew doing so would result in the vehicle jack-knifing. His heart was in his mouth as he screamed the warning one final time. "HOLD ON!"

*

"JESUS WEPT!" Mya cried as the brakes of the Land Rover wailed too. She, Mike, Wren, Robyn, Mila, Wolf and Muppet were the scouting squad. The lorry had been fitted with a snow plough, which had been effective, but some roads had been impassable, and on a couple of occasions, they'd had to take the lead and find alternative paths. The rest of the time, they had travelled behind the giant truck, content just to tailgate. But now contentment was the last thing any of them felt as their vehicle careened from side to side.

POP! POP! POP!

"Fuuuck," Mya said to herself more than anyone else as the sound of the exploding tyres rose above the screech. The steering wheel struggled for freedom, but she held on.

A deafening crunch boomed ahead of them, and the trailer of the truck began to jack-knife as the cab came to a sudden, jarring halt. "FUCK!" yelled Mike this time as he realised avoiding a collision was going to be impossible.

*

Jenny had managed to grab on to a lashing strap that was secured to the inner frame of the trailer in one hand, and her other arm was clamped around Meg, who scrambled to stay in her grasp as fear gripped her. "Ugghh!" The pain was immeasurable. It felt like someone was trying to rip her arm out of its socket, but she held on regardless as her beloved old dog looked up helplessly.

The deafening crash coincided with a climax to the agony, but now she and Meg began to slide in another direction as the trailer started to skid.

Screams and pleas continued to ring out as people collided with the inner walls. Shrieks of pain and panic sang a constant accompaniment to the grating dirge of metal against tarmac. Bodies flew, rolled and spun like they were in a giant washing machine drum. *This is it. We're dead.*

*

George was convinced he was going to die. Before he collided with the tree, he had visions of being harpooned by a sturdy bough or being crushed between the vehicle and the trunk. Other than the worst whiplash he'd ever felt and his throbbing ankle, though, he was still alive, still breathing. He looked across to Jules' two brothers, and they wore the same stunned expression as he. The horror was not over for them, however, as the cab began to move once more, this time due to the momentum of the trailer.

"Oh, dear God. We're going to go over," he cried, reaching out and gripping the wheel once again.

*

Everything happened so quickly, but Mya was used to making split-second life-and-death decisions. She knew locking the wheel could potentially turn them over, but she also knew that if they nudged the now almost tipping trailer, that could cause a lot more injuries and even deaths inside.

"Hold on tight," she cried as Wolf and Muppet both let out frightened yelps, reacting to the heightened panic in the car.

Mya dragged the wheel across, aiming into the woods on the opposite side of the road to where the cab had come to rest.

"SHIIIT!" Mike cried, holding on to his seatbelt.

"CRAAAP!" Wren yelled, reaching out and squeezing her sister's hand as the Land Rover went into a spin.

*

Emma had grabbed Sammy's belt when they had begun their slide towards the front of the cargo area. A split second later, she'd found a dangling lashing strap with her other hand, and now the two of them hung on with all the strength and determination they possessed. It had only been a brief fragment of time since this nightmare had begun, but somehow it stretched like elastic. Emma desperately wanted to close her eyes and just hang on for dear life, but she was in charge. She had to see what was happening and keep watch for danger regardless of how powerless she was to do anything about it.

Suddenly, the trailer began to slow, and relief flooded over her for a single beat, but it was short-lived as the unmistakable sensation of the lorry beginning to tip filled all the occupants with a fresh dread.

"AAAGGGHHH!"

It was impossible to tell who the loudest scream belonged to as dozens rang out all at once, but somewhere among them, she felt sure she could hear Jules' cry.

*

Andy and Rob both unbuckled their seatbelts at the same time. Andy flung open the passenger door, still not quite believing that they'd somehow managed to survive the crash. The cab was still only moving slowly as the impending disaster of the trailer tipping in seemingly slow motion still loomed.

He jumped down and ran clear. Rob did the same, and it was only then that George realised he should follow suit. The advanced safety features in the cab had saved them from the worst of the collision. The inbuilt crash zones, the absorption zones, the shifting steering column had saved him and his cab passengers, but they would do nothing to help those in the cargo compartment, and someone would need to help them when this hellish scare ride was finally over.

Sounds of torment filled the air as he barged open the driver's door and leapt to safety. The cab was shifting more now as the momentum had taken a fresh hold, and George felt all of his years and more as he jumped to the ground. A spasm of agony shot up through his ankle, but it was only fleeting as the pain in his head took over when he collided with a half-buried tree root.

There was much more at stake than his well-being,

though, and as he heard the terrifying shriek of the Land Rover behind them, he scrambled free and dived behind one of the giant pines.

*

"Fuck! Fuck! FUCK!" Robyn screamed as the Land Rover left the road and began to churn up dirt. It was obvious to all the occupants that their tyres had been lost in the spin. The shriek of the metal rims against the tarmac had added a new dimension of fear to their journey, and now they were in the middle of a tornado as what remained of their wheels carved giant circles in the dirt.

*

Emma, Sammy and pretty much everyone in the trailer who wasn't airborne or in a state of flux felt the sensation they had been dreading since the loud crunch.

"We're tipping. We're tipping," someone called out, stating the obvious.

The initial crash had slowed them down considerably, but the momentum of the trailer had continued to drive them, albeit in the wrong direction; but now, as the crashed and broken cab acted as an anchor, they could all feel the inevitable drawing near.

"LEFT SIDE. GET TO THE LEFT SIDE!" Emma yelled above the sound of the cries and grating metal. She let go of the strap, leapt up and charged to the other side. It was like climbing an access ramp that somehow became steeper with each step.

Others suddenly understood, and those that could gather themselves rushed across to join her.

Please let this work. Please let this work.

*

The Land Rover finally came to a stop, but the whirl of dust and dirt continued around them. The occupants of the car all experienced the sensation that they were still moving, but at the same time, they knew it was only because of the speed and force of their short journey. Despite their own discomfort and disorientation, they all dived out of the vehicle in perfect synchronicity, preparing to help with the aftermath, whatever that might involve.

*

Andy and Rob watched helplessly. Their hearts were pounding in their chests. Their brother and sister were in the lorry and they had no seatbelts. They had none of the safety features they'd been lucky enough to have in the cab. And now they were being thrown around in a giant metal box with dozens of others. At best, there would be broken bones. At worst … they couldn't think about it.

They climbed to their feet, their own hardships, strains and pains forgotten as they watched. The cab started to shift more dramatically once more as the trailer tipped.

*

Shouts accompanied the stamping feet and rush of bodies that converged on the left wall. It was as if all the air had been sucked out of the container as the occupants collectively held their breath.

Even cries of pain from the injured paused for a moment as they waited in grave anticipation to witness what happened next. Emma leaned against the wall as if she was pushing a car. Instinct took over from sense. Her weight on that side of the lorry was all that mattered. Any further actions she carried out were superfluous, but danger often has a way of putting reason on hold.

In the corner of her eye, she could see her little sister doing the same. She wanted to reach out and hug her, but if they got through this with their bones unbroken, there would be time for that later.

Like a lift having its cables cut, the trailer dropped once more with an almighty crunch as the metal rims of the wheels crashed against the tarmac. The whole structure wobbled for a few seconds before finally coming to rest.

Emma remained frozen in position, still pushing hard against the wall. It took her a little while longer to understand that they were safe. She climbed to her feet and let out a short nervous laugh. Others followed suit, and the fear and terror that had hung in the air like sulphur lifted.

An echoing clunk made them all jump, and it was only when the rear doors opened that they understood what it was, and nervous laughter rippled.

"Is everybody okay?" Mike asked, staring into the lorry.

Emma turned and looked towards the huddled bodies. "Is anybody hurt?" A few of them were holding their arms, shoulders and legs. Others had cuts, and one had a bleeding nose, but they were all conscious. "Badly, I mean."

"I'm not hurt, but I'm busting for a piss," Jules replied, and everyone laughed.

"Yeah. I get that."

2

Liz walked to the far end of the trailer and picked up her bag. "I dare say we're going to be here for a while, so if anyone wants me to take a look at them, I'm going to be outside where we've got proper light." She headed to the open doors, and others followed while Emma just remained for a moment.

"You okay, Sammy?" she asked. Sammy nodded, wide-eyed and still in shock.

"Jesus. What the fuck happened?" Jules asked as she walked up to the pair of them.

"I don't know. I'm just grateful everyone's okay."

"It's a miracle," Jenny replied, joining them with Meg panting heavily by her side.

"Oh shit," Jules suddenly blurted. "George and my brothers." She and Jon rushed to the open doors as fresh panic rose within them. As they reached daylight, the familiar figures of Andy, Rob and George came into view. "Oh, thank Christ," she said, jumping down and hugging each one in turn.

Jon followed her and did the same. "You okay?" Mike asked, turning towards Jules as he helped James down from the back. He was limping a little, but, in fairness, most people were, young and old alike. It was as if they'd been thrown into a giant malfunctioning bread maker and tossed around on a high-speed setting.

"I'm okay, darlin'," she replied, looking across to the Land Rover. "Are you?"

"Yeah. I didn't think we were going to be, but yeah."

Sammy appeared at the entrance, and Mike lifted her down. Then Meg and Jenny. Emma jumped down by herself as others gradually roused behind her.

Tommy was still pushing against the left wall of the trailer, believing if he stopped, the nightmarish journey would start again. "It's okay, Tommy. It's okay," Ruby assured him, but they all knew it would be some time before she could coax him out of the lorry.

Emma looked towards the Land Rover then turned to Mike and threw her arms around him. "I thought we were goners."

"Yeah. You and me both," he replied as he placed a guiding hand on Sammy's shoulder, and the three siblings got out of the way of the others trying to exit the vehicle.

Wolf and Muppet enthusiastically greeted Meg before the three of them went across to the side of the road and sat down to watch the proceedings as Liz and some of the nurses helped those who had sustained the worst of the bangs and cuts.

"I'm sorry," Jules said. "But I wasn't joking when I said I needed a piss." She broke away and started jogging towards the trees to the right of the road."

"Actually, neither was I," Emma replied, following her.

"Do you need a wee, Sammy?" Mike asked.

"I'm old enough to know when I need the toilet, thank you," she replied, a little irritated that her brother had asked her.

He put his hands up placatingly. "That told you, didn't it?" Robyn said as she, Wren and Mila walked up to greet them. They were all hugged out by George, and now, while he went across to talk to Mya, they joined their friends.

"Pretty much. Yeah."

They stood in a loose circle for a moment, occasionally looking across to the vehicles. "What are we going to do now?" Sammy asked.

"That's a good question, Sammy. And I'm guessing—"

"Mike!" Mya called out, and the four of them, with Wolf back by Wren's side, went across to join her and George. As they arrived, Mya bent down and picked something up from the road. "This was no accident."

They looked at the object she held carefully in her hand. It was the same shape but a little bigger than a jumping jack. It had been painted matt black, like the colour of the tarmac. The points were needle-sharp, and as they began to scour the ground, they could see many of them scattered around.

"Somebody did this to us?" Mike asked.

"So it would seem." Their eyes began to search the trees on either side of the road. "Looks like they specifically chose here as well. The road's wider than it has been for miles, and the big verges on either side mean vehicles can still get around if they need to.

"Shit, Em and Jules," Mike blurted before exploding into a sprint.

*

"Ooorrrggghhh. It's like the fuckin' Hoover Dam's bursting down there," Jules said over the sound of her stream.

"Nice. You've always had a gift with words, Jules," Emma replied as she crouched down behind a neighbouring tree.

"Well, I hope you have a nice piss because considering we're two vehicles down and you're our new leader, it's the last bit of peace and quiet you're going to get for some time."

"Thanks for reminding me."

"So, have you got any thoughts?"

"It's only just happened, Jules. Do you think I had a contingency in place for this?"

Jules sniffed. "Fair enough, I supp—"

When Jules didn't continue, Emma leaned out a little from behind her tree to look at her friend. "You okay?"

"It might just be paranoia, but I could swear I just saw those bushes move."

"What? Which ones?"

"Those," she said, pointing.

Emma followed the line and focused on a wide growth of shrubbery. Her eyes fixed on it for several seconds. "They're not moving now."

"Well, I can see they're not fuckin' moving now, but I'm telling you. They were a second ago."

Thundering feet drummed towards them, from where they weren't quite sure. "Crap."

"Jesus fuckin' Christ. This is just my luck. I'm going to get attacked by a horde of zombies while I'm trying to have a piss."

"EM? JULES?"

"Mike?" Emma called out.

"Are you okay?" he asked, running around the corner to find his sister still crouched behind a tree.

"Well, turn your head or something. What do you want?"

"This wasn't an accident. Someone made us crash."

A sudden chill fell over the forest as more pounding feet headed towards them. "Fuckin' brilliant," Jules mumbled to herself. "Come one, come all. The next time I try to have a peaceful piss, I'll sell fucking tickets."

"Jules thinks she saw something in the bushes over there," Emma said, finally finishing and pulling her jeans up.

"Over where?" Wren asked as she and Robyn both raised their bows.

Emma pointed, and the two of them advanced

slowly. Wolf was glued to Wren's side as they moved nearer to the spot.

Mike broke into a run, passing the two sisters and the German shepherd then leapfrogging the lowest section of the bushes before coming to a skidding stop on the other side.

It was a few seconds before the two sisters and Wolf joined him and a few seconds more before Emma appeared. "Nothing," Robyn said, lowering her bow.

*

There were multiple wet and still leaking patches below the truck. Steam was rising from the grill, and the front of the cab had caved. It was pure luck that the three occupants had avoided serious injury.

Mya had been tempted to follow the others into the forest after Emma and Jules, but she was confident that Mike, Robyn and Wren could handle any problems, and if they couldn't, they were intelligent enough to seek help. Everyone was out of the truck now, but the supplies were still strapped in securely.

Mila had retrieved George's walking stick. He only needed it when his ankle flared up, which had been less and less in the last few days, and the adrenaline had been surging through his system when he'd made his initial escape from the lorry, but as the threat of immediate peril dissipated, the pain became more acute. It had steadily been getting better and better, and there were times when he could go for several hours with no twinges. This would probably set him back a little though.

"This is a mess, ja?" she said, looking around at the frightened and shaken crash survivors.

"You've got a talent for understatement," Mya said, returning to join them after doing a quick sweep of the tree lines on either side of the road.

"I-I should have seen them. I should have—"

"Don't beat yourself up, George," Mya replied, plucking one of the small objects out of her pocket. "With the rest of the debris on the road, you'd need eyes like a hawk to see these things."

"Ja. Nobody could have avoided—scheisse!"

Mya and George both turned towards Mila then followed her eyes as a dozen more fearful exclamations erupted.

"Shit!" Mya echoed. Smoke was spreading from beneath the cab. For a moment, they were all frozen, unable to peel their eyes away from the horror show. There was a loud whoosh and a bright orange flash before another wave of sour blackness billowed out. Mya looked towards the open doors of the trailer. Thankfully, people already had their weapons and personal allotment of ammunition, but the remainder, alongside whatever food and supplies they'd scrounged together, was still in the lorry.

Muppet let out a frightened yelp as Mya burst into a run and leapt into the cargo compartment.

"Mya. No!" Mila cried as the smoke and flames began to spread exponentially.

*

"I'm not making it up," Jules said, fastening her belt as she eventually reached the others.

"No one's saying you are," Emma replied. "But there's nobody here now, is there?"

"I'm telling you—"

"There was someone here," Mike interrupted.

"What?" Emma asked.

Mike gestured down to the ground. The earth was dry next to the bushes, and as he pointed now, they could all clearly see two partial footprints.

"See. I told you," Jules said. "Some dirty bastard was watching the pair of us pee."

"I hate to break it to you, Jules, but I doubt if that was their ultimate goal."

"Mike's right," said Wren. "It was probably the same person or persons who made us crash."

"Emma. EMMA!" a voice called through the woods.

Emma was struggling to process everything. The crash was bad enough. Finding out that someone had caused it deliberately made the situation a lot worse. Her eyes were fixed on the fresh footprints that her brother had spotted, and now someone else was calling for her. *I get why Shaw had a freakout.*

"Yeah!" she called out, still not taking her eyes off the ground.

"The truck's caught fire, and Mya's still in it," Kat cried, appearing on the other side of the bushes for just a moment before tearing back to where she'd come from.

"Course she is," Emma muttered. "Why wouldn't she be?" She threw one glance back down to the footprints then broke into a run in the direction of the road.

*

This is crazy. This is fucking crazy. Mya had seen plenty of vehicle fires in her time. *Hell. I've caused plenty.* She knew how quickly they took hold. She knew how unpredictable they were. Sometimes it might take a good few minutes for the fuel tank to ignite. Sometimes it happened in no time at all. It was the very unpredictability that made them dangerous. But one thing was for sure. If the flames punched through the trailer, the jerricans of fuel and the small amount of spare ammo they had would make a bad situation a whole lot worse.

Some of the dynamo lanterns were still throwing out a little light as she carved through the industrial lashings that held their last remaining supplies in place. She heard a sudden noise behind her and turned to see Andy, Rob and Jon forming a line towards the open doors. "It's dangerous in here. This thing could go up at any moment," she said, not needing to warn them of the obvious but doing it anyway.

"We'd better be quick then," Andy replied as Mila, Ephraim, and Jack climbed into the truck, too, forming another line.

Mya grabbed one of the jerricans and ran to Andy,

who met her halfway, snatching it from her and passing it to Rob.

Mila joined Mya at the pile of supplies and grabbed the crate of ammunition, running back and handing it to Ephraim. The bursts and whooshes could be heard building in volume, and the front of the cargo container was already getting hot. When the final jerrican was removed, Emma and the others appeared.

"Get the hell out of there now. It could blow at any minute," she ordered, although she knew full well Mya was not one to take orders from anybody other than Beck.

However, Mila and Mya each grabbed a lidded crate of food before running towards daylight. They passed them to Mike and Jules then jumped down themselves and ran towards where the crowd of former Safe Haven residents all stood in bewilderment.

A thunderclap erupted from the cab, and even though everyone was expecting it, terrified screams still rose from many, followed by several sad and hopeless cries.

"So what the fuck do we do now?" Jules asked as she and her small group of friends just stared towards the pyre of smoke and raging flames.

"I'm still trying to figure that out," Emma replied.

"Well, we'd better get the hell out of here while you do," Mike replied.

"Jesus, Mike. Can you just give me a minute, for Christ's sake? It's only just happened. We're a safe enough distance from the bloody thing now. It's not like we're going to lose our eyebrows or anything."

Sammy had been comforting some of the others while they'd waited in line to get seen by Liz or a nurse. When the cab had exploded, she'd sought out her family, as scared as anyone but not wanting to show it. She slipped her hand into Emma's, seeking comfort.

There were conversations that Mike did his best to shield his little sister from, but given what was going on, he couldn't this time. He looked at Wren, Robyn, Mila and

Mya. They all knew what he was trying to say, they all shared his urgency to get away, but the five of them had experienced more than the rest of the survivors put together, and it would take them a little longer to understand.

Mike stepped forward and placed his hand on Emma's upper arm. When he spoke, it was in a soft tone. She, Sammy and Jules would hear, but it was unlikely that anyone else would, given the nervous chatter that murmured around the frightened crowd.

"Em. Every RAM that can see that tower of smoke is going to be heading in this direction right now."

A look of dawning suddenly appeared on his sister's face. "Oh, shit." It was obvious, and if she'd had just a moment to pause and breathe, she would have come to that conclusion. But everything was coming at her like balls from a cannon, and her mind was awash with all the problems facing them. "Oh, shit, shit, shit," she whispered this time, looking in one direction and then the other. "Err … the Land Rover. Is there any way we can get that going again?"

"The tyres are shredded, the rims are bent. She's not going anywhere," Mya replied.

"For what it's worth, we're probably better staying off the road," Wren said. "You always seem to get bigger concentrations of them on the roads."

"Yeah," Robyn agreed. "And in the forest, they could easily lose sight of the smoke and get distracted by something else, so, y'know … there's that."

"You're saying we should head into the forest?" Emma asked.

Robyn shrugged. "If it was me running the show."

"But, I mean, isn't it easier for us to get attacked without warning in the trees? And what about the people who laid the trap for us? They're going to be in there somewhere, too, aren't they?"

"Given our options," Mya began, "I say the forest is our best bet. We'll head in and try to find somewhere to hole up just so we can take a breath and think about what's next."

Sammy's hand squeezed Emma's a little tighter. "What do you mean what's next?" Emma asked. "We need to get to Glasgow."

"True enough," Mya replied. "But we've still got at least another twenty-five miles to go, and even if, by some miracle, we made it that far on foot, there is no way fifty-odd of us are just walking into the city. We need to come up with a plan."

"Mya's right," Mike said. "Let's just get everyone moving for now."

"Any suggestions as to which direction?"

"Well, the pervy bastard who was watching us was over that way, so I say we go the other way," Jules replied.

Emma shrugged. "I suppose that's as good a reason as any. Divide up the remainder of the ammunition and food between everyone and we'll head off."

"Okay," Jules replied, disappearing.

"We'd better go get the rest of our gear from the Land Rover," Mya said, gesturing to Mike and the others to follow her. When they were all out of earshot, she continued. "Okay. There is nothing about this I like."

"I would have thought you'd know as well as anyone what the dangers are of us staying put," Wren replied.

Mya opened the back, and Muppet was about to jump in, but she put her hand up to stop him. She took a surreptitious glance back to the crowd as Emma gathered them in order to explain what they were doing. "I'm not talking about getting out of here. That's a given. I mean whoever set this trap up for us had resources." She pulled the spiky ball from her pocket. "These things have been welded together and painted. We're not talking about a couple of scavengers who're just chancing their arms."

"Then why haven't they attacked then?" Robyn asked.

Mya reached into the car, grabbing her rucksack and

pulling it onto her shoulder. "My guess is they didn't think there'd be any more of us than who was in the cab and who was in the car. When they saw everyone climb out of the back, they probably got cold feet."

"That's good. That means we don't have to worry about them, at least."

"Or they might track us, pick us off a couple at a time. We're strangers in a strange land here. This is their backyard."

"It's always great talking to you, Mya. If I ever need cheering up, I always know that after a conversation with you, there's always death to look forward to."

"Hey, you're welcome. I just tell it like I see it."

"Okay. So, putting possible abduction and slaughter by our mystery highwaymen or women to one side for the moment. How are we going to play this?" Wren asked, nodding back to the others.

Mya looked at Wolf and Muppet then smiled briefly before her face became serious once more and she returned her gaze to Wren. "Well, I wish it was that easy. We can't put aside possible abduction and slaughter. We need to keep our eyes peeled for anything out of the ordinary. Thankfully, Muppet, Wolf and Meg are going to be our early warning systems for the infected, but we'll have to watch out for anything else."

"Everybody's just about ready," Emma said as she and Jules walked across. "A few people are pretty banged up after the crash, and George's ankle is playing up, so we're not going to be able to make a quick getaway if we need to. But everyone's armed one way or another, and after I explained about the smoke signal, they're eager as hell to get out of here."

"Have you explained that guns are an absolute last resort?" Mya asked.

"Most of the people with guns trained with the militia, so they know what they're doing. But everyone's got spears or hand-to-hand combat weapons of one type or another."

"I was just explaining that we need to be extra alert. It's not just the infected we need to think about. There are the people who did this, plus whatever else is lying in wait for us out there."

Emma looked back to the burning lorry as the flames continued to consume it. "Everyone's pretty jumpy at the moment, so I don't think anything's going to go unnoticed."

"We have got that going for us, I suppose."

"How do we do this then?"

"What do you mean?"

"Are we going to walk in one long line or in small groups or what?"

"I say one line. Stealth is everything, so we keep talking to a minimum. Wren and Robyn are on the flanks with Mila and Mike. One bow and one blade on each flank. You and I lead with Muppet. Jules and her brothers bring up the rear with Jenny and Meg."

"Why the fuck do I have to get stuck with my brothers?" Jules asked, causing the others to chuckle.

"Seriously," Mya said. "Keep your eyes on Meg. She's getting on, but she's got a good sense of smell. If there's anything creeping up behind us, she'll hear it. Your brothers can manage hand-to-hand combat well. If anything happens, they'll be able to give us enough time to mount a proper response."

"Okay," Jules replied. "Em wasn't joking about George. He's struggling."

Mya nodded. "We're not leaving anyone behind, so we'll just take it steady. If he needs to rest, we'll rest, although, knowing George, if his leg had fallen off, he'd claim he was still okay to walk."

"Alright," Emma said, taking a deep breath. "Let's get this show on the road."

3

Beck watched as the dark green liquid swirled around in his mug. For the entire duration of his time at Number Ten, he'd made less than half a dozen warm drinks. He'd poured plenty of cold ones, often on the rocks.

"Are you alright, Prime Minister?" Talikha asked.

Beck looked up distantly. He hadn't heard her come into the small galley and had no idea how long she'd been standing there, but he realised that if the expression on his face was mirroring what he was feeling inside, he desperately needed to do some damage limitation. A convincing but nonetheless fake smile cracked on his face. "Sorry. I was miles away. Can I make you a drink?"

She looked down at the mug. "You like my mint tea?"

"In the absence of normal tea, coffee or anything alcoholic, I can safely say that it's my favourite drink."

Talikha giggled. "I will take that as a compliment."

"You should," he replied, grabbing another mug and pouring from the teapot.

"Thank you," Talikha said as he handed her the mug. "I have had a lot of people make me drinks in my life, but never a prime minister."

Beck laughed sadly. "Let's face it. I stopped being that a long time ago."

Talikha frowned a little. "You will always be that."

Beck let out a long, deep sigh. There was something about Raj and Talikha that made him feel comfortable and more able to share. "That's kind of you to say, but I think recent events prove that I'm just a man who's completely out of his depth."

"You are talking about what happened in Glasgow?"

"Ha! How did you guess? You must be psychic."

"That was not your fault."

"I sent six of the bravest people I know on what was almost a suicide mission for a golden egg that didn't exist. It's nothing short of a miracle that they got out of there alive. If anything had happened to any one of them, I wouldn't have been able to live with myself."

"But it didn't."

"But it could have done. And all for what? For some empty trucks. I was peddling erroneous information, believing it was actually something that could help us, and it turned out nothing was further from the truth. It could have lost us our best people, all while I was safely sitting behind a desk patting myself on the back, thinking I'd done a good job.

"I was so sure. I was so sure it was going to be the answer to all our prayers. I was sure that information was going to save us."

Talikha took a sip of her tea and studied her companion for a moment before speaking. "And it was," she eventually replied.

Beck looked at her with a confused expression. "What are you talking about?"

"If Mike and the others had not gone down to

Glasgow they would not have met this Griz person. We would not be on our way to join his community now."

"Well … no, but that's no thanks to me."

"How is it not? They would not have gone to Glasgow in the first place if it wasn't for you."

"Well … no. But I didn't send them there for that, did I?"

"Whether you sent them there to meet Griz or not, meet Griz they did, and now we are going to join him. So, you are responsible for this change in our fortunes no matter how we arrived here."

Beck's brow furrowed as he tried to outreason Talikha, but all he could come out with was, "Err…."

"When we start down a new path, we have no idea where we will end up, but our final destination will always be up to us."

"How can our final destination be up to us?"

"Because our destination is only final if we choose to stop travelling. Everything happens in life for a reason. Our place is not to understand that reason but to accept it."

Beck stared at her for several seconds. "Okay. You're starting to blow my mind a bit here. I feel like I'm having an acid flashback or something."

Talikha laughed. "When we were in Candleton, we heard lots of stories."

"What kind of stories?" Beck asked.

"Stories about the organised crime gangs."

"Ah," Beck said. "Yeah. You'd hope that at a time when the whole world was going to hell, people might actually start pulling together a little bit. They became more of a problem than they ever had in peacetime."

"Your information. The information that told you the trucks in Glasgow were full. The information you believed to be true. I am just a vet's assistant, but might it not be possible that the contents of the lorries fell into the hands of these gangs? When Mike spoke to Raj and me, he said that all the container seals were in place. If the lorries left one depot full and entered another still sealed with the same code number but empty, it would suggest to me that a well-organised operation was in place to create the illusion they had not been tampered with. That does not sound like something one truck driver or even a dozen truck drivers could pull off by themselves. They would need storage facilities and lots of manpower." She shrugged. "Are those not things that a crime gang might have access to?"

"Well … yes. But, I mean, it's not like we can prove it, is it? It's not like we can forensically trace every can of beans back from when they were originally purchased to the point of disappearance. It's all a hypothesis."

Talikha nodded. "It is. But I know the man I am talking to now was convinced that the food that was meant to be in those trucks was in them. Otherwise, he would not have sent six of his friends down to Glasgow. I know he did it in good faith to try to help everyone. I know circumstances outside of his control stopped his plan from coming to fruition. And I know that, despite this, we are heading to our new destination because of him and his desire to help his people."

Beck looked at Talikha for a few more seconds, and a smile flashed onto her face momentarily before she took another sip of tea. "This is an ambush," he said. "You're freaking me out in my time of weakness with all this 'everything happens for a reason' stuff, and I'm in danger of believing it just so I feel a little better about myself." Talikha laughed this time, and the door to the galley opened.

"I think he was looking for you," Mel said as Humphrey barged in with his tail wagging. He leapt up at Talikha, almost knocking her over. His front paws reached her shoulders and his tongue lolled out of the side of his mouth before his face turned more serious and he sniffed her breath to make sure she hadn't been eating without him. He swivelled clumsily, and his pads landed on the small countertop, where he spotted a single dry cracker left on a plate from earlier. Without any forethought, he shuffled along the counter, knocking Beck backwards and nudging the half-full teapot to the edge.

Used to his single-mindedness and the trail of devastation that could ensue when it came to food, Talikha whipped her hand out, grabbing the handle of the pot and saving it from certain destruction.

At the same instant, Humphrey gently seized the cracker, flopped down to the floor and disappeared back out of the door before Beck had even gathered himself.

Mel was laughing as shock and confusion painted the face of the former PM. "What the hell was that?" he asked.

"That was Hurricane Humphrey," Talikha replied, carefully replacing the teapot.

"Trish asked me to tell you that they're about to start a fresh round of charades in there and she's been bigging up your miming prowess to everyone."

"As she should," Beck replied, smiling.

"I'll tell her you'll be along in a minute," Mel said before the galley door closed once more.

He waited until she was gone then turned back to his companion. "Thank you, Talikha."

She shrugged. "I have done nothing other than stated truths."

"We both know that's not the case."

Talikha smiled. "One day soon, you will realise."

Beck smiled now. "Are you coming to join us for charades?"

"I think I will go find Humphrey before he causes any more mayhem."

"Actually, that's probably for the best."

*

"So, I'm guessing you're my bodyguard," Wren said as she and Wolf walked along, scouring the forest to the south as they went.

"How do you figure?" Mike asked.

"Well, I'm the bowwoman, the important one.

You're here to make sure nothing happens to me."

Mike laughed. "That's the conclusion you came to from Mya assigning us to work together?"

"Well, it's the only thing that makes sense, isn't it?"

"You keep telling yourself that, Wren."

They walked along in silence for a few moments, checking that the procession of bodies to their left wasn't struggling to keep up. "Do you think they're following us, the ones who caused the crash?"

Mike looked over his shoulder. Jules and her brothers were bringing up the rear. They kept looking back too. There were few people Mike would trust in that position, but they were now close to the top of the list. "I don't know. I hope not."

"That's reassuring. Thanks."

"If they do follow us and make a move, we'll deal with them."

"How can you be so confident? I mean they could outnumber us two to one for all we know."

"I doubt it. But even if they do, you, Me, Robyn, Mila and Mya went into the Glasgow underground and we're still here to tell the tale. A bunch of highwaymen in a forest will be like a walk in the park."

*

"I heard you were quite the markswoman while we were in Glasgow," Mya said.

"I've just been practising a lot," Sammy replied. She walked along with her crossbow already drawn and loaded.

"Well, I heard you're a natural with that bow." Sammy tried not to show the satisfaction on her face as they carried on. "Wren told me that you took to it the first time you picked hers up."

"Wren and I spent a lot of time together back in Safe Haven."

"I know. She says you're like her little sister."

"She does?" Sammy said, breaking her search of the forest ahead and turning to Mya.

"Yeah. She reckons soon you'll be as good with your bow as Robyn is with hers."

Sammy let out a short laugh. "Nobody will ever be as good with their bow as Robyn."

"I don't know; Wren's got pretty good judgement."

Sammy looked behind her. Emma had dropped back a little to talk to Kat and Ephraim. "Nobody will tell me exactly what happened in Glasgow. I heard something about you going down into tunnels."

A flashback of the terror-filled episode flickered in Mya's mind. "It's not really something—"

"Let me guess. It's not really something that somebody my age should hear about?"

Mya smiled. "No. It's not really something I like thinking about. It was pretty scary."

"Mike said you're not scared of anything."

"Mike's being kind. I'm scared of plenty. Being scared keeps you alive."

"I was scared when the infected got into the grounds back at the centre."

"That's a good thing, Sammy. It's when you stop being afraid that things turn bad." They carried on walking for a little while before Mya continued. "I think I was just about as scared as I've ever been down in that tunnel."

"But you got through it."

Mya thought about the moment she had frozen, and it was only Mike running interference that had saved her life. "Just. But it's not something I ever want to go through again."

A pensive expression appeared on Sammy's face. "Thank you."

"What for?"

"Being honest with me. Most people still treat me like a baby."

"From what I've seen, you're anything but."

*

"I am so hungry," Robyn whined.

"Yes, of course, you are. It is probably fifteen minutes since you last ate. I'm surprised you can stand, let alone walk," Mila replied, zeroing in on a dark bush to their left and studying it for a moment before a bird took flight and her internal alarm relaxed.

"Hey, that's not true. It was ages ago. I can feel my stomach grumbling."

"Yes, and how kind, you vocalise its discontent just for me. I am so fortunate to be walking alongside you so I can share in your belly's disquiet."

"Okay, okay, sarky cow. I'm just saying."

"Yes, well, maybe you think less of your stomach and more about where we are walking and what might be waiting out there."

"I'll have you know that I'm multi-taskual. I can talk and do stuff at the same time, y'know."

Mila shook her head. "There is no such word as multi-taskual. Which is proof in itself that you can barely do one thing, let alone two."

"Oh yeah. Well, I saw the bird fly behind that bush you were so interested in about ten seconds before you even noticed the branches were moving."

"I am very happy for you."

"I'm just saying—"

"Yes, yes, yes. You are always just saying something."

"Fine. I'll stay quiet if you're going to be so arsey."

"Don't sulk."

"I'm not sulking."

"Your bottom lip always extends when you are sulking, and right now, you look like a disgruntled orangutang."

"Thanks very much," Robyn replied grumpily.

"Come, I was trying to make you smile."

"Oh yeah, with that legendary German wit."

"Lots of people find me funny."

"I hate to burst your bubble, but nobody finds you

funny. They either laugh because they feel sorry for you or they're scared of you."

"This is not true. I have an advanced sense of humour. It takes intelligent people to appreciate it."

"You're saying I'm not intelligent enough to appreciate your humour?"

"I am just making an observation."

"I think my explanation makes more sense. You're just not funny. You don't understand humour."

"Yes. You keep telling yourself that, dummkopf," Mila replied. "They continued walking for a moment before she sniffed once, twice, three times. "Oghh! You are a disgusting pig."

Robyn laughed, wafting the air at the same time. "See. Now that's funny."

*

"It's so lovely to have your brother and the rest of the gang back. Somehow life just doesn't feel the same when we're not on the cusp of death and living in terror," Ephraim said as he, Kat and Emma walked along.

"Are you saying my brother was somehow responsible for the truck crashing?"

"Not at all. Just making an observation. Cataclysm seems to follow him around like a lost puppy."

Emma and Kat both chuckled. "I thought you didn't believe in fate or predestination."

"I don't."

"Well, what you're saying is that wherever my brother goes, trouble won't be far away; ergo, my brother is a living synonym for impending doom, ergo it's predestined that misfortune and destruction follow him around, ergo predestination and fate do in fact exist."

Ephraim frowned for a moment, pushing his spectacles a little further up his nose. "Hmm. Now, that's interesting. It begs a thousand questions, doesn't it?"

"Or it begs no questions. We're living through an apocalypse. My brother, Mya, Wren, Robyn and Mila, they're always at the heart of everything because they're the ones who put themselves in harm's way to protect everyone."

"There is that, I suppose."

Muppet, Mya and Sammy stopped dead just ahead of them, and a loud growl began in the back of the mongrel's throat.

"On the other hand," Emma said, retrieving the hatchet from her rucksack. "You might be right."

4

At first, just a single creature appeared from the trees ahead of them. It seemed to have been drifting through the forest until the moment it saw them and they saw it. Then, all of a sudden, it broke into a sprint.

Its excited growls grew louder the closer it got, ratcheting up the tension. Everyone knew how quickly one became two, became four, became eight. They had seen it happen so many times before. There was no time off when dealing with the infected. There were no easy kills. There was no relaxation of the rules. They needed to be put down quickly and safely. You had to ensure they didn't bite you or scratch you. You had to make sure none of their blood or tissue got into your mouth or an open wound. In principle, it was simple.

When they were diving and clawing at you, when the monster had previously been someone you might have known or, worse still, loved, it became much harder.

Mya slid the crowbar from her rucksack and bent over to place a firm hand on Muppet's back, the signal for him to stay put. She took a few paces forward, putting herself between the impending danger and the rest of the group. A bolt suddenly whistled by her, and before the creature even reached the fifteen-metre mark, it was down. Mya turned to see Sammy on one knee, cranking the self-cocking lever and loading another bolt in the flight groove.

"Nice shot, Sammy," she said, immediately turning back to their direction of travel. Silence descended around them. Nobody moved; they just stared ahead, waiting to see if any more monsters emerged from the trees. A full minute passed before Mya raised her hand and gestured that they should continue going.

The procession moved off once again, but now the chatter had ceased. Everyone searched the trees for movement. Sammy plucked the bolt from her victim, wiping it on the clothes of what had once been a young man. His pallid face was scarred and scratched, and his clothes were torn as if he had been dragged through thorny bushes. The young girl turned away from him, closing her eyes tightly in the hope it would wash her memory.

She thought back to the lesson Wren had taught her so many months before during one of their lessons. "They're not people anymore, Sammy. They're just creatures trying to kill you."

"You okay?" Emma whispered.

"Yes."

"That was an amazing shot, Sammy."

"Yeah," Mya agreed. "Impressive."

Sammy closed her eyes again as a picture of the man her victim might once have been strobed in front of her. *He could have been someone's dad. He could have been someone's brother.* She gulped hard, trying to be strong.

*

"You taught my little sister well," Mike said proudly.

"I just showed her the basics," Wren replied. "The rest of it's all down to her."

"If you say so."

"I'm glad you and Grandad made up."

"It's not like we can really avoid each other, is it?"

Wren laughed. "No. I suppose not."

"Plus, I get where he was coming from. If someone coaxed Sammy into going on a deadly mission, I'd probably want to kill them."

"Yeah, the difference is Sammy's not even a teenager. Bobbi and I have pretty much had all the childhood we're going to have. Anyway, I'm glad you were the bigger man and made the first move because I know he's too stubborn. I don't know how I'd deal with two of the most important people in my life hating each other."

"I need to keep as many people as I can onside. There are already enough people who hate me. All it cost me was some tobacco, so it was a good trade."

"I thought you reasoned with him."

"I tried that at first, but it wasn't until I gave him the tobacco that he became okay with the idea of you and Robyn being plunged into a life-threatening situation. To be honest, it should probably have been my opening gambit."

Wren laughed. "It's good to know we're so important to him."

"Don't get me wrong. He'd be devastated if anything happened to either of you, but a couple of packets of Mild Virginia would probably perk him right up."

Wren laughed again and pushed Mike playfully as they walked along. "Arse."

*

Robyn looked down at her stomach as it gurgled once more and was about to complain to Mila when she caught movement out of the corner of her eye.

"Nine o'clock." In an instant, food was the last thing on her mind. She nocked an arrow, and Mila drew both swords. They worked well together; they always had.

A collective gasp rose from the rest of the convoy as first one then half a dozen infected charged from the north, making a beeline towards them. Robyn released her bowstring, and the arrow glided majestically through the air, cracking through the forehead of the frontrunner, who collapsed to the ground causing the second to stumble.

There was a clatter as knives, spears and other hand-to-hand combat weapons were raised behind. The scream of two children, louder than any sound that had come from the group since entering the forest, ensured that if there were any more infected in the area, they would be heading towards them now too.

Before the fallen beast had a chance to scramble to its feet, another arrow was flying, and Mila was in position ten metres in front of her friend.

*

Wren was about to run and join her sister when Mike grabbed her arm. At that exact moment, a growl rose in the back of Wolf's throat, and she turned to see at least ten more beasts tearing towards them from the south.

"Oh crap," she said, bringing up her crossbow and firing as the first clear shot presented itself. She pulled the self-cocking lever before the body of the first monster had even skidded to a stop. The second bolt was launched by the time Mike and Wolf ran forward. There was a part of Wren that wanted to cry out a warning *NO*. But the sensible part of her knew that at the speed the creatures were advancing, there was no way she would have time to take them all down with her bow.

Another bolt flew, but not from her weapon. She glanced to her left to see Sammy on one knee with Emma behind her. A split second later, a creature collapsed, and Wren turned to the direction of battle, firing again.

*

Mya's initial impulse had been to join Mike, but something stopped her. Muppet was not looking in the direction of either of the attacks but straight ahead. He was frozen, staring beyond the trees to what Mya had no idea.

Then she saw them, a small army of beasts rampaging towards her. The trees were thick up ahead, and it was impossible to maintain visual contact with all the creatures as they disappeared behind low branches and trunks. But there was no mistaking the fact that there were a lot more of them than the groups advancing on either of the flanks. *Shit!*

She placed her crowbar back in the rucksack and retrieved her Glock 17, knowing that the second she pulled the trigger, every RAM in earshot would descend on them, but also knowing that if she didn't, all hope of them getting out of this alive was gone.

There must be at least fifty of the bastards.

*

Swipe! Slash! Hack! Mila and Robyn worked together like a well-oiled machine. Mila was statuesque as the final beast fell. Her eyes were not on it but on the forest to the north as she searched out any more potential threats.

She saw nothing, but the frightened cries from behind told her there was more danger lurking somewhere. She spun around to see Robyn torn between rushing across to help her sister and running forward to confront the creatures charging towards them head-on.

"Scheisse!"

*

"Oh, fuck me!" Jules cried, dropping her rucksack and bringing up her rifle. "Jon, stay here with Jen and George. Rob, Andy, we need to help Mya."

"Err … Jules," Andy said. "We need to—"

"There's no fuckin' time to debate this." She was about to break into a run to the front when her eldest brother reached out and grabbed her.

"Jules," he said more forcefully this time.

"What? What the fuck is it?" she demanded.

Meg began to growl loudly, and a frightened cry left Jenny's mouth as at least two dozen more creatures closed on them. "Eleven o'clock," Rob cried, raising his rifle.

"Seven o'clock," Jon called out, doing the same.

"Shite," Jules said in little more than a whisper.

*

Wolf already had one of the creatures on the ground by the time the next pair reached Mike. With two powerful outward sweeps, he hacked through their skulls, causing both to drop. He strode forward three more paces and suddenly felt a presence at his side. Two more bolts flew, and two more creatures dropped as he and Emma faced the final trio of beasts. Emma brought her hatchet down with a thunderous crack as it split her target's forehead. The beast stopped dead for a moment in suspended animation. Its grey eyes locked open, its flaring pupils contracting to little more than pinpricks before it finally succumbed to gravity and dropped to the ground.

Mike whipped his machetes outward in a virtual action replay of his previous kills. Before the grabbing beasts had come to rest on the ground, he withdrew the blades and leapt forward, slashing down again to finish off the creature Wolf still had in a throat hold.

A scream erupted into the air, followed by another; then a sudden and deafening hail of gunfire began to boom.

"Oh shit!"

*

Muppet had burst into a sprint a few seconds before the first shot was fired. Mya did nothing to try to stop him. She had glimpsed behind before taking aim at the first beast, and she saw what Jules and the others had seen. The infected were converging on them from multiple angles and at alarming speed.

Crack! Crack! Crack! Ammunition was at a premium, and Mya understood that every bullet had to count. So far, each shot she had taken was a kill. She hoped the others who had weapons wouldn't panic and waste the little ammo they had. The barrage of fire behind her suggested this was not the case, and it wouldn't be long before what was left of the Safe Haven militia were using their M16s as clubs.

In the periphery of her vision, she could make out riflemen and women by her side, spreading out a little, hoping the dense wedge of charging bodies heading in their general direction would not deviate and zero in on them.

Crack! Crack! Crack! Three more dead, but many more down. She'd had a wealth of experience with situations like this. While others picked out any moving body, Mya's training and instincts drove her to the ones that would cause pile-ups. It was a method she'd used to buy extra time often, and it had usually worked, but the sheer wealth of beasts closing in, the lack of ammunition and the slowness of some members of the convoy told her that on this occasion, it was going to do little but delay the inevitable.

*

"Oh God," Jenny cried as her first shot entered the shoulder of one of the beasts attacking from the rear. It barely missed a step.

Crack! Her second shot tore through a low-hanging branch. Crack! Finally, she brought her target down. She wasn't sure how many rounds were left in the magazine, but she knew she didn't have a spare. Meg was about to bolt towards the advancing creatures, but Jenny pre-empted her, reaching down and grabbing her collar. She was just as likely to get hit in the crossfire as the two groups converged as she was to tackle one of the creatures to the ground.

*

"This is a fuckin' lost cause. There are too many of them," Jules cried as she brought another then another creature down. Andy, Rob and Jon had been taking careful, well-aimed shots, but even more beasts had been drawn by first the growls of their excited brethren, then the screams and finally the gunfire.

The two converging groups were only about thirty metres away now. When they met, it would coincide with reaching the rear of the convoy, and then it would be game over.

*

"What do we do? What the fuck do we do, Mike?"

Emma cried.

Wren had not paused once the creatures attacking from the south had all been put down. She sprinted towards the rear of the procession to try to protect her grandad. Sammy followed her without a second thought.

Mike just stood there for a moment. He was ready to fight, but not to the death. "There's no such thing as a no-win situation," he said to himself.

"What?"

"We're not losing anybody else. We've lost enough people."

Crack! Crack! Crack! Crack! Gunfire continued to erupt around them as death drew ever closer.

"That's a nice thought, but—"

"The grenades."

"What?"

"The grenades."

Emma's eyes flared excitedly. They'd rescued six M67 grenades from the weapons cache in Safe Haven. Shaw had three of them on the yacht with the spare weapons and a small amount of ammo. She had the remaining three. She dropped to her knees, flipping her rucksack around at the same time. She opened the flap, and Mike immediately picked up one of the objects removing it from its protective container and pulling free the transportation safety clip. Barnes had taken great delight in demonstrating how to use them. There was a part of Mike that never thought the day would come for him, but life had a funny way of turning out. Before Emma had a chance to say anything, he was sprinting to the front of the convoy, shouting behind him. "You've got about four seconds once you pull the pin."

*

Crack! Crack! Crack! Crack! Emma slid the rucksack back on her shoulder and began to sprint to the rear of the line, taking the grenade out of its container as she ran. *This is mental. This is absolutely mental.* It was. The grenades wouldn't take all of the creatures out. They might remove a handful at most. She had no idea how much ammunition had already been wasted, but it was guaranteed that any infected in the area who had yet to hear the gunfire would certainly hear the boom of an M67.

Wolf had tackled one of the front runners, but there were plenty more of them further back still emerging from the trees.

"Fuck it!" she said, ripping off the safety clip, whipping out the pin and lobbing the baseball grenade.

*

Mya had already used one magazine, and by her count, she was more than halfway through the second when something distracted her. At first, she thought it was a low-flying bird, but then it dawned on her exactly what it was as it flew towards the large group of creatures that had just emerged from the denser woodland. She threw a glance towards Muppet to see he had one of the beasts pinned to the ground behind a tree. He would be protected. Mike had told her about his love of cricket, and half a smile lit her face now as the grenade travelled further than most people would ever be able to throw it.

*

"WOLF!" Wren screamed when she saw the object in Emma's hand. The loyal German shepherd did not hesitate in obeying the call, and as the spherical grenade soared towards the clearing where a vast swathe of the would-be attackers were, he tore back towards his mistress.

Jules, her brothers and the other riflemen and women had done well, laying down a steady fire and diminishing the number of advancing beasts significantly, but another large group had just converged from the two approaches they were covering.

"GET DOWN!" Jules screamed.

*

Two deafening booms erupted within a second of each other, and for a moment, the gunfire paused. Instinctively, everyone had either crouched down or dropped to the ground covering their heads, but before the final echoes of the explosion had even dissipated, Mya was upright once more and taking aim at the much smaller crowd of creatures heading towards them.

Muppet still had his victim pinned instinctively; that was the first thing she had checked after the grenade. She felt a presence by her side and glimpsed Mike with his shotgun drawn. "There are a lot of people who've already run out of ammo," he shouted over the noise of those who were still firing.

"Yeah, well, I'm not going to be far behind them," she replied, taking three more shots in quick succession.

*

Five more infected had appeared from the north, but for the moment, Mila had those covered. Robyn had joined her sister at the rear of the convoy. The grenade had killed at least a dozen of the tightly packed beasts as they had stormed towards the Safe Haven refugees, and several more had been maimed, but another small army was still advancing.

Robyn took a deep breath, then another. Panic and fear swirled around her like a tornado. It was obvious some thought the grenade would miraculously solve all their problems and save them, but it was just a tool. The only way they had out of this was to fight like they had never fought before. She released her bowstring, nocking another arrow before the first had even reached its target.

*

"Shite!" Jules cried as her rifle ran dry. Seconds later, the same thing happened to Andy, then Rob. One by one, the other weapons fell silent until the only advancing creatures dropping were the ones Wren, Robyn, and Sammy were bringing down.

"What do we do?" Jon's shaking voice asked.

Jules was scared to her core. She'd been in tight situations before but nothing like this. When she'd started firing, she'd dropped her homemade spear on the ground, but now she picked it up again as another of the beasts fell, causing a few more behind to stumble.

"We fight. We fight like we always do."

*

Mya's Glock and Mike's shotgun ran dry at the same time. Mike knew he had another small handful of shells in his rucksack, but the time it would take to load them would negate any advantage they might give. He slid the weapon into his backpack and retrieved his machetes.

"Oh shit," Emma cried as her weapon emptied too.

Mike's face contorted into an animalistic snarl. "COME ON THEN, YA FUCKERS!" he shouted, exploding into a sprint towards the advancing creatures.

Mya and Emma cast each other bewildered glances before Mya grabbed her crowbar, Emma her hatchet and the pair tore after him.

*

This time when Meg darted forward, Jenny did nothing to stop her. Wolf had already got another beast on the ground, and no more bullets were flying. This was it. The one saving grace was the infected didn't attack animals, so whatever happened to Jenny, at least her beloved dog would be safe. She watched as Meg leapt, clamping her jaws around one of the creature's thighs, pulling it down to the ground with her, as another arrow and another bolt took two more out.

Jenny laid down her rifle and picked up the spear George, Jack and James had fashioned for many of them while still at the Skye Outward Bounds Centre.

This is it. It all ends today.

*

Mila had dispatched the first five creatures with the same exertion most would experience swatting flies, but now eight more charged at her from the same direction.

Breathe. Breathe. Breathe.

She had seen enough of what was going on to know this was no time for hesitation. One way or another, this would be a decisive battle.

Breathe. Breathe. Breathe.

An arrow suddenly appeared from nowhere and took out the second creature on the left side of the wedge, making two more fall behind it. She had no time to turn but knew it was her friend keeping an eye out for her.

Mila sprang forward. Whip! Sweep! Kick, parry. Slash! Hack! Hack! The first five were down as the remaining two gathered themselves and charged towards her. She crossed the replica katana blades above her head and the second the beasts were in striking range brought them down in perfect synchronicity.

There were no more infected heading her way, and before the pair of would-be attackers had fallen, Mila was sprinting across to join her friend.

*

Sammy was almost glued to Wren's side. The sound of gunfire for any child was a terrifying one, but she suddenly realised that the sound of the weapons emptying was far scarier.

In the periphery of her vision, she could see a line of people behind, bracing themselves with spears and whatever hand-to-hand combat weapons they had. She, Wren and Robyn had done a good job taking out frontrunners, causing mini pile-ups of infected bodies, buying them valuable seconds, but their arrows and bolts would not last forever, and it wouldn't be long before the beasts were on them. Suddenly, she didn't want to be here with Wren, as much as she loved her. She wanted to be with her brother and sister. But the time for that had been and gone.

A fear-filled tear trickled down her face as she launched another bolt. Her target flew back, and she cranked the self-cocking lever, placing another of the hand-carved missiles in the flight groove just as Mila blurred out of nowhere and launched what might be their last offensive.

5

Not much had gone through Mike's head when he had decided to make his charge. He'd heard his sister's cry of despair follow him as he raced through the woodland towards the approaching beasts, but he knew what this was. Anyone with a grain of sense knew what this was.

He had seen zen-like serenity sweep over Mila and Robyn when they were in battle mode. He envied them. For him, the tangled ball of blinking Christmas tree lights flashed ever faster the more hazardous a situation became, and now it was as if there was one giant multicoloured strobe in his head.

Swipe! Crack! Kick, punch, kick. Smash! Slash! Hack!

"Jesus!" Mya gasped as she and Emma reached him and the small pile of bodies around his feet as the next wave closed in. Whoosh, Crack! Her crowbar brought another to a staggering halt as she leapt forward, kicking out at the same time to catapult a second creature back.

Emma felt the shockwave jolt through her as the hatchet blade vanished into the forehead of her assailant.

She dragged it out just as quickly as another creature pounced.

"Waaahhh!" Before she had the time to react, the beast was on top of her, and she was falling back. *Shit!*

*

Mila could only control so much. There were a number of infected closing on the convoy from a wider angle. Sweep! Sweep! Crack! She kicked out hard, then again, almost pirouetting as she spun to dispatch her next two attackers.

*

Wren squeezed the trigger of her crossbow and cranked the lever, immediately placing another bolt in the flight groove. "This is hopeless. It's hopeless," Jenny cried, shaking by her side.

"Nothing's hopeless. We fight, and we keep on fighting," Wren replied, firing another bolt. "That's what we did all the time we were in Safe Haven, and it's what we do now."

"Fuuuck!" Robyn's cry came, and Wren looked across to her sister. Their eyes met. "I'm out."

For a split second, Wren didn't understand what she meant. Then her eyes focused on her sister's empty quiver. She reached for her own, and a feeling of dread consumed her as she suddenly realised she was down to her last bolt too.

*

Emma hit the ground, dropping her hatchet, and she felt the body of her attacker begin to scramble on top of her. Fear like nothing she had experienced before shuddered through her as she realised this would be her last day on Earth. Hughes' face flashed into her head, then Sarah's, then Lucy's, and finally Jake's. There were dozens more she had mourned the loss of, but now it was her turn. As much as she struggled, she could not throw the weight of the much bigger creature from her as it finally gathered itself and reared up.

It was like all her strength had left her. *I suppose it was only a matter of time.* The fear gave way to sadness as she realised the same fate would await her brother and little sister. She would be the first to go. They'd put up a good fight not to lose anyone so far, but now it was over for her, at least.

She looked into the creature's eyes, only just realising that it was missing one. The cavernous black hole that stared back at her sent another shiver of despair running through her. For some reason, that image made her think of hell. She had never been a particularly religious person. She'd flirted with the idea of an afterlife, but at this moment before her death, she wondered if an eternity of suffering awaited her. *Was this virus sent here to bring about the end for us all? Was this God's final joke, a way to root out the ones worthy of saving?*

The beast opened its lips in a slow-motion snarl revealing dirty yellow teeth. Its one remaining eye shot a jolt of icy malevolence into her veins as it moved its head closer. The creature's jaws moved up and down as if practising how it would tear the flesh from her neck when it finally reached her. Emma continued to struggle, but it was no good. A final sad whimper left her mouth, and she closed her eyes.

*

Mike had heard his sister scream, but he'd been fending off three more infected at that moment. As they lay on the ground at his feet, he finally glanced over to see the monster's mouth mere centimetres away from Emma's neck.

Mya booted another beast in the chest, launching it back while smashing a second against the temple with her crowbar. It provided the valuable pause he needed as he leapt across, dropping one of his machetes and clutching his sister's attacker by the scruff of its neck. It wore a thick leather jacket, and as heavy as the creature was, even after all this time, Mike hoisted it up and around.

Seizing the split-second respite, Emma rolled out of the way as the beast's stretching hands made a last-ditch attempt to grab at her.

Mike felt the strain on his muscles ease a little as the momentum from his sudden and explosive action drove the creature forward. Its head crashed against the trunk of a giant pine, and it slumped, dazed and confused for just a beat before having its skull smashed once more against the tree. Then again, and again, and again. The motionless body slumped to the ground, and Mike spun around, running forward and scooping up his machete once more.

He glanced across to Emma to see her standing there grasping her hatchet. There were tears in her eyes as they waited with Mya for the next wave of beasts.

*

When Jules had yawped her battle cry, she didn't know how many would follow her charge, but as she ran past Wren, Robyn and Sammy with her spear raised, she caught the movement of many more in the periphery of her field of vision. They finally drew level with Mila and came to a stop, angling their spears out in front of them as if they were attempting to halt a cavalry attack.

*

Ephraim and Kat were the first to join Mike, Emma and Mya. Their spears skewered two attacking creatures before they withdrew them once more and drove the bloody points through their heads.

Then, as the already established trio jerked into action once more, another dozen Safe Haven refugees joined them as they continued to hold off the assault of the infected together.

*

Nobody was more surprised than Jules when a line of spears joined her own in thrusting forward to fend off the attacking creatures. Some disappeared into stomachs and chests before being withdrawn to make their kills. Others struck the sweet zones immediately, ensuring the monsters would come to an abrupt halt.

"Forward. Forward," she ordered, as one after the

other, the creatures fell.

Robyn and Wren looked towards each other. They instantly understood what Jules was doing. The pair hovered just behind the line with their hunting knives drawn; then, as Jules and her small army stopped just past the first row of bodies they'd brought down, the sisters sprang into action, grabbing arrows and bolts from the fallen creatures, swiftly wiping them clean to ensure they got flight unimpeded by chunks of gristle or fat. Like children feverishly picking chocolate eggs on an Easter hunt, they gathered the missiles that might very well be the difference between life and death.

*

Mila sprinted forward. She was the vanguard of this attack. Each time she moved, Jules raised a rallying cry once more, and the rest of the spear line advanced. "Don't get in my way," she demanded as two of the former Safe Haven villagers lurched dangerously close to her arc of movement. She continued to whir and blur, leaving a trail of devastation in her wake.

Finally, there was something like an end in sight. There were no more creatures massing on the periphery. She threw another look to her left and right. She knew Robyn would be doing the same. The north and south approaches had stayed clear since their initial confrontations. She cast a glance to the east to see Mike and the others still in the throes of battle, but their defences were holding. No creatures had got through.

*

Mike and Mya locked eyes for the briefest of seconds. Despite Mike's reluctance to admit it, this had been a no-win situation from the start, and they both realised the same thing now. They had turned it around.

Slash, spin, strike, punch, kick, pivot, crack. *She's in a league of her own when it comes to these things*, Mike thought as he watched his friend explode into action once more.

"Aaarrrggghhh!" Emma screamed as she lunged

forward, smashing another creature through the forehead. Ever since she had been saved from the jaws of certain death, she'd had a point to prove. Vengeance simmered inside her. She had made peace; she had said goodbye. *How fucking dare they?*

She knew it was stupid in some ways. These aberrations had no thought processes, no agenda beyond that of feeding and infecting others. There was no vendetta, but for Emma there was as she swiped with her hatchet and kicked out once more.

*

Jules wasn't quite sure what was going on at first. There were only about twenty creatures left heading in their direction, but suddenly, a hail of arrows appeared from the trees to the north, and at least half the beasts fell to the ground while others stumbled. She heard a scream rise behind her and swivelled to see the same thing happening on the eastern approach.

"What the fuck is happening?" She turned around to see the remainder of the infected dispatched by Mila and her brothers as they rushed forward to help, but she felt no relief. Whoever had killed these creatures were well-armed. Would they be next?

*

Mike, Emma and Mya looked at each other wide-eyed as the last of the beasts charging towards them fell. Mike immediately dropped to one knee, ripped the rucksack from his bag and pulled out the shotgun and four shells, loading them feverishly as the archers who had taken down the remaining creatures stayed in the cover of the trees.

"Who's out there?" Emma called, her eyes looking in the direction the arrows had appeared from.

For a few seconds, there was no response and the tension mounted further. Then a single figure emerged, slowly followed by others. It was a man in his forties. There was a younger-looking woman by his side. They and the entourage behind them all carried bows and quivers. Several of their number broke away to collect arrows while the rest headed towards Emma.

"There'll probably be more," the man said. "If you want to keep your people safe, you need to come with us."

"No offence, and thank you for what you've done, but we're not just going to follow you because you say so."

"Fine," the man replied. "Stay here then, but there's a massive tower of smoke rising to the west and any undead that see it are going to be heading towards it. If you're in between them and it, it's going to end badly for you and your people."

"Please," the younger woman said. She gestured to the fallen beasts. "If we meant you any harm, we'd have let them finish you off, wouldn't we? There was a moor fire nearby a few days ago. That brought far more than usual to the area."

"For all we know, you could be cannibals," Mike replied before his sister could say anything else.

The man, the woman and any of the others in earshot all laughed. "Thanks for that. When I saw that smoke billowing with the potential to burn the entire forest down, I thought it was going to be some time before anything made me smile again," the man said.

"I've said something funny?"

It was the young woman who replied. "When we heard the firing, we thought we were coming out here to protect you from the cannibals."

"What?"

"Look," the man said. "We can discuss this when we're somewhere a little safer. If you want to live, you'll come with us now."

Emma took over from her brother. "We can't just foll—"

The whistle of further arrows made them all look up to see three more creatures fall to the ground. "As I was saying. We're not safe out here," said the man. "We came to help, but I'm not going to put my people at more risk than they already have been."

Emma turned to Mike then Mya. "Okay."

The man turned to a small group of his people. "Hang back a little and make sure we're not followed." They all nodded and disappeared into the trees.

The extended convoy travelled quickly and quietly through the forest. They came across only a small handful of infected, which Wren, Robyn and the other archers quickly put down. Eventually, they reached a large rocky mound. "If you've got torches, now would be a good time to turn them on," the young woman said as she and another woman disappeared behind a bush. Mike, Emma and the others followed. They watched as the pair heaved aside another expansive shrub that looked like it was growing from the earth but, in fact, was in a large trough.

When it was fully out of the way, it revealed a low cave entrance. The two women ducked and headed inside, and Emma joined them.

"I really don't like this," Mike whispered to Mya as they paused at the entrance.

"Tell me about it," she said, glancing down at Muppet, whose tail was wagging enthusiastically. "First sign of trouble, grab the girl. I'm pretty certain she's with the leader."

"What will you do?"

"Give you moral support."

"Gee, thanks."

"Support's all I've got because, other than your shells, we're out of bullets."

"When you're ready," the man said, coming up behind them.

Mya and Mike clicked on their torches and headed into the cave too. When they were all inside, the trough was pulled back into place, covering the entrance, and two heavy wooden doors were slotted into runners, one on either side of the opening. They were then pushed together and bolted into place. Thin streams of daylight could still be seen through slivers of gaps, but they vanished as a pair of heavy curtains were drawn.

"Curtains?" Mike asked.

"There's a private school not far from here. Frightfully posh," the young woman said, doing her best toff impression. "They had their own theatre, don't you know." She dropped the accent to continue. "We got all sorts from that place. Come on." She started heading further into the caves, and Mike and Mya exchanged another glance.

*

"Are you okay, Grandad?" Wren asked as she took his free arm. His walking stick clacked against the stone floor of the cave as they went further and further in.

He took a breath. The physical exertion of the journey and the events before had been a lot to contend with. Wren, Robyn and Mila had remained on the flanks all the while, but now, even though they were somewhere foreign and they couldn't be sure what the intentions of their hosts were, just being with his loved ones again made him feel a little better. Wolf brushed up against his leg almost as if he was asking the same question. "Yes, I'm fine, thank you. You…."

"Me what?" she asked as Robyn and Mila caught up to him on the other side. The tunnel had widened and heightened, and now people were walking along five, six, seven abreast as they went further and further down and in.

"You girls were unbelievable out there. I … I don't have the words."

"Yeah. We were pretty great," Robyn said, causing the others to laugh. "What do you reckon the score is with these dudes?" she asked in a slightly more hushed tone.

"They saved us when they didn't need to. So, this is a good thing, yes?" Mila said.

"Yeah, but like Mike asked. Why?"

*

"You alright, Jen?" Jules asked, dropping back a little

from her brothers and joining her friend and Meg.

Jenny reached out, taking the younger woman's hand tightly in her own. "I'm a liability out here."

"What are you talking about?"

"Other than wasting valuable ammunition, I did very little to contribute."

"Look. Not everybody's cut out for fighting. When we get to where we're going, I'm pretty sure there's no one who's going to make a bigger contribution than you. You kept everything running back home. The pub was the hub of Safe Haven, and you were the one who kept it all ticking. So don't you go getting all fuckin' morose on me."

Jenny couldn't help but let out a small laugh and held Jules' hand a little tighter. "You're a sweet girl, Jules. Always trying to make people feel better."

"I'm just telling the truth. We've all got our strengths. I mean that fuckin' mad bastard," she said, pointing her torch up ahead a little, bringing it to rest on Mike's back before lowering the beam once more to the ground in front of them. "When it comes to fighting like it's your last day on Earth, there's nobody who does it better. But can you imagine what would have happened if we had asked him to figure out the barter system or put him in charge of inventory? Safe Haven wouldn't have lasted five fuckin' minutes. Civil war would have broken out, and it would have been like *Lord of the fuckin' Flies*." Jenny laughed again. "We've all got strengths. Just because yours isn't shooting the infected, it doesn't mean you're not a fighter. It doesn't mean we're not all depending on you."

"Thank you, Jules," Jenny said.

"I told you. There's no need to thank me."

*

"So, anyway, formal introductions. I'm Della, and this is my husband, Clayton, Clay to his friends."

"I'm Emma. This is my sister, Sammy, my brother, Mike, and that's Mya."

"So, now everybody knows everybody, what is this

place and what did you mean about saving us from the cannibals?" Mike asked.

"You have to forgive my brother. He's not big on etiquette."

"Look, I get it," Clay said. "If a bunch of strangers had bundled me and my family into a cave, I'd be asking questions too, but we're nearly there, and we can have a proper chat then."

Mike and Mya cast each other another glance in the periphery of the torchlight. They carried on walking for a couple more minutes until the tunnel led into a sprawling cavern. At least twenty pop-up tents were spread around, and by the far wall, something glowed. "Let's head over to where there's a bit more light, shall we?" Della said.

The rest of the Safe Haven refugees followed, but Clay nodded towards one of his archers, and suddenly the armed escort dispersed.

"You've got hot water?" George asked incredulously as he saw the large tank standing just a few metres away from the solid fuel stove.

"We've got our own water supply too," Della replied, pointing her torch. They all turned to see a narrow, slow-running stream emerging from one end of the cavern and disappearing below ground a few metres later.

"So, you live down here?" Emma asked.

"It's one of the places we live."

"One of them?"

"We live in the trees too," she said, giggling. "Come, everybody, sit down." There was a loose semicircle of tree trunks laid out around the stove. Despite the size of the cavern and the obvious draughts, it was still possible to feel the heat thrown out by the fire that burned, and Della crouched down to throw two more logs in.

"The trees?" Mya asked.

Clay laid his lantern on the ground and sat down next to his wife as their new guests all took seats too. "Yeah. We—"

Clay grabbed Della's wrist. "I love Della, but she's the most trusting person I've ever met. We've brought you here at risk to ourselves because, in good conscience, I couldn't just leave you out there. The forest is going to be awash with infected for the next few hours at least. There's a lot of rain heading in from the west, so hopefully, that's going to stop the fire before it spreads out of control. I've invited you into our home, but I don't know you. I'm guessing by the fact you were using spears and clubs to fight your bullets ran out some time ago. Your archer and crossbow women seem very capable, but there are sixty of us, and we're all armed, and please don't think for a second I won't instruct my people to do what they need to if I sense that you present any kind of risk."

Mya leaned into Mike and whispered, "The ledge." No one else heard her, but Mike eased the rucksack from his back and placed it in front of him, giving him easy access to the shotgun and his machetes. There was a stone shelf about twenty feet off the ground. It was outside the arc of light provided by the stove, but several dark figures could be seen perched there. In the shadows, it was impossible to tell who they were or what they were doing, but Mike and Mya understood immediately that the reason Clay wanted everyone in the glow of the fire was so they would be easier for his archers to pick off.

Shit!

6

Emma reached out, placing her arm around Sammy. She had an uneasy feeling that went way beyond being stuck underground with a bunch of strangers. The adrenaline from the battle had dissipated a little, but something told her they weren't out of trouble; they were just in a different kind.

"Anyway," Clay said, "you'll want some peace of mind just as much as we do. But as I've invited you all into our home, I'd say it's only right that you go first, wouldn't you?"

"That's fair enough," Emma said, beating her brother to it. "Firstly, thank you. Thank you for what you did back there, and thank you for bringing us here." She waited for an acknowledgement from the other man, but when none came, she continued. "We were heading south, and someone made us crash."

"Made you crash?"

"Yeah. They'd laid these spiked ball things over the road. They were painted the same colour as the tarmac, so they were practically invisible. Anyway, they burst our tyres, and—"

"That explains the fire, I'm guessing."

"Yeah."

"It sounds like the mad monks," Della said, getting a glare from Clay. It was only fleeting, but it was plain to see for anyone sitting in the front row. She shrank back a little on her chair, realising she'd spoken out of turn once more.

"The mad monks?"

"We'll come on to that in a minute. Where were you going? Where were you coming from?"

Emma looked across at Mike and Mya. Both of them were willing her to be guarded with her responses, but given the circumstances, she didn't have many options. "We were going to Glasgow." She could see Mike's shoulders droop.

"Why the hell would you want to go to Glasgow? That place is awash with hundreds of thousands of infected."

Emma looked across at Mike again, and this time, she could see him shaking his head, begging her not to go on. She let out a long sigh and stared into the orange glow. "We were driven from our home."

"Your home? Driven by who? Why are you going to Glasgow?"

Emma went on to give Clay a potted history of Safe Haven and everything that had happened to them up to the point of reaching the Isle of Skye and Mike and the others meeting Griz. "And that's where we were heading when all this happened."

Clay and Della listened with interest, not interrupting her with questions once. When she had finished, Clay just let out a laugh and said, "The Skye Outward Bounds Centre?"

"Yes. What about it?" Emma asked.

"Small world, that's all. We used to go there a lot back in the day. I ran courses."

"Courses?"

"Yeah. White water rafting, rock climbing, spelunking." He gestured around him. "That's how I knew about this place."

"You seem to have it kitted out pretty well."

"You don't know the half of it," Della said, smiling, only for the smile to vanish just as quickly when Clay cast her another glare.

"And Beck's with you?" Clay asked.

"Yeah. He's on the yacht with the rest of our people."

Clay shook his head. "Well, I suppose the time for the unbelievable came and went when the dead started walking."

"Yeah."

"The day he gave his speech. That was when I started planning for this place. I'd found it a couple of months before. Hadn't explored it properly. They go on for miles do these tunnels. There's an underwater river further down. There are even cavefish in it. None of us have plucked up the courage to try them yet. To be honest, we haven't really needed to, but they're there if things get desperate." He turned back to Emma. "You say Olsen ran you from your homes?"

"That's right. Not just us but people all over Scotland. She plans to take the whole country back."

"Well, I dare say she won't be interested in our little corner of it."

"Yeah. That's what we thought."

"I was captured by her people," Mila said, causing all eyes to turn to her. "They use their prisoners as nothing but fodder for the infected. They chained us up across roads and gave us spears while their soldiers looted."

"Jesus," Clay said.

"You might think she is not your problem. But one day, she will be."

"Yeah, well. For the time being, we've got enough to contend with."

"The mad monks?" Emma asked.

Clay glanced at Della again before turning to Emma. "They're a consideration never too far away, but we keep our eyes open, and in the main, we've managed to avoid them."

"Who are they?"

"They live across at Dunnock Priory. About a mile or so away from where you crashed by the sound of it."

"I guess this whole end of the world thing made them question their faith."

A fleeting smile flashed on Clay's face. "I don't think they're actually the original inhabitants of the place. In my life, I've never seen monks with love and hate tattoos on their knuckles. There was a maximum security prison a few miles away from here. I get the feeling there might have been a jailbreak."

"You've had run-ins with them then?"

"We've only lost two people since this whole thing began, and it wasn't to the infected."

"It was to them?"

"Yes … and no." His head dropped as he thought back to it. Della reached out and took her husband's hand.

"They were a couple," she said, taking over. "Only just married before all this started. Dana and Darius. They were crazy," she said, smiling fondly. "They were into bouldering."

"Bouldering? What's that?" Jules asked.

"It's rock climbing without ropes."

Jules shrugged. "I thought it was some weird sexual thing for a minute."

The others laughed. "Please don't mind her," Emma said. "She doesn't get out much."

Della smiled before continuing her story. "They were out gathering mushrooms one day when they got caught. They were taken back to the priory. They threatened they were going to take their time with Dana, but they'd need sustenance to keep them going. They killed Darius in front of her. They kept her chained in the kitchen, and she had to watch and listen to everything. They carved him up like they'd calve up a pig. They bled him out into buckets. Joked they were going to make black pudding. They had a meat mincer, for God's sake. She had to watch him being ground up. The sick bastards forced her. Can you even imagine?"

"Jesus," Emma gasped, wrapping her arm ever tighter around Sammy.

"Anyway, the chain must have been rusted, or there must have been a weak link or something, because she managed to slip out when they were eating. She ran all the way back here. It took two days before she could bring herself to talk. She eventually told us what had happened and that there were about eighty of them. She said they had spears and clubs, and a few of them had truncheons, but there were others with guns. She said they all wore habits, but none of them looked like they knew the first thing about God. She described what they were like down to the scars on their faces and tattoos on their bodies. She said there was something weird, not right about them."

"Other than making people into black pudding and mincemeat, you mean?"

"She said they were wild. Their eyes looked but didn't see. She said they were unpredictable, strange, crazy. That's when we started referring to them as the mad monks. Given what they did and what they're capable of, it's a bit flippant, but the name stuck. We've come across the odd one or two since then and…."

"And what?"

Della turned back to the stove. "We can never let them find out where we are. If we see them, we kill them," Clay said.

"Sensible," Mike replied. "You can't take risks with maniacs."

"You said you lost two people," Emma said.

Clay nodded. "Dana didn't make it more than a few

days. We found her one morning hanging from a tree."

"Christ. You can't really blame her. Watching someone you loved going through that … it's … unimaginable."

"You haven't thought about going in there and taking them out of the equation?" Mike asked.

"Every day," Clay said. "But look, we're not special forces; we're not anything. We're all pretty fit. We've all spent every second of our spare time looking for the next adrenaline rush, but killing people? That's something else. We've had to deal with the few who we've run into, but it's not by choice. It's out of necessity. We can handle our bows. When I got the idea for this place, I made sure that everyone who was coming in trained with them. There were a lot who already knew how to use them, but a lot wasn't enough. I wanted everybody to be able to handle themselves. Shooting targets, even shooting the undead, that's one thing. But shooting a living, breathing human being that can fight back, that's something else."

"So, what happens if they ever come looking for you?" Mike asked.

"They've got no reason to. They don't know we exist. They found Dana and Darius, but they never let on that they were part of a bigger community. Anyway, we're pretty elusive most of the time. We're in touch with the environment around us, and usually they don't stray into this part of the forest. There's a river that runs by the priory. They grow vegetables in the grounds, and there's plenty of forest on their side of the road." He turned to Mike. "If they did ever find us, then I suppose we'd have to deal with it, but it wouldn't end well for anybody."

"After everything you've told us, why did you come to our aid?" Emma asked.

"Because in all good conscience, I couldn't knowingly let what happened to Darius and Dana happen to someone else." A single tear ran down his cheek.

"Thank you," Emma said. "Thank you so much."

Clay looked at her as if waking from a dream. He shook his head. "It's what decent people do, isn't it? I mean we've lost most markers in this life that can gauge what a decent person is, but not letting strangers get devoured by cannibals. That's got to be one, right?" A weak smile appeared on his face before it was gone again. "Well, look, at the very least, you can rest up here. I don't think it's advisable to head back to the surface for a while."

"Thank you again," Emma said.

Clay nodded. "People depend on me here. People look to me for answers. I took a big risk with everybody's lives heading out there to help you. Please don't make me regret it."

"I can assure you. You won't even know we're here."

"Della," Clay said. "Let's leave our guests to talk among themselves. I'm sure they have plenty to discuss. We've got work to do."

Della smiled at Emma and the others then climbed to her feet and followed her husband. Hushed conversations began among the survivors.

"So, what the fuck do we do now?" Jules asked.

Emma stood up and addressed the rest of her people. In addition to the glow of the stove, there were dynamo lanterns and torches casting enough light for them to see. Nearby, one of the cave dwellers had even lit a few candles on a waist-high rock. "I suggest everybody gets something to eat and drink while we figure out our next move."

People started to dip into their rucksacks while Emma and her small entourage drifted to a quiet but reasonably well-lit corner of the cave to talk.

"They're still there," Mya whispered to Mike, casting her eyes to the shadowy ledge once more.

"Yeah. What do you reckon?"

"The guy and his wife seem legit, but I've been wrong before."

"That's reassuring."

"What are you two talking about?" Jules asked.

"Just discussing the decor of this place. I love the whole gothic thing it's got going on," Mya replied.

"You're weird. Has anyone ever told you that?"

"Only once."

Jules laughed. "Duly noted."

"Okay," Emma began. "I think it's pretty obvious that there's no way we can head to Glasgow on foot, so we need to come up with a plan and fast. Raj and the others will be sailing up the Clyde late tomorrow afternoon, and we're the advance party, remember?"

"Well, it's obvious, isn't it?" Mike asked.

"What's obvious?"

"A few of us head to Glasgow to get the other truck we got going for Griz. We drive it back here, pick everyone up then carry on with the plan as before. While we're there, we can tell Griz to keep an eye out for the yacht just in case we're delayed getting back."

Emma laughed before her face turned more solemn. "Wait a minute; you're serious?"

Mike shrugged. "You said it yourself. We can't get everybody there on foot. This is the only logical option."

"You call that a logical option? Just a handful of us heading to Glasgow on foot. You're not just talking about a couple of streets this time. You're talking about the entire city. You'd have to travel through the whole city to get to where we're heading."

"She's right, Mike," Wren said. "We wouldn't stand a chance. A couple of streets was one thing, and just to refresh your memory, that nearly bloody killed us."

"Yeah," Robyn added. "Not to mention the fact that we'd pretty much been resting before we even set foot on terror perma."

"What?" Mike asked.

"What?" Wren echoed.

"Y'know," Robyn replied. "Dry land."

"You mean terra firma?" Wren asked.

"Whatever," Robyn replied. "I mean we'd been on the yacht until we hit that dock. What you're talking about is hiking twenty-odd miles on foot 'til we reach Glasgow then fighting our way through the city. That's mental."

Mike put his hands up. "Okay, I'm all about listening to other people's ideas. What have you got?"

Robyn opened her mouth to speak again, but nothing came out. "Well," Wren began, "maybe we could find another vehicle."

"Brilliant," Mike replied. "Where?"

"Well … I don't know, Mike. Maybe Della or someone knows where we might find one."

"Sure, 'cause there are probably loads of them kicking about in a forest, aren't there?"

"That was just off the top of my head. It beats going on a death march then taking on the city of the dead."

"The school," Mila interjected. "She mentioned a private school. They would have minibuses and other vehicles, yes?"

"It's possible," Mya replied before Mike could. "But the chances are the batteries would be dead. If there was any fuel left in them, then that could be like water now for all we know."

"I am not saying it would be like calling an Uber. But it is worth trying, yes?"

Mya nodded. "It beats heading out on foot. I mean it might come to that, but if there's any way of avoiding it, then it's worth a shot. What does everybody else think?" She looked around the small circle.

"If that's what everyone thinks, then sure, why not. It beats just standing around talking, but it could be a wild goose chase. It's not like these vehicles have just been sitting around for a week or two," said Mike.

"We got those two trucks going, didn't we?" Robyn replied.

"True enough. But we also…. Scratch that, Mya

and Darren also had to lug two batteries around with them so we could jump-start the trucks. And after that first one, do you remember how many we actually tried before we got another to fire? A lot of the fuel had gone bad, and that was in a well-sealed garage not exposed to the elements."

Silence hung in the air for a few moments. Jenny had joined them halfway through the conversation, but she'd immediately got the gist. Meg was almost sitting on her foot. Muppet and Wolf were both glued to their mistresses' sides as the tension and anxiety were palpable.

"What do you reckon, Jen?" Mike asked.

"Oh, no. You can keep me out of this. I think it was pretty clear from what went on out there that when it comes to this kind of thing, I'm completely out of my depth. Emma's in charge, but…."

"But what?" Emma asked.

"This isn't really your decision, is it?"

"What do you mean?"

"I mean you're needed. You've got fifty-odd people who are scared to death, disoriented, and wondering what the hell's going to happen next. If a group is heading out there, you can't be one of them, so ultimately, the decision lies with those who go."

Emma looked down to see Sammy standing between her and Wren. It was true. If Emma decided to go with them, then Sammy would insist on going too, and it didn't take a genius to read between the lines of what Jenny was saying. "You're right. It's up to whoever goes."

"Well, I'm not suggesting anyone after last time," Mike said, and the others all laughed.

"We'll go. Of course we will," Wren said.

"I said that without even moving my lips," Robyn replied.

"Ja. It is obvious. The five of us who went to Glasgow must go," Mila stated.

"It's not right," Jules said. "It's not right that it's the same people always putting themselves in harm's way. I'm going to go with."

"Just when I thought my life couldn't get any worse," Mike mumbled.

"Listen to me, y' wee prick. When we were stuck back at the Home and Garden Depot in Inverness, I—" Mike grabbed hold of her wrist and started dragging her away from the others. "What the fuck are you doing?" she demanded, trying to shake herself free. Laughter erupted behind them once more as the pair marched away.

"Listen to me," he said when they were far enough from the others and any other former Safe Haven residents not to be heard.

"The fuck do you think you're doin', dragging me away like that?"

"Because I know you. I know that if I try to reason with you in front of others, you'll stand your ground no matter what I say, but here you might listen."

"I wouldn't put money on that."

"We're out of ammo, Jules. I've got about six shells left for the shotgun, and then that's it. I've got my machetes, Mila's got her swords, and Wren and Robyn have their bows. What have you got?"

She shook her wrist free. "I've got a spear like everyone else. But if you think for a second I won't fight as hard as—"

"I know you'll fight. That's why I need you here with Em and the others. If anything happens, I need you and your brothers to put up a fight."

"Put up a fight? What the hell do you think's going to happen?"

"I don't know. But we've had bows trained on us ever since we walked in here."

"What? Where?" she asked, starting to look around.

"Shame Mya's not into the spy game any longer. She could have got you a job. Look, these people seem kosher, but we don't know for sure. Those monks or whatever the fuck they are, who knows, they didn't follow us back from the road? Who knows, they didn't get reinforcements and are heading here with their army now?"

"You're really putting my fuckin' mind at ease today, aren't ya?"

"I'm not saying they are. I'm saying we need fighters here as much as we do out there."

Finally, some of the bluster left Jules' argument. "But it's always you. It's always you and Wren and Robyn and Mila and Mya who are putting yourselves in harm's way. It's not right."

Mike reached out and took hold of Jules' hand. "I promise, when we're down in Glasgow, you can risk your life as much as you want, and I won't stand in your way."

Jules laughed and play punched him with her free hand. "I'm being serious, y' prick."

"I know. So am I. It's about more than trust, Jules. You, me, Em, Jen, the others, we've all been through something. We're more than family. We've got this shared experience that nobody on the outside will ever understand. It's like we're the same in some ways."

"Me the same as you? Now you are trying to scare me." Mike smiled. "You're right, though. I think I know what you mean."

"Knowing you were with Em back at the Outward Bounds Centre. It gave me peace of mind. I knew that together you'd be able to deal with whatever happened. I need you here. I need to know that you've got Em's back."

"I'll always have her back. I'll always have yours too."

"I know."

"Conceited wee prick, aren't you?"

Mike laughed this time. "I mean I know I will always, always be able to rely on you."

"Am I interrupting a moment here?" Emma asked as she walked up to the pair of them still holding hands.

"Yeah," Jules replied, letting go of Mike's hand and taking hold of his arm while placing her head on his shoulder. "We didn't quite know how to tell you, but I'm pregnant, and Mike's the father. We've just been discussin' how to tell everyone."

"Well, I know that can't be true. I'm still quite warm, and for that to have happened, hell would have to have frozen over."

Jules shrugged and let go of Mike. "True enough. So what have you come over here to tell us? Let me guess. The fire's spreading this way, and we're all going to suffocate to death down here."

"You're in a cheery mood. But very possibly."

"What?" both Mike and Jules said at the same time.

"Four more of Clay's archers appeared while you were having your tête-à-tête, and whatever's going on, it doesn't look good."

The trio all glanced over to the entrance of the vast cavern to see Clay, Della and a handful of their people talking by the light of an LED lantern. Clay ran his fingers through his thick head of greying hair. Almost as if he sensed eyes on him, he looked across to where the three of them stood. Even in the subdued light, they could see his face was troubled. He turned back to his people, and a muted conversation continued for a few moments until one of the women he was talking to shouted, "Well, that's all that matters then, isn't it?" before marching away.

"What do you suppose that's about?" Mya asked, walking up to join them. They continued to watch as the woman, surrounded by a small entourage, went to sit in a dark corner, where she burst out crying.

"I think we're about to find out," Emma replied as Della broke away from the group at the entrance and started across to them.

"Is everything okay?" Jules asked.

Della let out a shuddering breath before replying. "It never rains, but it pours, I suppose," she said, clearly distressed and trying to stop herself from crying.

"What is it?"

"Seems like we spoke too soon. We were telling you how well we've done to avoid the monks since Darius and Dana. They got two of ours."

"What? When?"

"The ones Clay asked to bring up the rear, make sure we weren't followed. On the way back here, they split into two groups of three." She nodded to the corner to the crying woman. "She was slightly ahead of the other two, and she managed to take cover so they didn't see her. There were four of them, which probably explains why they didn't make a move on you lot. But they must have been watching what was going on, and when they saw our people split up to do a last reccy before heading here, they decided to strike." Now Della started crying. "Keely was my best friend." Jules placed her arm around the younger woman.

"I'm sorry, darlin'."

"People are already blaming Clay for us heading out there."

They looked across to the corner where the crying woman was to see an even bigger crowd gathered around her now. "So, what's happening? Are you sending a party out to get them?" Mike asked.

"What?" Della looked at him, barely able to believe the words coming out of his mouth. "With all the infected out there too? It will be a miracle if they make it back to the priory alive as it is. All us going out there will do is ensure that more of us will die."

"So, you're just going to forget about them?"

"Mike!" Emma said.

"No," Della said, wiping her nose on her sleeve. "I told you, she was my best friend. I'm not going to forget about Keely or Rupert. But losing more people won't help anyone."

"This was your fault!" The shout boomed, and all heads turned to see another man standing face-to-face with Clay. "For what? For a bunch of fucking strangers, all because you had a crisis of conscience and something inside you said it was the right thing to do." The man made sure he kept his voice loud enough for others to hear.

"Please," Clay replied. "I—"

"We've managed to avoid those bastards all this time because we have strict safety procedures in place. But all that went to hell when you decided to play hero to a bunch of nobodies. Fuck the rest of us, as usual."

"That's not fair."

"No. I'll tell you what's not fair. Keely and Rupert have been taken. And we all know what's facing the pair of them, don't we?" the man said, looking around his dimly lit surroundings. "I told you it was a mistake to go out there, but you wouldn't listen, and now look."

"We can't just shut ourselves away. We can't just ignore it when there might be other people in trouble."

"The fight was practically over by the time we got there. They didn't need our help."

"What are you talking about? Of course they needed our help. If we didn't bring them down here, who's to say another army of infected wouldn't have found them?"

"And who's to say they would? But none of that matters, does it? Because your conscience is clear. It's cost us two of our own, but that means fuck all because Clay got to do the right thing. Our glorious leader put his mind at ease by helping a bunch of people who we're never going to see again after today."

"What if the situation was reversed?" Clay asked. "What if it was them who lived here and we ran into trouble? Wouldn't you hope that someone would help us if they could?"

"The situation isn't reversed. We had the foresight to set this place up. We ploughed money into it. We prepared. We—"

"WE?" Della screamed, marching over towards where her husband and the other man were arguing. Tears were still running down her cheeks, but they were tears of anger as well as sadness now. "It was my husband who set all this up. It was my husband who told everybody else about it. He was the one who organised the supplies, who bought the thousands of MREs we've been eating. He's the one who sourced all the dried and canned goods at a time when they were at a premium. He was the one who—"

"Like he did it for free."

"Do you have any idea how stupid you sound right now, Owen?" She gestured around to the tents. "Have we got a food supply hidden away that's not available to anyone else? Have we got a luxury villa down here in the cavern that we slope off to on a night while everyone else sleeps in their tents? No. Because Clay made sure everybody has the same as everybody else. The money you paid, the money everybody paid, was to secure the food and supplies we needed to last us as long as possible. And FYI, we helped out a lot of people who wouldn't have been able to afford it otherwise. The bikes, the bows, all of it cost money." Della gestured around her. "What benefit would it be to us to try to profit from this? We spent every spare penny on tools, materials and supplies."

"I still say that shouldn't make you and him the king and queen of this place."

"That's not fair. We're not, and we've never pretended to be."

"Well, how come we always have to follow you? How come it's your orders that mean we're down another two friends?"

"Do you really think this is the time to do this, Owen? Keely was my best friend. Do you think there's a single cell in my body that isn't screaming? And going out after these people was exactly the right thing to do." She gestured around. "Not just because of what Clay said, not just because we'd hope someone would do the same if the shoe was on the other foot, but because if we stop being human, if we forget about the things that made us look after one another in the time before, then what are we? What are we living for?"

"I'd say the time to think about reasons to live has come and gone, wouldn't you? I'd say just living is enough right now, but that's something that Keely and Rupert won't get the chance to do anymore."

Another torrent of tears streamed down Della's face. "Fuck you, Owen."

A huff of a laugh left his lips, and he turned to the others, many of whom had gathered around listening to the argument rage. "I think it's about time we had an election here, don't you?"

"If that's what people want, then by all means," Clay said, going to comfort his wife.

"I'd say it's what people want. I'd say if we'd have had one before now, then Keely and Rupert would still be here."

The fight left Clay in that instant. Anyone could see he was broken by the fact that his actions had inadvertently led to the abduction of their friends.

Owen turned his back on the couple and walked across to where a group was waiting for him. Hushed conversations ensued, and the tension in the giant cavern ratcheted up even more.

"We need to do something," Robyn said as Mila, Wren and Wolf came up behind her.

"I don't know if you've noticed, Robyn, but we're outgunned, or out bowed at least, here," Emma replied.

"I'm not talking about this. Whatever happens here happens. It sounds like they've had problems bubbling for some time. I mean we've got to do something to help that Keely bird and Rufus or Rupert or whatever his name is."

"You mean fight through a forest full of infected to get to a priory of what sound like criminally insane cannibals posing as monks to rescue two people we've never met? Count me in. That sounds like a hoot," Ephraim said as he and Kat joined them.

Robyn spun round, and Ephraim took half a step away as he saw a fiery reflection burn in her eyes. "Listen.

Mila and me have been there. We've been in that situation, waiting to die, counting out the minutes. Every time you hear footsteps, you think they're coming for you. You try not to think about what's going on, but it's impossible. And by the sound of it, it's even worse in that priory. I mean we had those crazy vegan chicks to deal with, and that was bad enough, but these psychos sound like they want a lot more than just to eat their prisoners."

Ephraim put his hands up. "I'm not saying it isn't horrible. What I'm saying is there are a lot more of them than there are of us, and in case you've forgotten"—he gestured to the rifle on his back—"we're completely out of ammo."

"He's right, Robyn," Emma said. "We got out of the forest by the skin of our teeth. Heading back out there is going to do nothing to help them, but it'll probably get some of us killed."

"Listen to Emma, please." George, Jenny and Meg had come over too, and it was Robyn's fretful grandfather who made the plea. "This is a lousy, terrible thing that's happened. But sacrificing your own life on some fool's errand isn't going to make it any better."

"Robyn is right," Mila said. "We must do something." She turned to her friend. "We will go ourselves."

"Okay," Robyn replied.

Wren grabbed hold of her sister's arm. "Bobbi. Think about this."

"I have thought about this, Wren. You weren't there. You weren't stuck in that room. You don't know what it was like."

Wren released her grasp and let out a long, deep breath, glancing down at Wolf for a moment before returning her gaze to her sister. "Well, if you're going, I'm going too."

Robyn threw her arms around her younger sibling. Jenny wrapped her hand around George's wrist as she heard a small cry of despair leave his lips. "Listen, darlings. I couldn't possibly understand what you went through in that hellhole, but think about this. There are people here who are counting on you. For all we know, Keely and Rupert might already be dead. The forest is swimming with infected. There's a massive fire still raging away. Heading to that priory would be suicide."

"Fine." Robyn shrugged. She looked at her grandad. She was getting used to the forlorn and self-pitying expression on his face, and at that moment, it did nothing but anger her. "I don't care what anyone says. I'm going."

"Wait a minute," Mike said, grabbing her arm as she began to walk away.

"Let go of me. I'm going," she replied, angrily trying to pull herself free.

"Wait a minute," Mike repeated, clenching his fingers a little tighter. "I'm coming with you."

"What?" Robyn asked, her surprise immediately dissolving any anger.

"What?" Emma asked.

"These people came out to help us. We owe it to them, but more than that, we owe it to Robyn and Mila. They've never hesitated to put themselves in harm's way when we've needed them. This is something they feel they've got to do, so I'm in. I know they'd do it for me in a heartbeat."

Emma looked at her brother for several seconds as a stony silence settled over them. "You're right," she said eventually.

"This is madness," George cried.

"No," Jules replied. "It's the right thing to do. Clay said it was the right thing to come out and help us, and this is the right thing too."

"Jules. Darling. Listen to what you're saying," Jenny pleaded.

"Mya. Are you with us?" Mike asked, ignoring Jenny's and George's mutterings.

"Did you think for a second I wouldn't be?" she replied.

"Okay," Emma replied. "Della!"

7

Time was of the essence. The best part of half an hour had already passed since Keely and Rupert had been taken. Emma's original plan had been to get directions from Della and Clay, but when she explained what they were doing, they volunteered to join them. They were the only ones. From the conversations they'd had since arriving back in the cave, it was clear that none of them would have ventured above ground in the first place if they'd had any idea how bad it was up there.

The group bypassed the pair of guards who were positioned just back from the doors. Nobody had ever found their cavern, but that didn't mean that they never would, and Clay insisted that two people remained on sentry duty in rotating shifts. This was how they had originally heard the gunfire. The duo looked up from their lantern-lit card game. News of what was happening had already reached them, and they were happy that they had a duty so they wouldn't even get asked to go along.

Clay had pleaded for volunteers, but Owen had muddied the waters, saying that demanding others go out and get killed wouldn't do anything to help Keely and Rupert, who, he reminded everyone, were only gone because of Clay's actions in the first place.

Mike and Emma had asked Sammy to stay behind with Jenny, but in reality, they felt just as nervous about leaving her in that cave with Owen and the others as they did taking her with them. So, when she had objected, she joined them, Jules, her brothers, Ephraim, Kat, Mya, Muppet, Wren, Wolf, Mila and Robyn. Seventeen of them were heading out, including the canines. How many would make it back, no one knew.

They did not go in the direction where Clay and the others had originally found them. Instead, they travelled in a wide arc of the battle site, believing the smell of the dead would act as a lure. They jogged quietly, keeping their eyes wide open.

Since they'd initially entered the cavern, it had started to rain lightly at first, but it was gradually getting heavier. It would take a long time to extinguish the blaze, but the dark clouds above suggested that this weather would linger for a while.

"What's that?" Emma asked, pointing to a tree as they continued to jog.

For a moment, Clay and Della didn't understand what she was talking about, but then they saw the rope. They had lived in the forest so long that they took things for granted, but to any newcomer, a rope dangling from the bough of a tree may look like a failed suicide attempt. "Ha!" Della said, reading the concerned look on the other woman's face. "Don't worry; we haven't got that desperate yet. We have those all over the forest. That's how we saw the smoke. They let us climb up high and see what's going on, but they allow us to hide too. We've got a couple of walkways up there that let us get from tree to tree. We've even got a few treehouses dotted around."

"Treehouses?"

"Yeah," Clay replied, taking over. "Some of them are

still a work in progress, but we felt having somewhere to escape to if the cave was ever found wouldn't be a bad idea. We've spent a few nights in them, and to be honest, they're more comfortable than the tents."

"That's smart."

Clay let out a sad sigh as he continued to run. "I try to be smart. I try to look after people. Not that you'd know that from everything that was said earlier on."

There was a short pause before Emma spoke again. "What are you going to do?"

"What do you mean?" Clay asked.

"I mean when we're gone. It doesn't sound like things are particularly amicable back there."

"This has been coming for some time," Della replied. "Owen's just been waiting for Clay to make a mistake."

"It wasn't a mistake," Clay snapped back.

"I'm sorry; I didn't mean it like that."

"I can't tell you how grateful we are for what you did," Emma said.

"I don't know how much we helped. You seemed to have things under control by the time we got there."

"If you hadn't taken us in, I'm not sure how well we'd have fared." She held up the homemade spear she was carrying.

"Something tells me you'd have done okay."

"You'd be welcome to come with us."

"What, to Glasgow?" Clay asked, horrified. "Della and I were the ones who discovered this place. We were the ones who set everything up. Why would we leave it?"

"I'm just saying you'd be welcome to come along."

"Why did you set up out here?" Jules asked. "I mean, by the sound of it, you guys put a lot of funding together. Why not buy a place in the country and put razor fences up and stuff?"

"When you own something, there's always someone who wants to take it away from you. There are no roads leading directly to the cavern. Nobody knows we're there.

Everybody down there is an outdoorsy type. That's how they've spent every free minute of their time. That's how they enjoyed their lives away from the rigmarole of work. It's perfect. It gives us shelter, there's a water supply, we've still got a tonne of MREs and dried goods. I invested every penny I had in stocking that place. We forage and we've even got a hidden veg patch on top of one of the ridges. We fish in the river, and barring a few drifters heading out of Glasgow in the early days, we've avoided people."

"Apart from the mad monks," Jules replied.

The enthusiasm that had been on Clay's face as he'd spoken about the place he and Della had built disappeared. "Up until today, they'd only got the upper hand that once. We'd managed to stay out of their way. We rarely venture to the road, but when we did, we saw the occasional clue as to what had gone on. You're not the first people they forced off it. It's months since the last vehicle came this way, but their trap had probably been there since then."

"We thought we saw someone in the trees. It felt like we were being watched."

Clay shrugged. "They might have been in the vicinity foraging or hunting. A lorry crashing would have been pretty easy to hear considering how little noise there is around here usually."

"I suppose."

A dog's growl, then the whistle of an arrow, made them all look up. A second later, a single RAM at the far end of the clearing up ahead dropped to the ground.

"Jesus, she's good," Della said as Robyn nocked another arrow, ready for any more infected that might appear. "I mean we've got people who are pretty accomplished, but none of them can aim and fire while they're still running."

"Yeah. She's something else is Robyn. All three of them are," Jules said, nodding to Wren and Mila too.

*

Robyn plucked the arrow from the forehead of the

dead RAM and wiped the bloody tissue off on the creature's clothing before readying her bowstring once more. "Thank you for saying what you did," she said.

"What do you mean?" Mike replied.

They had all slowed to a walk now in order to give themselves extra time to see approaching threats, and Robyn paused for a second, not sure if she had seen something beyond the nearest trees. When she was happy it was just more trees, she continued. "I mean that whole thing in the cave about having our backs."

"You don't need to thank me. It's the truth."

"Yeah, but thanks anyway."

"Y'know, Bobbi," Wren began. "When we get there, we might be too late."

"I know," Robyn said, straightening up and releasing another arrow. It glided through the trees, disappearing into the back of a creature's skull. Even though it hadn't seen them, it was still safer to put it down before it did, before it could alert others with its excited growls. "But we've got to try."

"Ja," Mila said. "We are all going to die one day. But there are good ways to die and bad ways. This is the very least we can do." Her mind drifted back to the tortured time she spent imprisoned in that room, just waiting for death. She had dealt with depression numerous times in her life, but she had never felt so hopeless. Then the day when she believed Robyn had taken her own life, she wanted to end it all too. The memories of what happened at that house would live with her for the rest of her life.

"We're going to have to be smart about this," Wren said, and Wolf nudged her, sensing her anxiety.

"When have we ever not been?" Mila asked. "We have never been reckless."

"Err—" Ephraim began.

"Shut up." Mila cut him off. "We have never been reckless."

"The hard part's going to be when we get to the

road," Clay said. "You said that you crashed where it widened at both sides. I'm pretty certain I know where you mean. Where we come out will be about a quarter of a mile north of there, but you do realise the chances of us crossing unnoticed and unpursued are pretty slim."

"I think our best option will be to cross as quickly as possible," Mya said, "then deal with whatever's trailing us on the other side. If we try to put up a fight on the road, we'll only attract more, and it will get out of hand."

"Whatever you say. The most infected we've seen up until today is about half a dozen, so I'm happy to bow to your experience."

"Shush," Robyn said, looking back and putting her finger up to her mouth. They all came to a stop, and for a moment, the only thing they could hear was the rain as it pattered on the leaves, bushes and ground around them.

"What is it?" Emma asked.

"Listen."

It took them a moment, but the familiar sound of the infected drifted towards them through the rain. "Th-that sounds like an awful lot of them," Kat said.

"Look on the bright side," Ephraim replied. "At least we'll die doing what we love. Getting ripped apart and devoured by an undead army of creatures that belong in horror films rather than the real world."

"That's not funny," Kat replied, punching him on the arm.

"How far do you think it is to the road?" Mya asked.

Clay looked around for a moment. "I'd guess about another hundred metres or so."

"Okay," Mya replied, and they huddled together. "We'll carry on for another fifty or sixty metres then run like we've never run before. Wren, Robyn, I want you on the flanks. If any of those things see us, every second is going to be vital. If you can slow them down just a little, it could be the difference between us making it through this and not. She looked down at Muppet, then at Wren. "Make sure

Wolf sticks with you. The last thing we want is for him to go on the attack before he needs to." Wren nodded and crouched down, kissing the German shepherd on the head before straightening up once more.

"I feel sick to my fuckin' stomach," Jules said as the full weight of what they were doing finally struck her.

"We're going to be fine," Emma said, reaching out and taking Sammy's hand. She knew she couldn't promise that. She couldn't promise anything.

"Okay," Mya said, "come on."

They set off at a jog once more. She and Mike took the lead with Muppet in between them. Emma, Sammy and Mila were next. Robyn took the right flank. That was to the north, where the majority of the creatures would be heading from if they were going to run into any. Wren took the left. The others moved in a loose arrowhead formation. The tension mounted with each stride they took.

The rain, the horde of creatures somewhere to the south and the drumming of their feet were the only sounds they could hear as they continued. Then, as if a starter pistol had gone off in their heads, Mike and Mya burst into a sprint. Muppet followed, then the others did too, realising this was it. The next seconds would determine if they'd make it to the other side of the road in one piece.

*

Fuck she can run fast. Mike sprinted flat out, clenching both machetes in his fists, ready. The trees began to thin, and up ahead, he could see the road. *It's clear. It's clear.*

He, Mya and Muppet exploded through the tree line and at precisely the same moment, four creatures crossed their path, immediately diverting towards them.

Shit.

*

Mya could see the outline of at least another twenty infected as the first four ran towards her and Mike. She could tell the rest of the group was starting to slow. "Keep going. Just keep going," she ordered, smashing down her crowbar on one monster while Mike hacked two others. She shoulder barged the fourth, knocking it flat, giving herself a second's pause to get a clear look at the northern approach. *Forget twenty, there must be at least double that.*

She whirled like a spinning top, cracking the scrambling creature she had knocked to the ground on the side of the head. It collapsed instantly.

*

Despite all Emma's impulses telling her she should stay with her brother until the rest of the group had made it across to the other side, she placed her hand on Sammy's back and sped up.

Mila ran even faster. With Mike and Mya no longer taking the lead, she would need to confront any creatures that might be waiting for them on the other side of the road.

She threw a quick glance to her right to see the army of infected that was heading towards them. Five, six, seven strides and she was entering the woodland once more. Her eyes shot from side to side, taking everything in, scouring for movement.

She carried on running and could hear Emma and the others behind her as they followed. *Need to find a good place to put up a stand.*

*

Robyn stopped. It had not been her intention. She had fired her bow while running plenty of times before, but as she saw the number of creatures approaching from the north, she knew there was no room for error.

Breathe. Breathe. Breathe.

"Come on. We don't have time." Mya's warning lingered in the rain-filled air behind her, but nothing would shatter Robyn's concentration. She released her bowstring and began to run again. Throwing a glance in the direction of the beasts, a satisfied smile curled her lips as she saw her target collapse, causing a pile-up. More still stumbled and staggered behind, buying her people valuable seconds.

*

Wren looked down at Wolf as he remained glued to her side. There was a bend in the road twenty metres to her left, the direction she was protecting the group from, and thankfully, not a single RAM was in sight. It didn't matter, though; despite her best intentions of focusing on her side of the road and only hers, she looked right and saw the mass of fallen bodies that were starting to scramble once more. It would probably be less than a minute before they were in the throes of battle with them.

*

Mila was already waiting with her swords drawn when Mike, Mya, Robyn, Wren and the two canines appeared through the trees. Emma had readied the rest of the group. Their various weapons were at hand, but they all knew it would be Mila who would be their best defence until the others arrived. Even though Clay and Della seemed adept with their bows, by their own admission they hadn't encountered many undead, and there was a world of difference between taking time and picking off the odd one and what was about to happen.

Mike came to a stop and swivelled around, standing side by side with Mila. Mya joined her on the other side, unsheathing her hunting knife while gripping the crowbar tightly in her other hand.

The rain continued to fall. Tip-tap. Tip-tap. Tip-tap.

She looked down at Muppet, whose attention was firmly set on the trees ahead. She glanced over her shoulder as the others edged forward to join them. Sammy stood next to Wren. On the other side, Robyn, Clay and Della all had their bows nocked.

Tip-tap. Tip-tap. Tip-tap.

*

What the hell was I thinking about letting Sammy come out here? A hundred doubts flashed into Emma's head. She looked at the spear in her hand. *Spear? It's a fucking pointy stick.* George, Jack and James had made them back at the Skye Outward Bounds centre to finish off any infected who tried to force their way through the fences. *Why didn't I send her on the yacht with Daisy?*

Tip-tap. Tip-tap. Tip-tap.

*

Jules turned to look at her brothers. She could tell they were all experiencing the same fear and dread as she was. *We were meant to be starting a new fuckin' life. Not ending this one. Please, God. Let us get out of this alive.*

*

A growl began in the back of Wolf's throat, and Robyn glimpsed Wren taking hold of his collar, stopping him from charging forward to protect them. Nothing had materialised through the trees yet, but it would only be seconds. Robyn turned, throwing a look over her shoulder to make sure nothing was creeping up on them before moving her eyes to the front once more.

Movement. No target yet. It was a branch about thirty metres back. Just a small judder that an untrained eye might not even have noticed, but Robyn did.

Then, not more than a beat later, a head and body appeared.

Breathe. Breathe. Breathe.

She released her bowstring.

8

Mike, Mya and Mila all charged at the same time. Robyn's arrow passed them as they ran towards the first few creatures to emerge into the clearing. Feet pounded behind as Emma, Jules and the others stormed forward too.

Crack! Squelch! Crack! Mya was the first to reach them, stabbing one potential attacker in the side of the head while swinging her crowbar around with the other hand. Both beasts hit the ground at the same time, just as Muppet appeared out of nowhere and flew towards another of the infected.

*

Arrow. Arrow. Bolt. Bolt. It was clear to Mila that Clay and Della were well out of their comfort zones. Their shots disappeared into a shoulder and a neck, doing little to cause their targets to pause.

The bolts brought down two creatures in quick succession, causing two more to stumble. *Wren has taught Sammy well.*

Four beasts lunged for Mila at the same time. She sprang to her right, her swords almost windmilling, slicing through the heads of her first targets before she pivoted and spun once more, taking down the next two creatures. Four down in less than a couple of seconds. She skipped forward, stopping dead on the spot with her blades down by her side, ready for the next.

*

Mike kicked out hard, booting one of the monsters reaching towards him back a good couple of metres while, at the same time, sweeping his blades out horizontally. It had only been seconds since the first wave of creatures had advanced, but at least ten were already on the ground.

Arrow. Bolt. Bolt. Arrow. Arrow. Three more dead. One down. A row of spears blurred into Mike's field of vision as Emma, Jules, her brothers, Ephraim and Kat all ran ahead.

*

Emma caught sight of Wolf launching at one of the incoming creatures. His paws crashed against the beast's chest, knocking it to the ground. He went tumbling but was up again in a second, clamping his jaws around the monster's neck.

The clearing reverberated with the noise of growls, pounding feet and the sounds of battle. Emma took a breath, held her spear tightly in both hands and sprang forward. The point disappeared into the eye socket of her attacker. Its outstretched arms instantly dropped to its sides, and as she withdrew the spear, the beast fell to the ground.

*

For the longest time in Safe Haven, Sammy had been cushioned from many of the dangers that faced her siblings. Mike had often gone out on scavenging missions. Emma had, too, but to a lesser extent. Then there were the wars they had fought with raiders. They never shared their experiences or the terror they faced, so Sammy never really knew just how bad things were.

The world changed forever in that kitchen when her brother and Lucy were murdered. In those seconds, her childhood ended. In those seconds, she understood there was no more protection from the horrors that lay in wait beyond the boundaries of their settlement.

Now, on a journey to start again down in Glasgow, terror had found them once more. Part of her wanted to cry. Part of her wanted to run away and hide and just be the little girl she deserved to be. But she knew she couldn't. She cranked the self-cocking lever on her crossbow and placed another bolt in the flight groove.

She was matching Wren action for action, and her mentor kept giving her words of encouragement as the pair stood side by side.

"You're doing great, Sammy. You're doing great." They both brought their bows up at the same time and squeezed the triggers.

"I missed." It was the first time one of her bolts had gone astray, and there was a quiver in her voice. Her family and friends were literally fighting for their lives. They were directly in harm's way as the beasts continued their onslaught.

"Doesn't matter. We all miss sometimes," Wren reassured her, loading another bolt. Sammy did the same but noticed she was shaking now. She felt a hand on her shoulder and turned to see Wren looking down at her. "We all miss sometimes," she said again. "Take a breath and find your target." She withdrew her hand and raised her crossbow once more.

Take a breath … and find my target. A giant suddenly appeared through the trees and charged towards Jules, who noticeably took a step back long before it reached striking distance.

Sammy squeezed the trigger and watched for a second as the small missile flew. She heard the crack even from so far away. The beast dropped like a sack of bricks. Jules looked over her shoulder, her frightened eyes locking on Sammy. A grateful smile cracked on her face before she turned back to the battleground.

"Shot," Wren said as they both reloaded.

*

The grunts and growls of the fighters, the whistles of the arrows, and the cracks as shattered bone caved all continued for a few moments more until the only person still moving was Mila. The last RAM standing limped towards her. Its foot was twisted at a cringeworthy angle, and if it had been a living human being, screams of pain would have accompanied each step it took. But this monster could feel nothing as it slowly trudged forward. Its pallid skin and grey eyes did not inspire the horror they once had. Mila took a stride and whipped one of her blades around. The beast's head somersaulted through the air thudding loudly against a tree.

Seconds before, Mike and Mya had taken care of the two creatures the dogs had brought down and now calm blanketed the bloody battlefield. They all just stood there looking around at one another, struggling to believe they had got through another confrontation with no losses. As happy as they all were, there was another part of them that dreaded the journey still ahead.

*

"If any group of people can look after themselves out there, it's your granddaughters," Jenny said, squeezing George's hand.

The Safe Haven survivors had all been quiet since the departure of the rescue party, but George more than most. He couldn't blame Mike this time. He'd heard the words come straight out of Robyn's mouth. There was no coercing. Their current hosts had not helped the situation. Mutterings suggesting there was no way Clay, Della or any of the rescue party would ever return hung in the vast cavern, causing all of the newcomers to regret ever climbing onto the lorry and leaving the Outward Bounds Centre in the first place.

"You've heard what they're saying," George said eventually, nodding in the direction of Owen and his followers as they all talked among themselves.

"They don't know what they're talking about," Jenny replied confidently as she stroked Meg more for her own comfort than the adoring mongrel's.

"These people at the priory. Sounds like they've avoided them like the plague, and with good reason. And who knows how many infected are out there now? There could be hundreds … thousands."

"Yes, and Wren, Robyn and Mila have all had more experience than anybody in how to avoid them and how to deal with them."

"There's only so long someone's luck can hold out."

Jenny looked around at the other faces. Nearly all of them shared George's grim expression. "That's true," Jenny admitted, "but luck has nothing to do with it." Suddenly, some of her fight was coming back. "Robyn, Wren, Mila, Mike, and Mya are all seasoned and proficient fighters. They're fit, healthy, and strong. Wolf and Muppet are like two early warning systems if ever any of the infected are around. They're with Clay and Della, who probably know this forest as well as anyone. And although Emma, Jules and the rest of them might not possess the same weapons skills as the others, they're just as fierce when it comes to battle. We're the lucky ones, George." She looked around at the faces of her audience as they all now listened. "We're lucky to have them. It's not an accident that they've lasted as long as they have. It's not a quirk of fate. It's because they're bloody good at what they do. So just remember that the next time you're talking about luck."

The crackle of the fire was all that could be heard for a moment as her words hung in the air. George was about to say something when Owen and a small delegation of others joined them. He looked a little uncomfortable for a moment as the glow of the flames revealed a man being forced to make decisions he did not want to make to achieve his newly acquired status as leader-in-waiting.

"Look. There's no easy way to say this," he began.

"Go on," Jenny replied as all eyes and ears turned to their conversation.

"It's doubtful that Clay, Della and your friends are coming back."

"Now look here," George said, grabbing his stick and standing up. "You don't know—"

Owen put his hand up. "It might be a big cavern, but sound travels. If, by some miracle, they make it through the forest to the priory, the chances of them getting back from there are negligible. They'll be massively outnumbered, and we know for a fact that they've got guns. Your people," he began, adding an afterthought, "and our people won't make it back."

George collapsed down on the tree trunk as if the words from this relative stranger had confirmed all his fears.

"Well, you don't know our people," Jenny replied.

"Listen, whatever false bravado you can conjure, you should save it. We're not monsters, we're not going to turf you out with only a few hours until evening. But tomorrow morning, you'll have to go. We don't have the food or the resources to keep you here. Survival is a struggle already without having a bunch of strangers unfamiliar with the territory to babysit as well."

"Listen to me," Jenny said, standing up and walking over to him with Meg by her side. "Those people are our family, and we're not going anywhere without them."

"And you listen to me. In the absence of Clay and Della, I'm in charge here, and I say that tomorrow morning, you're packing up your stuff and getting out of here, with or without them." Owen turned to leave, and one by one, his people followed.

Jenny walked back to where she'd been sitting and flopped down. Nobody spoke, but Meg gently placed her head in Jenny's lap to comfort her. "They'll be back," Jenny said to herself more than anyone else. "They'll be back."

*

"I have never known an animal poop as much as this

goat," Talikha said, emptying another dustpan of manure over the side.

"I have to say, it's a strange choice of pet," Trish said. She'd come up on deck a few minutes earlier just to clear her head, and the two women had engaged in polite conversation before Daisy decided to wander across and relieve herself right next to them.

Talikha smiled, stroking the goat's head briefly. "She is not a pet. She is family. She belonged to Mike and Emma's gran. She lived through Fry, she lived through Troy, and now she has lived through Olsen."

"You're saying that as if we've seen the last of Olsen."

Talikha cast her eyes back out to sea. "We can hope."

"You don't really believe we have, do you?"

Talikha let out a long, deep breath. "I believe that whatever is destined to happen will happen."

"Uh-huh. I could get the prime minister up here to order you to tell me what you think."

Talikha burst out laughing, covering her mouth, and then turned to Trish. They were not exactly close, but there was something about Talikha that Trish really liked and vice versa. "Is that something a prime minister can actually do?"

Trish shrugged. "He used to tell me he could, so it was just easier to let him believe it than not. Y'know what men are like. Well, maybe not your man. Raj is like perfect. But normal men I'm talking about."

They stood in silence for a full minute before Talikha spoke again. "I believe some of us will cross paths with Olsen again."

"Some?"

Talikha returned her gaze to Trish. "Some will go looking for her."

"You're not serious."

"Do you believe she will stop in her endeavours?"

It was Trish's turn to think for a moment now. "I met her once, y'know."

"Oh?"

"Yeah. A more tightly packed bundle of vileness and hate you would struggle to imagine. She used people's fears and insecurities like fuel. She thrived on conflict and craved power like no one I'd ever come across."

"You did not stay in touch then?"

Trish chuckled. "I loathed her from the moment I met her, and I'm sure the feeling was mutual. But in answer to your question, no. I don't think she'll stop, but I would think Glasgow would be a long, long way down her list of priorities. It would require a massive concerted effort and a lot of manpower and resources to head in there, and while she's taking over the country one village at a time, I think she'd struggle."

"So, you think this is just buying us time?"

Trish shrugged. "A lot can happen. When we made our escape north, Olsen wasn't even on our radar. A day's a long time. A week's a long time. A year's a long time. Who knows what's going to happen, but for all our sakes, I hope none of our people decide to go looking for her. That would be inviting trouble."

"Mike is not someone who forgives."

"Mike's an impressive young man. But he can't go up against an army by himself. He needs to look after his family now. We've suffered a big defeat, and we need to consolidate. We've been given another chance to start again, and we need to take it. If Olsen is waiting for us somewhere down the line, then hopefully we'll be in a much stronger position than we are now to deal with her, but like I said, a lot can happen."

"Mehehehh!" Daisy exclaimed grumpily, and they both looked down to see Humphrey had wandered across to join them. He was sniffing around Daisy but backed off as she stamped her foot. His wide googly eyes looked frightened for a moment, and he went to stand by the side of Talikha, peeking out from behind her legs.

The two women laughed. "Always as brave as a lion.

I have seen him protect us from the infected, but where this goat is concerned, he is like a little mouse."

"I suppose we've all got our own fears."

Talikha leaned over and tussled the Labrador retriever's fur. "Good boy. Good boy," she repeated reassuringly, and Humphrey sauntered away with his tail wagging.

The two women looked out over the waves once more. "I wonder how Emma and the others are all getting on. I would think they'd be approaching Glasgow by now, at least."

"Yeah. Another hour and they'll probably be sitting with their feet up, drinking Scotch and deciding who's going to sleep where."

"Probably."

*

"Granted, I'm no expert, but that doesn't look like any fuckin' priory I've ever heard of," Jules said as the others just stared down the hillside. They were at the tree line of the forest, and a lush green bank sloped down to a river with an old wooden bridge leading to the other side. Beyond it was what looked more like a compound than a priory. The grand building stood in the centre, but a vast chain link fence topped with razor wire encircled it. There was a road on the far side, which disappeared into more woodland, and in the grounds were what appeared to be dozens of vegetable patches, which continued on the other side of the fences.

"They've got vehicles," Mya said distantly, panning her binoculars around as far as she could before the line of sight was blocked by the black walls of the magnificent-looking building. "Army vehicles."

"Army?" Jules asked. "You're saying there are soldiers down there?"

Mya didn't answer for a moment. Instead, she angled the binoculars back to the fields where dozens of men laboured. Some wore normal civilian attire, others military clothing, others prison-issue garments, while a few more had black habits on. She zeroed in on one of the men in uniform. Although she couldn't make him out too clearly, there was something about his appearance and overall demeanour that told her he was not the original owner of the clothes. "Somehow, I don't think so."

"But the vehicles."

Mya shrugged. "Maybe they thought they'd found somewhere safe to hole up for a while. I mean a priory full of monks who grow their own veg. That should be pretty safe, right?"

"What, and then when their guard was down…."

"That would be my guess."

"You can't be sure of that," Kat said. "I mean anything could have happened. There might be soldiers down there. Maybe they—"

"Hughes told us all sorts of stories about the conscripts," Mike began. "There were a lot of career criminals who exploited their positions in the conscripted forces to syphon off vehicles, munitions, food and supplies. If it was prisoners who descended on this place and wiped out the monks who used to live here, it's not a stretch to think they had pals who were looking for a place to set up off the beaten track."

Mya thought back to the empty trucks they had risked their lives to get to. In a time when everything hinged on mankind sticking together in order to survive, so many had just looked after themselves, exploiting every weakness to profit while others went hungry. "I suppose that's another possibility."

"Well, it's not like we're going to do a *Panorama* special on them, is it? They're not going to let us go down there and do interviews, so who they are and how they ended up here doesn't really matter. What matters is that they've got Keely and Rupert, and we need to get them back," Emma said.

"You make a good point."

"That place is like a fortress," Della blurted, her wide eyes barely able to mask the terror she was feeling.

"I don't mean to be a negative Nelly," Ephraim announced, "but even without binoculars, I can see that there is no way we're going to make it within a hundred metres of that place without dying horrible, horrible deaths."

"Why do you think that's being negative?" Robyn asked. "Arsehole."

"Look. There isn't a person here who questions your bravery, will and determination. You, Wren and Mila are all forces of nature. But there has to come a point where you measure all of that against reason. Nothing short of a tank is getting through that fence and nothing short of an army is taking out ... well ... that army down there. They've probably got guns and enough ammo to kill us a hundred times over, and as much as I'm grateful to your grandad for furnishing me with this splendid spear"—he lifted it up and nodded towards the homemade weapon—"it's not really going to be much of a defence against someone with an assault rifle."

"So, what are you saying?"

"I'm saying as horrible and ghastly as it is and it feels to leave two innocent people down there, we have to face facts. There are people back at the cavern who need—"

"Nothing's changed," Robyn replied. "I didn't think this was going to be easy and guess what, I was right. I'm not leaving them down there."

Ephraim pushed down his impulse to be sarcastic and demeaning to her and took a breath. "If we go down there, we're going to die. I'm sorry to be so blunt, but it's true."

"Please listen, Robyn," Kat said. "We won't be able to get anywhere near that place, and if we try, it's all over for us, for your grandad, for Jenny, for everyone."

Wren had remained quiet by Robyn's side, and even though she knew Ephraim and Kat were talking sense, she wanted to remain loyal to her sister.

Ephraim took over once more, picking up on the younger sibling's doubts. "And I don't wish to sound cruel, but these aren't RAMs we're talking about. What do you think will happen when they get their hands on Wolf or Muppet?"

A shivering breath left Wren's lips, and for a second, Mya brought her binoculars down and glared at Ephraim before continuing her vigil. "Bobbi," Wren whispered, placing a hand on her sister's shoulder.

"You don't know what it was like," Robyn replied, bursting into tears. Wren tried to place her arm around her, but she pulled away. "Waiting in that room," she continued, "day after day wondering if it would be my last breakfast, my last dinner, wondering if they'd come for Mila or the others who were trapped there with us." More tears flowed down her cheeks.

"Bobbi, it's—"

"We can't leave them there. We can't. Nobody deserves that; nobody deserves to die like that." She wiped her face. "Go back. Go back with the others. Go back to Grandad. He doesn't need to lose both of us."

"Listen to what you're saying, Robyn," Ephraim pleaded. "You've just said he doesn't need to lose both of you. You're admitting this is a suicide mission. I think you need to take a breath and think about this."

"We cannot leave them down there." It was Mila who spoke now.

"Oh, good grief. Will someone please talk some sense into these girls?" Ephraim replied. "Emma. You're our leader. Please, do something. Say something. Do you want Sammy's last memory to be a living nightmare?"

Emma looked at her little sister, who was clearly on the verge of tears too, and then up at her brother, who was a few metres away with Mya. He was looking through the binoculars now, and Emma's eyes lingered on him for a few seconds before he passed them back to the other woman.

Jesus. They're still set on heading down there.

"We came out here to rescue these people, but there are limits to what we can do," she said. "Heading into a situation that will save no one but get us killed isn't heroic. It's irresponsible and just plain suicidal." She looked across to her brother again. "Mike. Are you going to back me up on this?"

The others, including Robyn and Mila, suddenly looked across to Mya and Mike as they continued to survey the priory. "Hmm?" Mike asked, not having listened to a word of the conversation.

"I said are you going to back me up on this?"

"Back you up on what?"

"Jesus, Mike. Haven't you been listening to a word that's been said?"

"Why? What did I miss?"

Emma closed her eyes and shook her head.

"Why don't you put your binoculars down for a minute and come over here?" Jules said, sharing Emma's frustration.

Mya answered for him. "We've found our in."

Nobody understood what she was saying, so Jules pressed for clarity. "What the fuck are yous talking about? Our fuckin' in where?"

Mya lowered her binoculars and looked across at her. "The priory."

"Well, that's a relief. I thought you were just wasting your time over there. I'm guessing you haven't been listening to a word we've been saying either."

"Did you hear what she said?" Mike asked.

"Yeah. And did you hear what we've been talking about?"

Mike and Mya looked at each other then walked across to join the others. Muppet had been glued to Mya's side the whole time she was surveying the priory, but now he lay down next to Wolf as the others talked.

"You said there's an in?" Robyn asked, causing the

hearts of everyone else to sink.

"We've seen four men disappear down the embankment on the other side and not come back up. Then we saw another two with rods make their way from further up the river and just disappear."

"That's it?" Jules asked. "You lost sight of half a dozen of them, and that's proof you've found a way in."

"It might be a storm drain; it might be a secret tunnel. These old places will have all sorts."

"Okay, for argument's sake, let's say you've found a way in. How does that change the fact that there are loads more of them and they're probably armed to the teeth while we're carrying fuckin' twigs to defend ourselves?"

"It would give us the element of surprise."

"Oh, well, the element of surprise. Why was I worried? We'll give them all a hell of a jump, and they'll just put their hands up and hand Keely and Rupert over. Brilliant plan."

"I thought so."

"Please tell me you're joking. Please tell me you're not seriously considering this."

Mya placed the binoculars in her rucksack. "At the very least, it's worth going down there and taking a look."

"Course it is. It's not like we'd be conspicuous or anything, is it? All seventeen of us can just go on a merry jaunt down the side of the hill. It'll be like something out of a fuckin' Enid Blyton book. Shame we don't have cucumber sandwiches and lashings of ginger beer."

"Okay, I'm confused. So, are you saying you like the idea or not?"

Jules shot an icy stare towards Mya before turning to Mike. "Tell me the pair of yous aren't serious about this."

Mike glanced towards Jules then at his sister before his eyes fixed on Robyn and Mila. "We're going to have to wait until nightfall."

"I'm sorry," Andy said, looking at Mike then Robyn and Mila. "But I'm not letting my sister and my brothers go down there." Everyone was taken aback. Andy had never spoken on behalf of his family, especially his sister. "We'll stay up here until morning for you. If you're not back by then, we'll head back to the others. We'll try to get them to Glasgow somehow, but…." He was clearly emotional as he spoke.

"But you think we will all die," Mila said, finishing his thought.

"I don't want to sound like a twat or a coward. But I love my family, and I'm really sorry about your friends," he said, looking at Clay and Della. "But for all we know, they might be already dead, and heading in there is probably going to get all of us dead." He shook his head. "I'm sorry. I won't do it.

"I came here with every intention of fighting alongside you. I don't know quite what I expected, but it wasn't this."

"Jesus, Mike," Jules said. "You've got me agreeing with my brother. Don't you see how dangerous this is?"

Mike ignored her question and turned to the others. "This isn't exactly what any of us had in mind when we set off, but I totally get it if you don't want to head down there. Nobody's going to think any less of you. Everybody here has earned a right of refusal for this one. Everybody here fought tooth and nail for Safe Haven. They've fought tooth and nail for everything. It's probably wise that a few people stay back just in case."

"Mike," Emma said, seeing the frightened expression on Sammy's face. "Can I have a word?" Without waiting for a response, she grabbed hold of his arm and marched him out of earshot of the others. "What the hell do you think you're doing?"

"What do you mean?"

"You've got a responsibility. We've got a responsibility to our little sister. This is a suicide mission. You know damn well it is."

"All I know is no amount of talking is going to

persuade Robyn or Mila not to go down there, and I won't let them go alone."

"By the sound of it, Mya's pretty hellbent on killing herself too, so you won't have to." It was only as the words left her lips that she realised how callous they were, and her head dropped. "I didn't mean it like that. I know she's trying to do the right thing. I know Robyn and Mila are as well, but we seriously need to think about this."

"There's nothing to think about for me, Em. When I was in Glasgow, I'd have been dead a dozen times over if it wasn't for them. If we leave here without them, the chances are we won't make it to our new life. Would I prefer not to be even talking about this? Damn right. But here we are."

"So, that's it. After all the discussions and promises about coming to joint decisions, about including Sammy in our choices, you're just throwing it all out of the window?"

"You came out here with me. You said it was the right thing."

"Yeah, but … but I didn't expect it to be like bloody Colditz down there."

"Em. What is this? I don't understand."

A glint of sadness sparkled in Emma's eye. "I'm scared, Mike."

"You're scared? This fucking petrifies me," he said, letting out a nervous laugh. "When Robyn and Mila first told me the story of how they were kept in their rooms just waiting to be butchered, it gave me nightmares for a week. I still dream about it now and again, and trust me, there's lots of competition in my head for the most gruesome nightmare award."

Emma couldn't help but let out a small laugh. "So why not head back to the cavern? Why not pick Sammy up, and all three of us will run as fast as we can back to Jenny and the others and get the hell out of here? Why would you put yourself through that?"

"Because it's the right thing to do. And the second we stop doing the right thing because it scares us is the second we stop being who we are."

Emma stared at him for a few more seconds. "I hate you. Just in case you were wondering."

"Nah. I pretty much figured that out a long time ago."

"Dick."

"Love you, Em."

"Dick," she repeated before smiling weakly. "Love you too. This is mental. This is totally mental."

"You'll be safe with Jules and her brothers. Maybe climb into the trees. That way, you'll avoid any infected and hopefully any of those bastards down there if they're out and about."

"Screw that. I'm coming with you."

It was Mike's turn to look surprised. "What about Sammy?"

Emma shrugged. "Like you said, without Robyn, Wren and Mila, without proper weapons, we're not going to make it to Glasgow anyway."

Mike thought for a moment. "Maybe we can convince her to stay here with Jules."

"Good luck with that. The problem is we opened the door to all this. We made her part of the decision-making process."

"You're right. Sammy," he called over to his younger sister. When she joined them, it was clear to see the troubled look still etched on her face.

"Listen, Sammy," Emma began. "Mike and I have been talking, and we don't really like the idea of you going down there."

The younger girl looked at Emma and then Mike. "Are you going down there? If you're both going down there, then so am I. I'm not going to be left alone."

"Well, Jules and her brothers are staying. You wouldn't be alone."

"If you're both going, then I'm going," she said, turning and marching across to join Wren without allowing either of them to reply.

"Dammit," Emma hissed.

"Are you sure I can't convince you to stay here with her?" Mike asked.

"How many times do we have to go through this?"

"We're not just talking about being killed, Em. We're talking about—"

"Thanks, I'm not an idiot. I know what we're talking about." Mike looked back to the others and sighed. "What?"

"I'm trying hard to do the right thing, only I'm not sure what the right thing is here."

"You know what the right thing is."

"I do?"

"This happened to Keely and Rupert because of us. There's no way Robyn or Mila are going to let this go, and after everything they've done, there's no way we can let them go in there by themselves. So, it's pretty obvious what we have to do, isn't it? We'll just have to do our best to make sure one of us stays with Sammy at all times, and if things start getting hairy, then we rethink."

"Things are already hairy."

"You know what I mean."

Mike looked over to his little sister. "She is pretty amazing with that crossbow."

"She's pretty amazing in a lot of ways."

"Yeah."

"There are no good options here, Bruv. So, we just have to take the one that we can manage the best, which means having her glued to us."

Mike looked up towards the sky. It was grey, getting darker by the second, and nightfall would not be far away. The rain was steady, but from their position under the canopy, they were well shielded from the worst of it. "For all we know, they might already be dead."

"Yeah. But we won't know a thing until we're down there, will we?"

9

Keely had tried to be strong, but it was hard with Rupert sobbing away by her side. The stories about this place, about these people, had assumed an almost mythical status, and with time the true level of horror that Dana had expressed about the priory was forgotten, but now it all came flooding back.

They were by themselves for the moment, and that was something to be relished at least. The pair occupied two large dog crates, far bigger than the one that her beloved golden retriever had when she was growing up. These were probably for a Great Dane or something similar. But a human could not fully stand up in one nor lie down without bending their legs significantly. They were in a corner of a sprawling kitchen, and several people had come and gone since their arrival.

It probably hadn't been that long, but the fear stretched every second out to an eternity.

"It's okay. It's okay, Rupert," Keely said, squeezing

her fingers through one of the small gaps in order to reach out to his cage in the hope that he would reciprocate and they could at least have some physical contact, even if only a fingertip or two. But it was no good. His head was bowed, and she could see his salty tears glisten in the light of the fire from the range that someone had relit not five minutes before. They had left the door open as the kindling and logs caught, and that gave the two prisoners some light, at least as the dismal day outside finally began to wane.

"None of this is okay," Rupert eventually replied. They had lived together on and off for five years before the fall of mankind. Keely loved him in a fashion, but it wasn't the burning and passionate love she had dreamt of finding as a teenager. They had split up a number of times only to drift back together weeks or sometimes months later.

It was hard. Their social circle consisted of the same group of outdoorsy adventurer types, and after a fun day kayaking or rock climbing followed by a few more bevvies than either of them should have partaken in, it seemed only polite to keep each other warm in the bed of whichever guesthouse the party was booked into.

There was a lot that irritated Keely about Rupert though. His unwillingness to take responsibility for his own actions, his self-pitying nature, his constant whining, but this was something else. There was a part of her that had hoped he'd man up in a situation like this and maybe even want to protect her, but instead, he had been crying pathetically ever since they'd been dumped in the cages. For all his adventuring and hard physical pursuits, mentally he was nothing more than a scared little boy, and there were certain circumstances in which Keely might have found that vulnerability endearing, but all she wanted to do now was shake him, despite her best attempts to try to make him feel better.

"Please don't cry." She stopped reaching towards him and instead curled her fingers, grasping the cold metal of the crisscrossed bars.

"We should never have gone out there. This is all Clay's fault. He should be here, not us," he replied before a shuddering breath left the back of his throat.

"There were people in trouble. It was only right—"

"Owen would never have forced us to go out there. Owen wouldn't have asked us to do a final sweep of the area to make sure there weren't any lurkers before we went back to the cavern. Owen wouldn't have—"

"Owen would never do anything," she snapped, shutting him up. "You and Owen are like peas in a pod, never prepared to put yourselves out, never prepared to organise or work, but always there to pick apart what others try to do." She regretted the words as soon as they came out of her mouth. It was something she'd wanted to say during their last big argument, and this was hardly the time or the place, but she hoped a reality check might give him the jump start he needed to at least stop being pathetic.

"You're such a bitch. These might be our last few minutes together, and that's what comes out of your mouth. If it wasn't for your beloved Clay, none of this would have happened in the first place."

They both turned away from each other like sulking infants. Good-humoured calls and shouts came from somewhere else in the massive building, but once they died down, the only sound to be heard was the crackle and hiss of the fire as even Rupert's crying quietened for a few moments.

Suddenly, the heavy wooden door to the kitchen opened and in marched a grizzled-looking figure, about six feet four inches tall. He wore khaki trousers and a black T-shirt. Tattoos painted his lower arms, and a scruffy salt and pepper beard hid part of a scar on his face. Behind him stood four others, two men and two women. The women wore military garb while the two men were dressed ironically in habits. It was clear from their demeanour that they were not the original owners of the garments. They did all carry rifles, however, and they seemed far more at home with and used to these.

The tall man looked from cage to cage. "Bring them both," he said, turning and heading back out of the kitchen.

Keely locked eyes with one of the women who cast a wicked smile towards her. Two of her front teeth were missing, and the rest were nicotine stained. "No. NOOO!" Keely screamed as the padlock was unfastened. The screech of metal as the cage door opened told her that her greatest fear was about to come true. "NOOO! PL-EA-SEE." The pained cry did nothing to deter the actions of the four guards. Instead, they began to snigger as the two men walked across to Rupert's cage and unlocked it. He did not scream; instead, the sobbing, which had been more or less continuous since their arrival, became heavier.

I could run. I could run and try to find a way out of here. It was Keely's initial thought as the freedom of the large kitchen and then the grand corridors gave her a taste of what might lurk behind one of the doors they passed. The two women held her upper arms in a vice-like grip. *They're strong, but I'm stronger. I could shake myself free and run. If they got a couple of shots off before I lost them, then at least I wouldn't have to face the horror that's ahead.* They walked along, the occasional open door letting in enough of the dying light to see where they were going. In the prolonged spaces with no natural light, candles illuminated the path. *I could do it. I could do it. I could—* then reality suddenly hit her as Rupert's pathetic cries echoed. *I can't leave him.*

She slumped into a steady rhythm, almost being dragged along until, finally, they reached a formidable arched oaken door. THE GUV was scratched into the wood, painted over in red. *Guv—slang for sir or short for governor, as in the governor of a prison. Very witty.*

One of the women pushed the door open to reveal the giant who had briefly appeared in the kitchen sitting behind a desk that looked like it might have taken a thousand hours to craft. On it rested his feet and an ashtray. The room was thick with blue smoke and a half-empty packet of cigarettes sat next to it.

It had been the longest time since Keely had seen cigarettes. It was a point of personal shame for someone who took such pride in her fitness that she occasionally partook in a sneaky ciggy on a night out, and as she looked at them now, she longed to suck in that evil blue smoke that was so bad for her just one last time.

She was pushed down into a waiting chair on the other side of the desk, and Rupert was forced into one next to her. He let out a small yelp as his coccyx crashed against the hard wood, and the guards laughed again. "What are you going to do with us?" he cried, staring across at the big man on the other side of the desk.

"Do you still need us, Beano?"

The tall figure raised his head towards the woman who had spoken. "Wait outside," and without hesitation, the four of them disappeared.

He's unarmed. We could overpower him, climb out of the window and run. Keely's thoughts of escape dissipated once again as another sob left Rupert's mouth. He would be both unwilling and unable to help her, and there was something about this man that oozed menace. He didn't appear to be armed, but he looked like someone who could snap a neck just as quickly as his fingers.

"What do you want with us?" Rupert asked weakly.

Beano broke his gaze with Keely and instead stared at the other figure sitting across from him. For a while, he didn't talk; he just looked, making Rupert wish he hadn't spoken. Then finally, he climbed to his feet and walked over to another door. He opened it up and went inside, disappearing for just seconds before returning to his desk with their two bows and placing them down.

What is this? Is he letting us go? What the hell's going on?

Beano took a step back and folded his arms. "We found you today with these."

"They're our bows," Keely said, stating the obvious.

"They're your bows," Beano replied, nodding. "A

few months ago, we found two drifters. At least, that's what they said they were. We had no reason to believe otherwise, but somehow, their story didn't ring true to me. One of them got away, and we searched and searched and searched, but we couldn't find her." He headed back across to the cupboard and retrieved two more identical bows. "Look familiar?" he asked.

Keely immediately lowered her head. If he'd placed one of their quivers on the desk along with the bow, she'd have nocked an arrow and taken her chances, but she knew what this was. He wanted information, and whatever horrific fate awaited them once they left this room, there was something about this man that told her it was nothing compared to what he'd do to get the truth.

*

"How are you doing?" Vicky asked as she joined Shaw in the small galley.

"People keep asking me that," he replied, smiling as politely as he could.

"I think it's fair enough given the circumstances, don't you?"

"I suppose," he admitted.

"And?"

"I'm okay … I will be okay, at least."

"I get it. I really do, probably better than a lot of people. When we were in Loch Uig, and then when we escaped to that forest, people were always looking to me, asking me what next, what next, what next. What next? How the fuck should I know what was next? Just getting out of Loch Uig was as far as my plan took me. How the hell was I supposed to know what we would do from there?" Shaw nodded and smiled appreciatively. "It didn't matter though. They still never fucking shut up."

"They were lucky to have you."

"Nah. I was lucky to have them, but it was hard to appreciate that at the time. There wasn't a day that went by when I didn't wish I could have just got the hell out of there.

I mean not just that situation but the responsibility too. I'd be lying to you if I said I didn't think about ending it more than once, and if I'd seen an opportunity where I could have just turned my back and walked away, I'd have taken it."

"I doubt that. You're made of tough stuff."

"And you're made of the toughest."

"I think there are plenty who'd disagree with you."

"If anybody disagrees, fuck them. They can come and speak to me. You've got our people through the worst times, and if anyone deserved to have a bit of a freakout when their best friend died, it's you."

"Your friends died too."

Vicky suddenly looked sad. It was true. She'd lost those closest to her, but for the time being, she wasn't thinking about it. She would grieve later. She'd grieve later for all those they'd lost, but her mission at the moment was to help get everyone down to Glasgow safely.

"Yeah. And down the line, I don't know how I'm going to deal with that, but right now, I just want to get everybody to where we're going."

"I'm glad you're here with me. We have no idea what we're going to face when we get down there. I hope everything goes as smoothly as we planned, but knowing you're here makes me breathe a little easier."

"That's nice of you to say. I watched you and Barnes for the longest time. I can see Denise doing the same."

"Is she like your protege or something?"

Vicky laughed. "Not quite. But she's got potential. Finlay and Rory are okay too, but she's got a bit more of a spark. I'm glad we've got the three of them here. Denise is a quick learner, and none of them shirk responsibility. If something happens when we get down to Glasgow, they're good people to hunker down with."

"Where are they now?"

"Where do you think? Beck's like a one-man cabaret show. They're listening to him with all the old folks."

"I'm not convinced some of those people will be

happy being called old folk."

"You know what I mean. Ruth and Richard are down there with them too. They really haven't been themselves since we left Safe Haven."

"A lot of people haven't been themselves. I hope things will get better when we settle."

"We can hope, I suppose."

Shaw smiled. "Yeah. Listen, I'm not going to get into it now 'cause it won't be long before it's dark, and some people will be thinking about getting some rest. But I think we need to come up with a contingency plan for tomorrow if Mike and the others aren't there to meet us at the dock."

"Yeah. I've been thinking about that too. You want to talk about it over breakfast?"

"Yeah. I'd like that."

Vicky smiled. "Me too."

*

Liz hadn't spoken much since they'd arrived at the cavern. She'd checked in with George to see if he needed more painkillers, but the rest of the time, she had sat on the outskirts of the semicircle and just listened.

When Owen had made his announcement, she had probably been the least surprised of everyone. She had been in the bunker with Beck and Trish and had learnt to spot treachery in a mile of mist. It was usually born from fear or stupidity or both, and Owen and his cronies had those attributes in spades. *They'd have made outstanding politicians.*

She finally broke the silent vigil she'd been keeping next to the three young women who had been her nurses first in the Outward Bounds Centre then in Safe Haven. Other than Trish, they were the closest thing she had to friends. She'd never really had time for friends before the outbreak or during it, but it gave her some modicum of comfort to have familiar faces surrounding her.

After Owen's little speech, however, she felt a need to step up. Jenny was a brilliant organiser, somebody who could help keep all the cogs running, somebody people listened to and respected, but she wasn't a strategist. Actually, coming up with a plan, especially one to save them, was not something she felt comfortable with, and despite her bravado, Liz could see it on her firelit face and hear it in her voice.

She wandered over and perched down beside her. "They're going to be back."

"Hmm?" Jenny said.

"Mya and the others, they'll be back."

"Yes. Yes, of course, they will."

"I mean it. Did you know Mya was trapped in Paris by herself at the beginning of the outbreak? She made it all the way to the Channel and fended off dozens of those things single-handedly. Something like this will be a walk in the park for her. And the fact that she's got Mike and the others along for the ride makes me feel sorry for those mad monks or whatever they are."

"Well, yes, absolutely. That's what I've been saying," Jenny replied, looking at George.

"The thing is, though," Liz went on. "She'll never overplay her hand. She won't take unnecessary risks. She'll wait for the right time to strike, so it really wouldn't surprise me if they're not back by first light, and unfortunately, that's going to be a little too late for us because Captain Cowardice over there wants us out of his hair."

"Do you think I should talk to him?" Jenny asked. "Do you think I should tell him that they might not be back by morning but they will be back?"

Liz looked down at Meg, who still had her head resting on Jenny's knee. "That really won't do any good. He's drunk on the attention he's getting at the moment, and any confrontation might just empower him to throw us out sooner."

"Okay. So what are you suggesting then?"

"Maybe we start talking to some of the others. He's got his fawning gang following him around, but you can tell there are some who think he's as odious as we do."

"You think we should try to start an uprising?" Jenny asked, a little shocked.

"Oh, good grief, no. That would end in disaster. The ones who weren't with him would certainly bond with him if they thought we were trying to act as usurpers."

"Okay, so what then?"

"Maybe we try to figure out if there's somewhere around here that we can go that doesn't leave us out in the open. Maybe there's another cave or an old abandoned farmhouse or something. Let's face it, none of us are fighters in the same way that the others are. We might be able to fend off a small handful of these things, but if we faced what we did before arriving here, we'd be done for."

Jenny leaned back, stroking Meg's head with a little more force as she relived the lowlights from the battle they'd endured before arriving at the cavern. "And what then?"

"Well, we wait. We hope that whoever we got the information from will tell Mya and the others where we went and they'll come and find us."

Jenny looked around the cavern. It was true what Liz had said. There were some who shot Owen and his gang death stares as they huddled together. "I suppose it's worth a try, but…." She didn't want to carry on. She didn't want to carry on with the question that no doubt was on the lips of everyone who had heard Liz speak.

"But what?"

"But what if they don't come back?" she whispered.

It was Liz's turn to lean back a little now. She crossed her legs and clasped her hands around her knee as she looked into the flames. "Beck, Trish, Shaw and the others are all expecting us down in Glasgow. They're depending on us, and we have an obligation to try to get to them."

"What, by ourselves?"

"If that's what it comes down to, yes. By ourselves."

10

Daylight was fading fast, aided by the thick cloud cover. While they'd been keeping a vigil of the priory, about a dozen infected had appeared from the other side of the forest, presumably following the tower of smoke but honing in on the grand building once it came into view. Sentries on the other side of the compound had taken them out with spears as they approached the fences, but riflemen and women stood with their weapons raised and ready if any broke through.

In the dark, the smoke would not be visible, and although none of them were in sight of the pyre, it was debatable whether the fire would burn much longer, given the amount of rainfall.

"I think this is the longest I've ever seen you sit still in one place," Wren said, planting herself on the rock next to her sister." Wolf pushed in between their legs, placing his chin first in Wren's lap then Robyn's.

"Every second we're up here is one more second they're closer to ending up in a stew or as sausages or as … I don't know, but I hate this waiting."

Wren glanced across to Mike and Mya, who had been taking it in turns with the binoculars ever since they'd first discovered their prospective way into the property. "We can't just go down there in broad daylight, Bobbi. We'd get picked off one by one."

"I know, but … this waiting is killing me."

"Showing up. Going down there. Getting in there. Facing those bastards is going to have to be enough. We have no way of telling if Rupert and Keely are still alive. They might have killed them as soon as they arrived, for all we know. But us being here, now. That's going to have to count. Being prepared to fight, prepared to act, that's the best we have to give."

Robyn nodded slowly. Her tortured gaze revealed where she really was, and it pained Wren to see it. She wasn't sitting on the rock beside her; she was trapped back in that little room waiting to die, waiting to suffer unimaginable horror, the ultimate desecration of her flesh. It turned Wren's stomach just thinking about it.

"Wren is right," Mila announced, and both sisters jumped, turning behind them to look at their German friend. "Yes, yes, I know. I should wear bells or wind chimes or squeaky clown shoes or something. But my point remains. She is right. If they are still alive, we do them no service by getting ourselves killed. When night comes, we will go down there. We will fight until we have won or until we are dead. Rupert and Keely have one hope, and that hope is us."

"And what if that's no hope in hell?" Robyn asked.

"Then, at least, they will not end up there alone."

*

This is unreal. This can't be happening. Keely's eyes kept drifting to the bows longingly. She was one of the better archers in the group. *Hell, I'm the best.* It didn't matter though. Nothing mattered at that moment because it was as clear as day what was happening and what would happen. Yes, she was with Rupert, and if truth be told, she didn't think that much of him right now, but she hoped he would never betray their friends the way he was being pushed to.

"I'll ask you again, how many of you are there and where do you stay?"

"You're crazy," Keely said, finally breaking the silence. "Just because you found two people with bows a few months back and we've got bows ourselves, you think it's related. I hate to tell you this, but the world turned to shit, and people armed themselves and supplied themselves the best they could. We've come across dozens of people armed with bows and all sorts since we've been on the road."

"On the road?" Beano asked, narrowing his eyes and then turning to Rupert, who had remained silent other than the odd shivering breath leaving his lips.

"Yeah. We started off in Carlisle when everything happened, and we've been working our way north ever since."

Beano smiled. "Just the two of you?"

"Yeah."

"On the road heading north?"

"That's right."

Beano nodded. "I see. And what have you been eating, thin air? Where have you been sleeping, the fucking clouds?"

"What do you mean?"

"When my people found you, they said all you had on you were these bows and quivers. You'd think if you'd been on the road for so long, you might have had a rucksack or a sleeping bag or something to eat, at least."

"W-we were out hunting. We'd set up camp, and we were looking for food."

"I see. And all that gunfire that we heard. What was all that then, firecrackers?"

"I-I don't know. I don't know what that was." She gestured to the bows on the desk. "It obviously wasn't us, was it?"

"You," he said, turning to Rupert, who was hunched over a little in his chair, staring down at the floor, rocking back and forth. "I've got a built-in bullshitometer, and it's going fucking crazy at the moment. Your girlfriend here hasn't done either one of you any favours with what she's told me. You've got a chance to put it right. If you're honest with me – and trust me, I'll know if you're being honest with me – I'll let the pair of you go."

"I was telling you the truth," Keely insisted. *Please don't fall for this, Rupert. Please.*

The sad and pathetic breaths and whimpers stopped for a moment as Rupert looked up towards their captor. It had gotten noticeably darker outside since they had entered the office, and the other man lit a lantern, placing it on one side of the desk. He fixed Rupert with his stare, raising his eyebrows expectantly as if he was waiting for the truth to be told. Rupert glanced towards Keely, whose eyes were pleading with him to stay silent, and then he turned back to Beano. *There's no way out of this. Maybe if I do tell him, he'll go easy on us. If I don't, he'll kill us for sure, and it won't be quick.* The seconds of hesitation dragged on, and Beano spoke again.

"Listen to me. This place is finely balanced. Yes, I'm in charge, but I'm only in charge as long as I keep people fed and safe. Nothing is free these days. You two came in here, and I can absofuckinglutely guarantee you that word has gotten out that you were carrying exactly the same bows as the people we found a few months ago. We asked them the same questions that I'm asking you now, and they told us zip, but I could tell they were lying. Lies aren't something I can trade in, but the truth. Truth is as good as gold."

Rupert continued to stare. "Wh-what do you mean?"

"I mean that if you tell me what I'm asking you, then I've got something tangible. I've got the truth. In return, I'll let you and your little bit of skirt here be on your merry way. I can tell my people we made a trade. But if I get nothing, then all I've got is you, isn't it?"

"Y-you'll let us go?"

Oh, Jesus, no, Rupert. You idiot. Keely's head dropped. By just uttering this question, it was all over. It was an admission that everything she'd said had been a lie. It was an admission that there were others. It was an admission that Rupert was stupid enough and cowardly enough to trust this man with a joker tattoo on one arm and a fire-breathing dragon on the other.

"I give you my word. If you're straight with me. If you tell us what I want to know, I'll let you both walk."

The room fell silent, and as much as she tried not to, all Keely could think about were her friends back in the cavern. They had shared every loss and every victory like family over the last few months. They had got each other through the worst of times, the end times, and they were still standing to tell the tale. *I could leap across the desk and stick my thumbs through his eyeballs. No. It's a wide desk, he'd have plenty of time to see me coming, and he doesn't look like someone to shy away from a fight.*

"Your word?" Rupert asked, willing himself to believe the other man. "You'll give us your word?"

The lantern's plastic—would barely scratch him if I cracked it over his head. Her eyes darted around the room feverishly, looking for something, anything that could stop this. *They're not friends. They're family.* Her mind drifted back to the night Della had held her while she was crying. She'd fallen asleep in her arms. Everyone had experienced nights like that since the fall. It was finding a picture of her family in her rucksack that had set her off. Seeing her mum and dad smiling, seeing her sister pulling a face. It reminded her of all the good times that she'd never have again. It had reminded her of everything she'd lost. She had started sobbing and not been able to stop. Not Rupert but Della had clutched her and soothed her, occasionally kissing her on the head like a loving sibling. It was the people who got you through those moments that were impossible to forget. Della got her through that night when all sorts of crazy thoughts had been bouncing around in her head.

Keely looked down at the chair she was sitting on. It was old and sturdy; she shifted a little, trying to gauge its weight. *Too heavy. No way I'd be able to leg this thing at him.* Hope began to leave her as she could taste inevitability in the air. *Even if I managed to take him out somehow, there are those thugs on the other side of the door.*

"I've already told you, haven't I?" Beano said with a hint of irritability in his voice.

For a moment, Keely had no idea what he was talking about, and then her mind was back in the present. Rupert had asked once again if the other man would be true to his word. She looked across at her partner, and any shred of pity she had felt for him when they were together in those cages was gone. *He's buying into this. He's going to sell the others out.* At that moment, Keely couldn't recall a single reason why they had stayed together. She saw nothing to love in him, nothing to admire in him. She saw nothing but a weak, gullible, self-serving coward.

"Keely as well?" he asked, turning to her as an afterthought, remembering probably for the first time since they'd stepped into the room that she was there with him.

"Aye. Your bird'll go with you."

Half a smile lit Rupert's face as he genuinely believed he'd found a way out for them. He couldn't read the simmering hatred behind Keely's eyes as she stared back at him. He turned to look at Beano once more and took a breath. "We're with—"

Keely rose out of her chair, spinning like a top with her left arm extended. The blade of her hand smashed against Rupert's Adam's apple with hurricane force, and bile rose in the back of her throat as she felt it buckle beneath her strike. Rupert fell forward, spluttering blood from his mouth as he desperately tried to suck in air through the collapsed channel. He brought both hands up to his throat as he struggled and writhed on the ground like a fish out of water.

Keely stood over him, her hand now down by her

side as he continued to squirm. *What have I done?* She stared in disbelief. The thought had been fleeting. One minute it flashed into her head and the next she was doing it. There was no processing in between, and now she had killed the man she loved … in a way … sometimes. But however confused her feelings were for him, it did not detract from the fact she'd taken his life—and that was bewildering in itself.

She slowly drew her eyes away and looked over the desk towards Beano, whose expression was locked in disbelief for a moment before a booming laugh erupted from his mouth. He leaned back in his chair like some mad king whose jester had just whispered the funniest joke he'd ever heard in his ear.

Keely's shock turned to confusion as she stared at the other man, who now slammed the desk with his left hand while holding his belly with his right. The door burst open as the echoing clap of the wood caused concern to the waiting guards. They all stared down at the floundering prisoner, and once their initial shock subsided, they began to laugh too.

What is this? I'm dreaming. This is all some kind of horrific nightmare, and I'm going to wake up any minute. She looked down at Rupert again, and the shock turned to regret. *What have I done?* The grating gargle that came from his broken throat was a thousand times worse than his pained sobbing or any sound that she'd heard for that matter. It was the sound of death—the death she'd caused.

"Fucking belter," Beano guffawed as the others continued laughing too, not quite sure what they were laughing at but not wanting to show their leader the discourtesy of laughing alone.

Keely looked towards the big man as he leaned over the desk, just watching Rupert spasm. There was nothing ironic in his laughter. He found what had happened genuinely funny, and the mad glint in his eye turned to something else as he wiped a tear from the corner. Tears of a different kind rolled down Keely's face as the horror overload became too much for her. She gawped in disbelief at the hysterical figures in the doorway. Their faces were magnified and distorted as she searched each one in vain for the smallest grain of humanity.

"What happened?" one of the men at the door asked as the male prisoner finally fell still.

"Y'should have fucking seen it. He was about to spill his guts, and she Karate chopped the poor fucker in the throat. Bam. Straight fucking down he went," Beano managed to say before dabbing another tear away. "She's a fucking beauty. Nobody's made me laugh like that in an age."

"So what do we do with her?"

Beano carried on laughing for another few seconds before he finally calmed down enough to speak properly. "This one isn't going to tell us fuck all. Take her back down. The boys can have a crack at her after dinner." He walked around the desk and kicked Rupert's corpse. "Get this one down to Chef before he starts stinking up the place. Tell everyone there's going to be meat on the menu for a couple of weeks at least." He turned to Keely and winked.

It was only then that the meaning of everything Beano had said caught up with her. *The boys can have a crack at her after dinner. There's going to be meat on the menu for a couple of weeks.* Her breathing became erratic, and as soon as she felt two firm hands grab her arms, she started to howl as they dragged her out of the room. "NOOO. NOOO. NOOO!"

By the time she was thrown back in the cage, multiple candles and lanterns burned away in the kitchen. The door clanked shut, and the padlock clicked closed while the other two guards dumped Rupert's body on a thick wooden counter next to what looked like preparation stations. The door to the kitchen flew open once more, and in walked a figure almost as tall as the one called Beano. He wore a white apron over a chef's jacket and white trousers. All were equally tarnished by the red-brown stain of blood. The floor was cold and tiled, but he wore nothing on his feet, and even in this light, Keely could see his toenails were yellow and overgrown to the point of curling over.

There was nothing about the figure that didn't cause vomit to rise in her throat. "What the fuck are you doing?" he growled in a gravelly East End voice not dissimilar to Beano's.

The guard who had spoken in the office answered nervously, suggesting to Keely that they were just as scared of this man as they were of the other. "Err … the Guv wanted us to bring him down here. Said he'd make good meat." The man's smile was weak, not sure if what he'd said would throw Chef into a rage.

"How many fucking times?" he demanded, marching up to the body and placing his fingers on Rupert's wrist. "How many fucking times do I have to tell you that I need to be the one to slit them while they're still breathing? It's the only way to ensure a good flow."

"I-it wasn't us, Chef," one of the women said. "She did it." She pointed towards Keely, and the chef turned towards the cage for the first time since entering the room. "She did it? She did it? Why's she doing anything?" He almost ran towards the small cuboid prison and smashed his fist against the door, causing Keely to scream and the whole structure to shudder. "Why are you doing anything?" he screamed, and in that instant, Keely saw madness in his eyes. She was the first to break the gaze, looking down like a frightened dog, hoping not to get a beating. "Get him on the hook," Chef ordered, straightening up.

"But Beano wants us to—"

"I don't give a fuck what anyone wants you to do. My kitchen, my rules. Get him on the hook now. And get the bucket underneath him."

The four of them sprang into action, first undressing the dead man then using a length of rope to bind Rupert's feet together before lifting him in unison and latching him on a sharp metal hook that hung over a large grate. "There you go, Chef," one of the women said.

"The bucket. The fucking bucket," Chef barked, folding his arms and glaring at the guards. Two of them went across to a cupboard and pulled out a vessel the size of a family laundry hamper. They placed it beneath Rupert's upside-down corpse and stepped back while Chef grabbed a knife from the rack and walked up to the hanging body. He drew the blade across Rupert's throat and blood began to stream out. "Look at that. It's barely trickling. See what you've done?" he shouted over to Keely as she continued to cry.

"Can we go now, Chef?"

"Huh?" he replied, looking down at the bucket with disappointment engrained on his face.

"Can we go now?"

"Yeah. Fuck off, the lot of you."

Without any further pause, the four guards withdrew as quickly as they could and didn't look back.

Keely just sat there in the cage, watching the blood slowly drain from Rupert's body. "They think they'll be getting meat tonight. Well, they won't be getting any meat tonight," Chef said, walking over to the range and pulling the lid off a giant pan. "They don't know what's involved. There's an art to getting the most from an animal."

An animal?

"If you know what you're doing, you can use everything. Offal, trotters, ears." He glanced across towards the cage, and Keely lowered her eyes. There was not a huge amount of light in the kitchen, but Chef's psychotic glare sent shivers running through her. "Black pudding. Long time since we've had black pudding here. Not so many come this way anymore. Not as many cars as in the early days. Of course, we got it when we found Jenkins had been stealing from the pantry." He burst out laughing as he stirred the contents of the giant pan before moving over to the other. "Aye. Good pudding he made. Sausage, bacon, loin chops, ribs." He stared across at her once more. "It was summer, and we had a barbecue. Made burgers too. They were a disappointment." He shook his head. "Too much salt in the mixture." He looked towards Rupert once more as the blood continued to trickle. "You should have let me slit him. That was a mistake. You should have let me slit him."

Keely began to sob, and Chef rushed over to the cage. "There, there. Don't cry. You'll know for next time. I do all the slitting. Don't cry; you'll get dehydrated. You don't want to get dehydrated." He spoke the words tenderly, like he only had her best interests at heart.

He's insane. He's completely insane.

"Don't worry, you'll know next time." He reached out, caressing the door of the cage as if it was his daughter locked inside. Then he turned and walked back to the preparation station, where he picked up a handful of mushrooms and began to chop them.

Keely peered through the gaps to watch him through her tear-filled eyes. He placed the chopped mushrooms in one pot, then some more in the other, before shoving a few in his mouth. "Oh Jesus," she whispered, and as quiet as she was, Chef turned towards her before grabbing another scoop and slicing them. *No wonder they're all crazy. They're eating psilocybin mushrooms like they're fucking portobellos. They must be tripping twenty-four-seven.*

11

The workers in the grounds and many of the sentries at the gates had drifted inside long before the final throes of daylight had died. Mya and Mike had kept their vigil under cover of a giant Scottish pine and behind a growth of bushes. The others had stayed back, waiting for darkness to come and doing their best to remain positive about the task ahead.

The rain had come in fits and starts throughout the afternoon and early evening. Torrents had been followed by mild flurries, but now there was nothing but damp air to keep them company until their mission commenced.

With each passing minute, the enormity of what faced them magnified. After careful consideration, Jules and her brothers had decided not to be the odd ones out and as dangerous as they believed the plan to be, they would walk shoulder to shoulder with the others and face whatever might come.

In their zeal to do the right thing, logic had been given a holiday, and the reality of the seventeen of them breaking into the priory, saving Keely and Rupert, and then escaping in one piece dawned like a stormy winter's morning. This wasn't going to end well for all of them, if any.

"Bobbi," Wren whispered, "I just want to say that—"

"Save it, Sis. I know. I know how mad this is. I know how dangerous this is, and I'm not asking anyone to go with me, but the only way I'll be able to live with myself is if—"

"I just want to say I'm with you one hundred percent."

"Oh."

"Whatever happens. I've been thinking about this, and if it was you and me down there and we'd helped rescue someone, then I'd hope they might have the guts to come after us."

"Thanks, Wren. Y'know, it's totally okay if you don't come. I'm not happy about any of this, but I can't even think what they might do to Wolf if they get hold of him."

"Don't, Bobbi." She said the words with a shiver in her voice. It had been the main thing on her mind since they'd first set off.

"I'm just saying."

"I know, but don't."

*

"I don't think I've ever been so scared in my life," Della admitted as a small huddle of them sat under the protection of another giant tree.

"Stick around us for a while. You'll find it's a normal state of being. If you're not scared out of your wits, worried for your loved ones and sure that today's going to be your last, then you're just not paying attention," Jules said, and Della and the others laughed.

"You're funny."

"Who's joking?"

*

"Y'know," Mike began, handing the binoculars back to Mya, "this is a pretty good base."

Mya took the field glasses and zeroed in on the small shed that acted as a sentry box by the gate. A couple of candles burnt away inside, and two scruffy-looking men played cards at a table. There were lights on inside the priory, but everywhere else was dark apart from when the patrolling guards flicked on a torch to check something out, but that was rare.

In all likelihood, very few RAMs would happen upon this place in normal circumstances. It was well off the beaten track and surrounded by trees, which would shield it from discovery most of the time. Due to the massive tower of smoke, more infected than the norm had stumbled across it today. This had lessened in the last hour or so of daylight, and Mya guessed the reason was the fire may have been extinguished by the rain or at least doused enough not to send up a giant plume.

"Yeah. Let's hope we don't find out how good and we can get in and out without losing anyone."

"No. I mean I think it would make a good base for us."

Mya let out a small giggle. "What are you going to do, charm them into leaving?"

"Charm's never really been my strong point."

Mya felt Muppet nudge her leg, and she lowered the binoculars for a second to stroke him. It was dark enough to begin their journey down the hillside, and there was an air of apprehension surrounding all of them now, the canines included. Mya reached out and squeezed Mike's arm. "Okay, reality check, Mike. You do understand that we're heading to Glasgow. This little detour is just that, and I don't want to burst your bubble, but we're probably outnumbered by about five to one. From what I've seen, a lot of them have got weapons … I mean weapons with bullets, not crowbars and machetes. This is a rescue, and I really hope we can pull it off because there's actually a pretty good chance that we could get captured and face the same fate as Keely and Rupert. Thinking that we could launch a full-scale takeover is…."

"Insane?"

She could hear the smile in his voice. "Just a little bit."

"Listen, those vehicles could be the key."

"What do you mean?"

"As it stands, if we make it out of here, some of us are going to have to head to Glasgow, get the other truck and head back up here for everyone else."

"Yeah."

"So, what if we make this about getting the vehicles?"

"I don't understand."

"There are two army trucks down there as well as a Ford Transit van. There should be more than enough room in those to get our people down to Glasgow. If we make this look like it's about getting the vehicles, they're going to be preoccupied with that, which should act as a good subterfuge for finding Keely and Rupert and getting them to safety."

It was Mike's turn to hear the smile in Mya's voice now. "In the meantime, we bust open the gates and hope all the noise makes any infected who are in the area head towards the priory so they've got more than enough to deal with."

"Yeah, and who knows, the next time we come back here, this place might be ripe for the picking."

"Where's all this coming from? I thought you were happy with the idea of settling in Glasgow."

"I told you I was going to make Olsen pay. We can't do that down there. We can't walk into someone's home and make them a target."

"Just by us being there, we're making them a target if word ever got out, but…."

"But what?"

"But I know what you mean. We do need somewhere." She placed the binoculars in her rucksack and turned back towards the others. If she hadn't known where they were gathered, she would have struggled to see them in the dim glow of the cloud-covered moon. "We've got a new plan," she announced before briefing them on Mike's idea. When she was done, Emma was the first to speak.

"I like this idea much better. The prospect of all of us bumbling around the priory looking for Keely and Rupert wasn't something I was looking forward to."

"Okay," Jules said. "So, who goes with who?"

"The fewer people in the building the better," Mya replied.

"I'll go into the priory," Mike said.

"Ja. I will go too," added Mila.

"That's three of us then," said Robyn, turning to her sister. "You go with Mya."

"No way. I'm going with you," Wren snapped back.

"Listen. They're not going to be able to pull this off with empty guns and spears. Plus, it makes more sense if Wolf and Muppet stay outside. Hopefully, we're not going to run into any infected, but who knows?"

Wren wanted to argue, but everything her sister said was true. They wouldn't be able to make this work without both of them playing their part, and that meant splitting up. Sammy was very good, especially for someone of her age, but when it came to killing living, breathing human beings, who knew how she'd cope in a pressure situation. Likewise, Della and Clay had already displayed their limitations. She let out a long sigh. "I don't like the thought of us splitting up."

"Me neither. But to be honest, I like this plan a hell of a lot more than the other one. Now, come on, the sooner we do this the sooner we get out of here."

*

"How is he?" Jenny asked as she sat down beside

Ruby. Tommy was rocking back and forth rhythmically. He'd been doing so ever since they arrived. First the crash and then the battle with the infected in the woods had sent him to a place where he hadn't been in the longest time. The siren-like wail that often came from his mouth in times of distress had become a long, empty silence.

Most were happy about this. Silence meant that the infected wouldn't hear him and subsequently wouldn't be drawn to them. But silence scared Ruby to her core. She had witnessed it before. Twice in his life, Tommy had receded so far inside himself that he had become unreachable. He just sat and stared at the flickering flames of the fire, the occasional blink being the only sign he was still alive.

"Not good," Ruby said eventually.

"Has Liz seen him?"

Ruby smiled sadly. "Liz is a great doctor, but there's nothing she can do. I've been here before. He might snap out of this in a heartbeat, or it might carry on for months. Hell, it might carry on forever."

"Maybe when we get down to Glasgow, and things become a little more settled, he'll start feeling better."

"I don't envy you."

"What do you mean?" Jenny asked.

"I've seen you going around trying to cheer everyone up, trying to make it seem that things aren't as bad as they actually are."

"We need to stay positive."

"It's a nice sentiment."

Jenny looked across at Tommy once more as his eyes remained glued to the fire. "I've been speaking to a couple who live here. They say that there's a ridge to the east. There's a small cave beneath it that should keep us sheltered from the elements until the others come back. They said that they'll tell them where we are."

Ruby started laughing. "You really think they're coming back, don't you?"

"I've known Mike and the others a lot longer than

you have, Ruby. I know what they're capable of."

"If they've got any sense, they'll leave us here. They'll head to Glasgow by themselves and start afresh."

Others gathered around who had only been half listening to the conversation started paying more attention. "I realise you're upset, Ruby, but—"

"Me being upset has nothing to do with it. They're out there with knives and spears. They're in this massive forest with God knows how many infected on some hopeless quest to save a couple of strangers who are probably already dead. If any of them have any sense, they'll realise they're on a fool's errand and just get the hell out of here, leaving every last one of us behind. If they haven't, then you can wait in that cave as long as you want, but nobody's going to come for you."

Her words seemed to echo as they left her lips, and more than just the few gathered around them were listening now. "They'll be back," Jenny said, more to reassure herself than the others. She reached out and gently stroked Meg's head. "They'll be back."

*

They waited until the patrolling guard disappeared from view once more then ran down the hillside in single file. They stayed low and kept silent, traversing the wooden bridge as quietly as they could before backtracking and heading down the riverbank on the other side. They walked along for a moment until they reached the point where Mike and Mya had watched several of the priory's inhabitants disappear. Just as they had suspected, it was an overflow storm drain. A substantial metal grate covered it, but, as Mike discovered, a fast, hard pull made it open like a heavy door with rusty hinges.

It was waist high, and because of the gravelly surface of the riverbank, the dogs needed lifting in. A steady stream of water trickled out, and they all felt the same cold, damp discomfort in their trainers and boots as they climbed in. Only Sammy was able to stand up straight. The others hunched over a little as they began their journey into the darkness. One by one, they flicked their torches on but maintained their silence.

Mya had expected to see at least one guard, but when they had entered the tunnel with no trouble, her paranoia edged up a level. She searched beyond the light that her torch beam drifted, regularly looking towards Muppet to see if his acute sense of hearing or smell had detected anything.

They continued along, sloshing in the water as they went, all filled with the same fear, the same apprehension. The occasional outlet trickled into the tunnel. These would be from the fields inside and outside the compound. The priory had originally been built in the seventeenth century. Crops of junipers grew on the hillsides, and historically, these would have been used to manufacture the priory's gin, which was the main source of income for the monks. But they had also lived as self-sufficiently as they could, growing much of their own produce. Being positioned in what was essentially a large, wide valley, good drainage was vital to ensure the fields didn't flood, and no doubt this tunnel was born from the labour of hundreds of monks over time.

The incline of the tunnel noticeably steepened, and suddenly, they weren't walking in water anymore. A few more paces and there was enough room for them all to stand upright.

Mya came to a stop, raising a hand as her torch beam came to rest on five steps leading up to an ancient-looking wooden door. Still, nobody said a word, but it was obvious from her expression and the readying of her crowbar that she believed anything could be beyond it. She started climbing, and Robyn joined her, nocking an arrow ready for whatever they might face.

Rather than a handle, there was a gate latch, and Mya pressed the wide round button down, releasing the mechanism. It clinked loudly, making her wince a little as the sound reverberated through the tunnel and would surely echo on the other side too. She turned off her torch, as did the others, and pulled the door inwards, revealing continued blackness.

She switched her torch back on and panned it around to see bags of coal and piles of chopped wood.

"This must be the coal cellar," Andy whispered.

"Hundreds of millions of sperm and he was the fastest fuckin' one," Jules muttered, resulting in a small ripple of laughter despite the tension.

"Keep it down," Mya hissed as she and Robyn led the way to the next door. Again, they all cut their torches as she released the latch. This time, it opened up into a much wider space. A furnace roared away in the corner. From it rose pipes leading up the walls and out. A steep staircase led to another door. "Shit. I don't like this. We could be coming out in the middle of the dining room for all we know."

"Do you want to go back?" Emma asked.

Mya thought for a moment and looked down at Muppet and Wolf as they sniffed around. "Hell, we've come this far. Just be ready for anything."

"Wait a minute," Mike said.

"What?" Mya replied.

He pulled the shotgun and the remaining shells from his rucksack. "If I need to use this in there, I'm probably already dead. But hopefully, it'll help you cause a distraction."

Mya looked down at the weapon and nodded appreciatively. "Let's hope I get to return it to you on the other side."

They all started up the staircase. The handrail had rusted away to nothing in places, but they took each step carefully, almost as if it was their last, which, given the circumstances, it could well be.

Mya paused once again at the door at the top. This had the same style of handle, and she pressed and pushed cautiously, turning off her torch once more before opening it fully. The others did the same, and as a cool breeze of air hit them all, they understood that there were no more pauses, not more what-ifs. This was it now. They were in it, and what happened from here was everything.

12

Chef continued to work away, adding this and that to the simmering pots on the range. Occasionally, he'd glance across at the cage, but he seemed to be lost in his own little world, often coming out with random phrases as if in answer to a question nobody asked. "Every day they go out with fishing lines. Every day they come back empty-handed," he muttered to himself.

Keely just watched him from the far end of her cage. The drip, drip, drip of Rupert's blood had become far less rhythmical, and it reminded her that her own time was running out. The door to the kitchen swung open, and three men barged in.

"Wah-hey," one of them said as the trio swaggered over to the cage.

"No one told us she was a looker," another replied as he sprawled his hands over the top, looking down at Keely, who recoiled, scooching as far away as she could. "How about we give her a little taste test before the others—"

"Get away from me." Keely tried to sound brave,

tried to sound like she could do something about it if the men took her, but she knew it was a lie. She looked at the faces that surrounded her. In the glint of the candle and lantern light, she could see the same glaze in their eyes, the same distance in their expressions. *Are they all out of it? Are they constantly dosing so they're always high?* She looked back to the tubular mushrooms as Chef scooped up another handful and placed them in the pot.

"Sounds like she might be a fighter. I love the ones who fight," the first one said, reaching towards the padlock. "Chef. Where's the key?" he asked, turning around.

"Beano said after dinner. He said she was after-dinner entertainment," Chef replied.

"Yeah, well, we're wanting a bit of before-dinner entertainment, so where's the fucking key?"

"After dinner," he said again.

The other three laughed. "He's fucking out of it." The ringleader looked around the kitchen. "Over there," he said, pointing to a set of keys on a hook by the door. "Go get them."

Oh, God. Please, no, please.

*

The furnace building and coal cellar were adjacent to the priory. It was in a dark courtyard behind the main building, and after piling out of the entrance, they had lingered a few seconds, saying their goodbyes and adjusting to the night once more before splitting up.

Mike, Robyn and Mila almost hugged the building, staying below window ledges as they skirted around, trying to find an entrance.

Mya and the others kept low too, but they knew where they were going. They waited at the north rear corner of the priory, lingering in the darkness like malevolent spirits waiting to pounce.

*

To an untrained ear, it sounded like nothing more than a wisp of wind. To anyone familiar with the crossbow, it signified something far more deadly. The moon was still shrouded by clouds, like a torch under the bedclothes, only casting a faint hint of light, but Wren picked her target well.

The patrolling guard dropped like a stone. Rob and Andy immediately ran forward, grabbing the fallen figure and dragging him into the shadows. Mya pulled the SA80 from his shoulder and checked his body for anything else that might be useful. There was nothing, but at least they had the rifle. She handed it to Andy. "Let's hope you don't need to use this."

"Thanks," he said, taking it gratefully. The fact he'd been chosen by Mya to carry the only other firearm displayed a level of trust he'd not known for much of his life, but now he had proved countless times that he could be relied on in tough situations.

*

Mike straightened up, as did Robyn and Mila. They'd found what they were looking for. A ground-floor window was open just a few centimetres. The stench of tobacco drifted out into the night, and a muted conversation could be heard from inside as they continued to hug the wall.

"I hear two voices," Mike whispered.

"Yeah, but there could be ten people in there for all we know," Robyn replied with her bow already nocked.

Mike took a breath and edged a little closer to the window before stretching his neck to catch a split-second peek. He shrunk back immediately, processing what he'd seen before looking again.

There were two men sitting at a desk next to the door. An LED lantern glowed as they both looked down towards a small object in front of them. He couldn't hear the topic of the conversation, but that didn't matter. He gently took hold of Robyn's arm and guided her into position next to him before they both ducked back once more. "What do you think?" he whispered.

"They're really close to the door," she replied. "Getting the first won't be a problem. But I can't guarantee the other won't escape before I can get a second shot off."

"We haven't got any other options. Soon, all hell's going to break loose, and this is our one chance."

"No pressure then."

"You can do this, Robyn," Mila said, squeezing her friend's hand. "You can do this."

*

Mya and the others clung to the wall as they made their way to the courtyard at the front of the building. This was the easy part. The hard part would be getting to the glorified shed, which acted as the sentry box next to the gate, without being spotted. They would have to break cover and use the vehicles to hide behind, hoping they could take out the guards before an alarm was raised.

"What now?" Jules whispered.

"Now we—" Mya's words cut off as a figure shone his torch directly towards her. All the time she and Mike had been watching the place there had only been one patrolling guard, but now here was a second. His rifle was slung over his shoulder, and in the periphery of torchlight, she could see a look of shock on his face to rival her own.

Time stood still for a moment, but finally understanding dawned and the guard jerked into action, frantically reaching for his rifle and opening his mouth to shout at the same time.

He collapsed backwards, the warning failing to rise from his throat. Instead, a bloody gurgle bubbled as soon as he hit the ground. Jon and Rob lunged forward, dragging the figure around the corner.

At that moment, there was a break in the clouds, and the moon shone down, illuminating the figure on the ground as he struggled through his last moments of life. The sound of gargling blood sent shivers through all of them. They did not have to imagine the pain of such a death. Instead, they got to see it, and a small cry left Sammy's mouth.

"I'm sorry," she said, still with her bow raised.

When the others had seen the figure fall, they had all assumed it was Wren who had made the shot. They all felt relief and gratitude at that moment as the guard would, without a doubt, have pinpointed them for the other sentries. Emma placed her hand on her sister's shoulder. "It's okay. You did good. You saved us."

"Pl-ea-se." It came out as a disjointed, bloodcurdling whisper as the figure continued to writhe on the ground, starved of oxygen, drowning in his own fluids.

"I'm sorry," Sammy said again, sobbing as her victim continued to struggle. He was in his early twenties, and with the best surgeon in the world, there was no hope of saving him now.

Suddenly, Mya dropped to her knees, clamping her hands around the suffering figure's head and twisting. There was a crack, and the guard fell silent. "Put him in the bushes over there," she said to Jon and Rob, gesturing to several growths of shrubbery near a large window that overlooked what was once a sprawling lawn but was now a potato field.

*

Five, four, three, two, one. Robyn stepped into the shaft of light cast out of the window by the LED lantern. She released her bowstring and reached for another arrow as the first disappeared into her target's back. One, two. The figure slumped over the desk, and it was only then that his companion saw the projectile sticking out of his back. Three, four. He did not look to the window. Instead, he lunged for the door and five. The second arrow cracked through the back of his skull. He remained standing for the briefest moment before falling backwards and crashing onto the carpeted floor.

"Shot," Mike said as he and Mila stepped into the light to see. He was about to lift the window up a little more when they all froze as the sound of another voice drifted towards them. They glanced at one another with bewildered expressions until they finally understood what they were hearing.

"Holy shit!" Robyn exclaimed, raising the window and hoisting herself over the sill and into the room.

*

Mya reached out and gripped Sammy's arm. "You don't cry. You just saved us. That was a good kill. If you hadn't done what you did, it would have been all over. Now reload your weapon and get ready because this part was a breeze compared to what comes next."

Sammy took a deep breath and wiped her eyes before cranking the self-cocking lever and placing another bolt in the flight groove. She felt Wren and Wolf move up beside her.

"It's okay, Sammy," Wren said, stroking her back reassuringly.

"He…." The young girl couldn't continue, and Emma placed a comforting hand on her from the other side.

"Okay," Mya said as Rob and Jon rejoined them. "Single file, keep your eyes on the sentry box. You see them lifting their heads and you hit the ground. Wren, Della, Clay, this is all down to you. If they set foot out of that door, you need to take them down quickly and quietly. Otherwise, this is all over before it starts. Now, we're heading to the vehicles. Keep low and stay quiet." Without another word, Mya angled her head around the corner and launched into a run.

*

Mike and Mila followed Robyn into the room. They ignored the dead bodies; they'd seen enough in their time and there was nothing particularly special about them. What was special was the pocket radio on the desk.

"... supplies and a working wind turbine. We have a community that's growing all the time. If you can make it to Edinburgh by road, we have ten safe sites positioned around the city with enough food and water to last until we get to you. We send out armed patrols once a week looking for survivors. We are the Edinburgh Castle community, and we want to help.

"This is the Edinburgh Castle community. If you're listening to this message, then you're still alive, and that's something. Congratulations. We have supplies and a working wind turbine. We have a…."

"Jesus," Mike said as they all continued to look at the small orange transistor radio.

"This is your home," Mila said.

Robyn didn't answer. She just picked up and listened to the small radio as the message repeated over and over. "Hey, look," Mike said eventually. "I realise this is a big thing, but we're kind of in the middle of something here."

Robyn broke her gaze from the small orange box and raised her head, noticing Mike for the first time since he'd joined her. She blinked once, twice, then rolled the wheel on the side of the radio until it clicked off. She put it in her pocket and shook her head as if trying to snap out of a daze.

The sound of footsteps from the corridor outside shook them all from their thoughts, and Robyn plucked the arrow from her first victim's back, wiping it off and nocking it ready for anyone who put their head around the corner.

They listened carefully as the steps got closer and closer. Instinctively, Mike reached out, hitting the button on top of the lantern and making the room dark.

"It's just one person," he whispered as he looked at the dim orange glow from the hallway outside as it reached under the door.

The footsteps got nearer still, and then, without warning, Mike leapt towards the door, flinging it open and diving out into the corridor. He grasped the shocked figure, punching him in the face and dragging him back into the room before a single word left his mouth.

*

Mya stood guard with Muppet behind the military truck as, one by one, the others joined her. There was another truck between them and the main priory building, meaning they were invisible to both it and the sentry box, giving them the tiniest respite before they made their next move.

Wren and Wolf brought up the rear, making sure everyone was safe before the final leg of the plan.

"Okay," Emma said, remaining glued to her little sister's side.

"Now we check to make sure the keys are in the vehicles," Mya replied.

"I suppose that would help."

"I'll do this one. Rob, you the next. Emma, do the Transit van."

Without questions, without hesitation, the three of them immediately got to work while the others waited in nervous anticipation, sandwiched between the two army trucks just waiting to be discovered.

*

The man's eyes were wide and glaring in the glow of Robyn's torch even before he saw the bodies of his compatriots. Mike held him firmly by his jacket, and when his arms began to flail in a desperate attempt to escape, Mike punched his captive in the face once more.

"Where are the prisoners?" Mike growled, doing his best Batman impersonation.

"I-I—"

Punch. "Where are the prisoners?" he demanded once more, this time pushing the man up against a wall and clamping his thumb and forefinger around his neck.

The man's attempts to escape Mike's grasp became weaker as he realised he was outmatched. "I-I haven't seen them," he wheezed, and Mike released his grip a little.

"That's not what I asked."

"Th-the kitchen. That's usually where they keep them."

Usually? Jesus. How many times have they done this? "Where's the kitchen?"

The man's eyes danced unnaturally. "The hall. Down the hall. At the end," he said, raising his finger and pointing. "D-don't hurt me. Please."

He's telling the truth. There's something weird about the scrawny little fucker, but he's telling the truth. Mike clamped his hand around the other man's neck tighter than ever before, whipping one of his machetes from the rucksack and hammering it down, splitting his skull open. A single trickle of blood streamed down his forehead, and he slumped to the floor. When Mike withdrew his weapon, the wound pumped like a broken dam, covering his victim's white T-shirt and pooling around him.

"Uh, gross," Robyn said, stepping back.

"We need to check these three to see if they're carrying anything useful," Mike said.

"Go on then. I'm not stepping anywhere near that."

Mike pushed the slumped figure onto his side as more blood than ever gushed from the wound. There was a penknife in one of his pockets, which Mike grabbed. Something rustled in one of the other pockets, and he pulled out a small homemade envelope. He angled it towards the lantern as he opened it up. "That explains a lot," he said, examining the contents.

"What the hell are those?" Robyn asked.

"Dried shrooms."

"What?"

"Magic mushrooms. No wonder they called them mad monks."

"How do you know what they are?"

"These were popular at the institute."

"I forgot you were inside."

Mike smiled. "Yeah. He looked a bit spaced out but not totally gone. I know a few guys who used to microdose on these things to get them through the day. They were a little out of it, but they could still function. There were others who just went wild on the things. There are all different kinds, and some can mellow you out; others can turn you into a raging psychotic if you OD."

"You took plenty then."

"Funny," Mike said, smiling as he placed the

envelope in his pocket. He checked the other bodies but found nothing then turned to his two companions again. "Okay," he said, placing his fingers on the door handle. "You ready?"

"Ja. Let's do this," Mila replied.

*

Mya levered just the slightest gap in the passenger side door before crawling up and into the cab. She raised her head to glimpse the sentry box. Both guards were still playing cards. She reached over to the ignition and her heart sank a little to find it empty. She leaned up once more and lowered the sun visor. There was a momentary jingle as a set of keys dropped onto the driver's seat.

A breath of relief left her lips, and a smile formed on her face. It was only fleeting though. Her cab suddenly lit up, and she froze. *Shit. They've seen me.*

*

"Wait a minute," Robyn said, reaching out and grabbing Mike's arm.

"What?"

"Aren't we meant to be waiting for the diversion?"

"The plan was never to wait for the diversion. It's going to help us, but our mission stays the same. Ideally, we want to get to the kitchen before it all kicks off or the corridors are going to be teaming with these bastards." He kicked one of the dead men on the ground.

Robyn shrugged. "Yeah. I suppose you're right."

"Come," Mila said. "We have wasted long enough. It is time to act."

*

It was worse than waiting for a guillotine blade to drop or a trap door on the gallows to open. With each key the trio of lascivious maniacs tried Keely came closer to a horror beyond anything she could imagine. There was a part of her that wanted to translocate her mind, just shut herself off from everything that was happening and hopefully return to her body when the sordid vileness and ugliness were all over. Maybe she would last long enough in the cage as their entertainment to find a way to escape before they finally decided to use her as an ingredient. There was another part of her that wanted to stay alert, to fight with everything she had. She could use the hate and anger that welled inside her to try to beat them, try to get away. *They're high as kites, for Christ's sake. I've got to be able to use that.*

Click.

Oh shit. No, no, no, no.

The padlock fell to the ground, and Keely took a breath, dreading what would come next.

13

The cab got brighter and brighter, and it only took Mya another second to understand that this was no torch or lantern; this was not another foot patrol that had inadvertently stumbled across her. It was a vehicle approaching the gates. She raised her head once more to see the outline of a covered army truck as the two guards abandoned their game in the sentry box to open the entrance and greet them.

"Fuuuck!" She shuffled back out of the passenger door, nearly falling over Muppet as he eagerly awaited her.

"What the fuck is that?" Jules asked, only seeing the light illuminate the courtyard, not seeing its source.

"There's another truck approaching. We need to go, and we need to go now."

Emma and Rob appeared simultaneously. Both held the keys in their hands. "We need to go," Emma said.

"Yeah. No shit. Let's hope these things have got fuel and they work."

"That's a fuckin' cheery thought," Jules said as the sound of the driver and one of the guards laughing told them all that there were just seconds left before they were discovered.

*

Keely stared through the gap over the trio's shoulders as they each reached into the cage. Chef was holding his head. "You shouldn't play with your food. Mother always used to say that you shouldn't play with your food."

Holy shit. They're all totally insane.

"Come 'ere then. Come on, darlin'." The man who spoke had a shaved head and a tangled, dirty beard. Like the others, his eyes were wild, dancing in the glimmer of lanterns and candles. He reached to grab hold of her shin, but Keely kicked out hard with her other foot, connecting with his face. He shot back, falling onto his buttocks, and the other two descended into fits of hysterical laughter before another hand extended towards her.

"GET THE FUCK AWAY FROM ME!"

*

Keely's cries echoed down the hallway, and Mike, Robyn and Mila launched from a cautious walk into a sprint. It was mere seconds before they burst through the kitchen door, and all eyes shot towards them.

Chef glared, unsure whether this was reality or some shroom-induced hallucination, but not waiting to find out, he grabbed a cleaver from the rack and charged.

"AAARRRGGGHHH!"

Their eyes were initially drawn to Rupert's body as blood dripped from it into the waiting bucket. The smell of death hung heavy in the air, but their attention didn't linger on the freshly slain carcass long as the crazed giant stormed towards them with his glinting blade.

At the exact same second, the three would-be rapists reached for their weapons.

Scheisse!

*

Gezim was one of the few inhabitants of the priory who didn't indulge in the fungi that were prevalent in the valley and on their side of the forest. The things seemed to grow everywhere. If he'd known about this place back in the day, he could have made a fortune for himself. He'd been a lieutenant for one of the biggest crime syndicates in Manchester, dealing in everything from girls to cloned phones to heroin. He'd always wanted to work for himself rather than someone else, but time caught up with him. When the outbreak happened, he was serving eight to ten for people trafficking.

He never partook in any of the wares of his former employers, however, and he continued to adhere to this ethos inside and even after arriving at the priory. So, as he slowly set off from the gate once more and entered the courtyard in front of the main building, he knew that the scurrying silhouettes he was seeing were real and not a figment of some drug-induced daze.

What the hell?

*

Two solid bangs from the back of the truck told Mya everyone who was meant to be on board was onboard. She remained hunched over for a moment, staying hidden from the headlights as Muppet sat in the passenger footwell; then she turned the key in the ignition and listened as the engine coughed and spluttered. *Come on. Please come on.*

She could see the butt of the shotgun protruding from her rucksack on the passenger seat, and she knew the four shells in that were all that stood between them and capture. She wouldn't have time to reload. She wouldn't have time to do much at all.

Finally, the engine rumbled, and she placed her foot down hard on the accelerator, making it roar even louder. Mya sat up straight and, for the first time, revealed herself to the occupants of the other truck and probably the guards at the gate too. She hit the clutch, ground the gear stick into first and released the handbrake.

"Here goes nothing, boy," she said, rolling down the window and reaching across for the shotgun before turning the wheel, revving even harder and sliding into second.

*

Robyn was the first to fire. Her arrow entered the chest of its target, catapulting him backwards but doing nothing to deter the other gunmen. Mila rushed towards them, but Mike understood there was no way for her to reach them before they got a shot off. He withdrew his machetes and flung one in the direction of the first man while stretching out the other towards the behemoth in the chef's uniform charging towards him. The extended blade did nothing to deter the giant chef, and Mike leapt back as the cleaver swung down with Goliathan power.

*

Mila dove for cover as the first rifle crack boomed. The kitchen was large, but its old stone walls made the sound reverberate down the hallway.

Crap. Robyn's second arrow William Telled the gunman. If he'd had an apple on his head, it would have split it in two, but he ducked just in time, anticipating the shot, and now he fell to one knee, raising his gun once more.

*

The third member of the trio picked himself up off the ground. He'd landed heavily on his SA80, and if it wasn't for all the naturally occurring chemicals circulating in his system, the pain from the broken ribs he'd just incurred would no doubt have been unbearable, but as it was, he'd avoided the machete flying towards him, and now it was his turn to seek a little justice.

*

"This is my kitchen. What are you doing in my kitchen?" Chef growled, and Mike could only stare for a second into his mad eyes. The hulking figure swung the cleaver again, making the air around it whistle, and Mike edged back further. The weight of the blade and the speed and strength of the swipe meant that his machete would be chopped in two if he used it to defend himself. *Need to strike when he's off balance.*

*

This is surreal. Keely wondered if she had been slipped some of the mushrooms without her knowing. She had been hoping for a miracle, and here it was. She crab-walked forward out of the cage, pulling her right leg back as far as she could and kicking.

Her boot made contact with the rifleman's back, and although his weapon boomed once more, there was no danger of the shot hitting anyone as he went sprawling, and the bullet disappeared into the ceiling.

*

Beano was about to head down for dinner when he'd heard what sounded like a gunshot. He'd stepped out into the hallway as he did every night at this time. He always ate with his brother, the man everyone referred to as Chef, but who to him would always be Badger. He'd waited just a few seconds; then another shot had rung out and he knew he wasn't hearing or imagining things.

That's the kitchen. That's the fucking kitchen. "The kitchen. It's the kitchen," he shouted at the top of his voice as he ran past the large dining room. The doors were open, and the conversations and laughter inside told him that the occupants either hadn't heard the shots or they weren't concerned by them, but he continued nonetheless, his strides getting wider, his speed increasing.

"Beano? Beano?"

He glanced back to see one, two, three figures emerging from the doorway. "THE KITCHEN!" he shouted.

*

Gezim slammed the brakes on the truck as the other vehicle sped towards him. "Let me guess," his passenger in the cab said. "Chef's gone crazy on the brandy again. Remember the last time he—"

"This isn't that," Gezim said, his brow furrowing as the other vehicle continued in their direction. The lights of a truck behind it and the Transit van turned on as well. "Is it an evacuation or something? Have the infected got in?"

A figure suddenly leaned out of the driver-side window, her long black hair flowing behind her in the wind.

"What the fuck is this?"

"I—"

BOOM!

*

Beano skidded to a stop, still several metres away from the kitchen. That shot had most definitely come from outside. Had the strange acoustics of the old building confused him? Had he believed the gunfire had come from the kitchen when all the time it was the courtyard? *Was it the shrooms?* He didn't consume half as many as some, but there were times when he blacked out, when he didn't quite understand what he was doing.

"That came from the gate," one of the men who had followed him down the hallway announced.

Indecision gripped Beano for a moment, but another rifle report suddenly made the hallway quake. "That fucking didn't though."

*

The vehicle was beginning to veer as Mya squeezed the trigger again. If she'd have had a Glock, she'd have been able to shoot and steer, but beggars couldn't be choosers. Her heart lifted a little as the second blast shattered the windscreen of the other truck, and she heaved herself back in, taking the steering wheel and straightening up. She glanced in the mirror to see Andy and Emma following her, and a small smile eased onto her face, grateful that they'd got the other vehicles started.

*

Gezim looked down, and the lights flitted around him as the advancing truck swerved wildly.

Something dripped over his eyes and face. He could smell and taste copper, and he immediately knew what it was. His foot had slid off the clutch, and the truck had stalled. It now rolled forward slowly. He wanted to reach out and pull on the handbrake, but all he could do was look at the blood staining his T-shirt. Out of the corner of his eye, he could see his friend slumped forward, and he could hear the confused cries of his passengers in the back as the sounds of gunshots and roaring engines echoed around the sprawling courtyard.

*

Automatic gunfire erupted, and Mya ducked down, sliding the gear into third and pressing harder on the accelerator. Tink, tink, tink. The bullets crashed against the front of the truck, and some punched holes in the windscreen. She raised her head for a second, risking becoming a target, but a second was all it took, and she shifted the wheel, aiming her vehicle directly at the two firing guards. Their resolve held for another second before their screams of fear filled the air and they dived for cover.

*

Robyn released her bowstring again, this time aiming lower, ensuring that if her target ducked, she'd still get him. The man with the already broken ribs shrieked in pain as the arrow entered his stomach; he staggered back, dropping his weapon and colliding with the cage as his friend, now rising from the floor once more, stopped dead.

He couldn't understand why at first, but then he saw the bloody sword blade withdraw from the other man's gut and the katana-wielding Boudicca kick out, causing her victim to crash to the ground.

He tried to remember something from his childhood, a happy memory, anything to replace that image, but he could think of nothing. The sight of his dead friend and the sound of his lifeless body collapsing would be the last things to go through his head.

*

Chef swung again, even harder this time. *Now!* Mike lunged while the big man followed through. He brought his machete down hard and fast as the other man brought his arm up in defence. The blade cracked into the bone, but no utter of pain left the giant's lips.

"Shiiit!" The next thing he knew, Mike was flying back as Chef swatted him like an annoying insect. He crashed into the wall, banging his head hard against the stone.

Robyn released her bowstring once more, and the arrow disappeared into Chef's stomach. Her mouth dropped open a little as the big man started towards her, unperturbed by the object sticking out of his belly. "Shit!" She echoed Mike's word as the giant loomed ever closer.

The door to the kitchen burst open, and a figure eerily similar to the insane creature marching towards her lurched into the room, followed by three other men. They all had their weapons drawn and a sense of impending doom shrouded Robyn and Mike.

*

Mila launched into a run to cover the few metres between her and the new arrivals. *Too late. I'm too late.*

Her eyes widened to the size of golf balls as she saw all three weapons aim towards her at the same time. *I'm sorry, Robyn. I'm sorry.*

*

From being the focus of everyone's attention moments before, Keely almost felt invisible now. Her contribution to the battle had been kicking one of her would-be attackers off balance.

She'd stayed low, crawling around some of the kitchen units and preparation stations, utterly confused by everything that was happening but determined not to lose her one chance to escape at the same time. When four more men had exploded into the room, taking everyone by surprise, she was sure that her last chance to gain her freedom had flown, but as desperation hung in the air and the blonde, sword-wielding woman made a fiery but hopeless last-ditch attempt to try to save them, she knew she had to do something.

Keely leapt to her feet, grabbing one of the bubbling

pans from the top of the range. She could see all four men about to fire their weapons. *Got to try. Got to try, at least. They came here to save me. Got to try, at least.*

A banshee-like wail left her mouth, and all four turned to see the source of the ear-splitting sound. The boiling, bubbling liquid flew through the air as if it had a purpose, and a second later, they were the ones to be howling like wild creatures as the lava-like concoction adhered itself to their faces and bodies. Three of them dropped to the ground, leaving only the tallest man standing but hunched over, trying his hardest to wipe the steaming liquid from his blistering skin.

*

It was as if the other men had not even entered the room. Chef continued towards Robyn, his face locked in a rage-filled grimace. She scrambled, reaching to her quiver for another arrow but knowing it would probably be in vain. Mike, still on the floor, lunged, sweeping his machete out hard and fast. He'd fought plenty of men bigger than him in his time, but he'd never faced one like this. "Run, Robyn," he said, hoping but not sure his plan would work. The blade disappeared through the back of Chef's boot, and Mike yanked it out again just as quickly.

The giant collapsed down on one knee as his Achilles tendon was severed. A lion's roar left his mouth as he looked up to the heavens, cleaver still in hand.

"You fucker!" he screamed, swiping towards Mike but being in too much pain to move from the spot.

Mike rolled again and again, casting a glance towards Robyn to make sure she was safely out of the madman's grasp. To his relief, she was and had backed away far enough to nock another arrow.

*

There had been several times in her life when Mila had been convinced she was going to die. Most of them had been since she'd met Robyn, but when all four guns had pointed towards her, she had been certain it was all over.

Keely's actions had not saved them, but they had bought them time.

She sidestepped the wild figure of Chef, still desperately trying to make contact with Mike despite the younger man being farther away than ever. She skidded to a stop on the shore of the bubbling sea that had splashed from the giant stockpot, which now rolled on the ground. The four men were still crying out in agony, trying their hardest to douse the fiery torture that continued to light their pain receptors.

Whoosh, swipe, flash. It took less than two seconds to silence the cries of the first three. The bigger man, the one who looked a lot like the chef, continued to back away, still hunched over, still cradling his face. He couldn't open his eyes; it felt like they had been welded shut by the glutinous brew.

He had involuntarily inhaled the mixture, too, and on top of everything else, his nostrils burnt and swelled, making it almost impossible to breathe through his nose. "Badger. Badger. I can't see." The croaked words fell on deaf ears as his brother had become fully consumed by the fury that flared within him.

*

Mya glanced in her wing mirror once more. The two sentries were still on the ground. She could see the noise had brought dozens more figures running from the main doors. They wouldn't be able to get clean shots off because a truck carrying some of their own and the two guards were positioned in between them and her own band of escapees. "I think we did it, Muppet. I think we did it."

The euphoric feeling was short-lived as she saw the Ford Transit slow to a halt. "What the hell's she doing?"

She knew Emma was the driver, but she had no idea as to why she would be stopping. She pressed on her own brake too, and Andy pulled up behind as they watched in their mirrors.

*

Ever since Mya and Mike had seen the vehicles, there had been more than one part to this mission. But the most important thing for Emma was seeing her brother again, safe and well.

She took a breath of cool air as she climbed out of the Transit. The sentries were still scrambling on the ground as more and more figures stormed out of the priory. *God, I hope you're okay, Mike.*

She had overheard her brother talking about this place as a possible base, somewhere to call their own, a secret stash away from the people in Glasgow that would allow them to build the resources they needed to fight back against Olsen and retake Safe Haven.

While they were there in the woods, lurking in the rain with no real weapons and no real hope, it was just a pipe dream that seemed further away than ever. But they had fulfilled the first part of their mission, and somehow, the rest of the plan seemed just as possible now.

She reached into her bag and withdrew the final grenade, removing the transportation clip and pulling out the pin. Sporadic gunfire began, urging her on, and she lobbed the ball-shaped device as hard as she could before turning and diving to the ground.

For a moment more, the gunfire continued, pinging the rear doors of the Transit, churning the ground around her, and then, suddenly, an explosion made the air and earth quake around her.

*

The boom from outside did nothing to stop Chef. Beano continued to stumble and stagger, looking for a few seconds to recover, but everyone else still standing in the kitchen turned in the direction of the explosion.

Mike leapt to his feet as Robyn fired another arrow, which entered Chef's side. Still, he didn't go down, and he shuffled forward on one knee towards Mike, swinging his cleaver.

"He's like the frikkin' Terminator or something,"

Robyn cried. "He won't die." She nocked another arrow ready, but Mike charged forward, dodging the swinging cleaver once more. He plunged his machete into Chef's chest, and for a moment, the seemingly unstoppable figure stopped, but then he grabbed Mike's wrist in a vice-like grip. His eyes bulged as he glared at the younger man, and Mike began to wonder if Robyn was right.

The giant swung his weapon again, but Mike twisted around, grabbing the other man's hand. *This isn't possible. This isn't possible.*

*

Mila skidded. The stewy sludge was spreading further by the second, but it was hard to see in the limited light. Beano had not been able to open his eyes since it had hit his face, and he was in the middle of a lake of the stuff.

Frantic shouts erupted from the corridor as people searched for their leader, not knowing if this was a full-scale attack or just a vehicle theft. Mila steadied herself and then drove one of her blades straight into the stomach of the floundering figure.

"Urrrggghh." He dropped to his knees, lowering his hands from his swollen face to the wound. "Ugghh." Another grating gasp left his throat before he collapsed.

*

Emma scrambled to her feet, glancing over her shoulder as she ran back to the van. The glorified shed they'd used as a guard house was on fire. The gates were just jags of shredded metal, and, hopefully, every creature in earshot was heading out of the forest to find out what was going on.

She leapt into the driver's seat, slamming the door behind her. The wheels spun and screeched as the convoy got underway again. She glimpsed the ensuing chaos in the wing mirror and then turned to Sammy in the passenger seat. Her sister was holding on to her crossbow as if it was a comfort blanket.

"It's okay, Sammy. We're out of here."

"What about Mike?"

Emma looked in the mirror once more. "Mike and the others will be fine."

*

The voices in the corridor were getting louder, and as Mike stared into Chef's crazed eyes, a chill ran through him. The lantern and candlelight made them glint eerily. *Need to end this.* He brought his head down on the kneeling figure's face with his full weight. There was an echoing crack and an explosion of skin and cartilage. Blood spurted all over Chef's face. He released his grip on Mike and the cleaver as he fell back, crashing onto the hard stone floor.

"The fuck? What the fuck? What the fuck?" he muttered over and over, reaching up to his nose. His injured leg, still gushing blood, was trapped beneath him, and none of them were sure how he could be locked in that position without howling in pain.

The noise outside grew louder still, and Mike raised his machete once more, this time bringing it down hard, cracking through the giant's skull. Still, his eyes remained open. Still, he glared towards his attacker with venom.

"You've got to be kidding me."

"Holy shit. This is really creeping me out," Robyn cried, placing another arrow in her bow.

Mike levered the blade out of his victim's head and then brought it down with even more power. There was another loud crack as a second bloody crater opened up in the big man's skull. His eyes widened further, and Mike threw a concerned glance towards Robyn, who was staring on in terror. He turned back to see Chef's eyes finally close and his body go limp. "Thank Christ for that," he said, yanking the blade out.

He ran across to grab the machete he'd flung earlier then took hold of Robyn's arm while looking towards the other two women, who were both still bewildered by what they'd just witnessed.

"BEANO?"

It sounded as if the shout was just a few metres outside of the door.

"Come," Mila said, and the four of them jerked into motion once more.

*

Mya brought the truck to a stop. There had been a rush to get everyone loaded on board, and the initial plan to have either Della or Clay upfront with her had not panned out. It seemed, however, that the residents of the priory had enough to do for the moment without following in hot pursuit. She walked around to the back of the covered wagon.

"I'll need someone up front with me for directions to this school."

"I'll come," Della said, climbing out and walking to the passenger side to discover Muppet comfortably coiled up in the footwell.

"Don't mind him," Mya said, climbing in.

"Oh. Okay," she replied, doing her best not to stand on the mongrel's tail. No sooner had she closed the door than they were off again. She looked in the wing mirror to see the other vehicles following.

"I still can't really believe what I've just seen. Do you think the others are okay? Do you think they found Rupert and Keely?"

"If anybody could, it's those three. Emma throwing that grenade would have alerted anyone who hadn't heard the gunfire, and to be honest, if that was me, my main priority would be getting that entrance secured before any infected got into the grounds."

"So you think they're okay then?"

"We'll find out tomorrow, won't we?"

14

Keely had snatched the keys out of the discarded padlock and was examining them in what little light there was by the outer kitchen door. She tried one to no avail as the others stared at the inner entrance expecting it to open at any moment.

"Got it," she said, and a rush of cool air hit them as they ran out into the night. Keely closed the exit quietly behind them, locking it once more.

"What now?" Robyn asked.

It was dark outside, but there was just enough light for Mike to see where they were in relation to the coal bunker and furnace building.

"This way," he said, starting to run. "Keep your eyes peeled."

The four of them sprinted as fast as the dark would allow around the back of the building. It sounded as if hell had broken loose at the front, but that didn't stop them from being vigilant. The three former Safe Haven inhabitants had been in plenty of situations like this, and they knew that nothing should be taken for granted.

"You were with the people in the forest," Keely said. "I don't understand what you're doing here. Where are the others?"

"We'll explain everything when we're out of here. Right now, you need to trust us," Mike replied.

They reached the entrance to the furnace building and entered. One by one, they clicked on their torches. "Don't rely on the handrail," Mila warned. "It is not safe."

It was only a minute before they were in the tunnel once more, and they all paused to catch their breath. "I'm sorry about Rupert," Robyn said.

Keely started to cry. Everything had happened so quickly, and however confused her feelings for Rupert were, seeing what happened to him was horrific. "I don't want to sound like a dick," Mike began, "but you're going to have to hold off on mourning him until we're out of this. We don't know if any of those mad bastards are out looking for us, and even if they're not, there are a shit load of infected in this general area."

Keely sniffed loudly and then wiped her eyes and nose on her sleeve. "I'm probably crying out of guilt more than anything. It was me who killed him." The others looked towards her with confused expressions. "He was going to tell them where the rest of our people were. I didn't mean to. I just meant to shut him up. He didn't deserve it, and he didn't deserve what happened to him next."

"Yeah, well, like I say, we need to keep our wits about us; otherwise, we might have a gruesome and painful death to look forward to."

"Nice, Mike," Robyn said.

Mike shrugged. "Okay, are we ready?" They all nodded before the four of them were moving again.

*

"You realise that if you stroke him any harder, you might actually dislocate his neck?" Ephraim said as he and

Kat sat opposite Wren.

They were at the rear of the truck where more of the subdued moonlight was visible. "Oh," she said distantly, pulling her hand away from the German shepherd in mid-movement. "I suppose my mind's elsewhere."

"Robyn and Mila will be fine," Kat said.

"Not that you're bothered, but Mike will be too," Ephraim said, almost laughing.

"What's that supposed to mean?" Wren asked.

"Ignore him," Kat replied.

"Yes. Ignore me. I always get crotchety when I've had to go on a mission to save a couple of strangers with nothing more than a pointy stick to defend myself."

"You volunteered," Wren replied.

"Given a choice of staying in a dank, dark cave and suffering through hours of 'Ooh, I do hope they're alright. Do you think they're going to be okay? What if they're not back by morning?' and a thousand other half-formed thoughts that should be left to develop to full fruition in one's mind before being spoken, I'll opt for the promise of almost certain death every time."

"You're a dick."

"It's been said before. It will be said again."

"Yeah. You're a dick."

Kat laughed, and they fell into quiet contemplation for a moment before Wren spoke again. "I hope they're okay."

"And suddenly, the cave is seeming more attractive by the minute," Ephraim replied.

"Did I mention that you're a dick?"

Ephraim took a breath. "Listen to me. In the time I've known those three people, they have managed to astound and flabbergast me with their will, determination, skill, strength and sheer bloody-mindedness on an almost daily basis. I doubt that there is anything they can't do if they put their minds to it. And I don't say those words lightly. You know I don't like dishing out praise."

Wren thought for a moment. "I suppose you're right."

"And it wasn't like we just left them to it and crossed our fingers, was it? Stealing the vehicles, killing some of their guards, destroying their sentry box, and—" Ephraim cleared his throat and did his best Michael Caine impression "—we only went and blew the bloody gates off." He chuckled quietly to himself.

"What?" Wren asked.

"From *The Italian Job*," he replied, the self-satisfied smile still evident in his voice.

"What's *The Italian Job*?"

"Oh, kill me now."

"Wren's too young to know what you're talking about. And it was doors, not gates," Kat said.

"Okay, but surely she's heard of Michael Caine."

"Course I have. But what's that got to do with anything? And why did you say that bit about the gates in a funny accent?"

"I was doing Michael Caine."

"That was nothing like Michael Caine. It sounded like you were having a stroke."

Kat burst out laughing.

"People used to plead with me to do my impressions at parties."

"I can believe they pleaded with you to stop."

"And who'd invite you to any parties, anyway?" Kat asked.

Ephraim sat back in his seat. "Well, I'm so glad I bothered now. I'm glad I bothered to try to make you feel better. It was so worth it."

Wren leaned across and placed a hand on his knee. "Thank you, Ephraim. I appreciate what you said."

He sniffed sulkily. "You're welcome, I suppose."

"But that was nothing like Michael Caine."

*

They wanted darkness or as close to darkness as

possible to get back up the hillside to the forest, but from the moment they crossed the bridge, the moon broke out from behind the clouds. All four of them kept looking back to the priory. They couldn't see the fire, but the odd flicker of burning ash rose from the other side of the ground, which reassured them that the priory's inhabitants had more to think about than them.

"Shit!" Robyn hissed as two RAMs broke from the trees. The noise from the last few minutes would have had all those in earshot looking for its source, but this pair of creatures had seen the four of them and were closing in fast. Robyn raised her bow, but Mike stopped her.

"Mila and I will deal with any infected. It's best that you save your arrows." He and the German swordswoman accelerated up the hill meeting the two dark figures as they charged towards them. Crack! Swoosh! And they were down.

Without missing a beat, they continued towards the forest, grateful to finally reach the tree line but, now they were there, realising that the darkness was no longer their friend. The sound of thundering feet raced towards them, and they all looked around frantically, trying to find its source. A single creature lunged out of the blackness, taking them all by surprise.

Keely screamed, dodging it at the last second. Mila jumped forward, slicing down and around. Its head above the ear frisbeed beyond a clump of bushes, and its body collapsed to the ground. Mila wiped the blade off on its clothes before returning it to the scabbard on her back.

"We will not make it to the cavern in the dark."

"Crap. I hate sleeping in trees." Robyn looked up towards the unwelcoming black branches above her.

"It is better this than dying, yes?"

"I suppose."

"The sooner we get off the ground the better. More will be coming."

They carried on walking for a few metres before the

sound of more infected drifted towards them. Enough light from above shone into a small clearing for them all to see the outline of a giant sycamore tree. "This is good. We will sleep here."

"Oh yeah. I'm sure we'll all sleep like babies."

*

"George. George!" Jenny placed her hand on the older man's arm and gently shook him. His eyes shot open, and he just stared into the fire for a few seconds before looking towards Jenny. "You were having a nightmare," she whispered, doing her best not to wake up those still deep in a slumber.

"I…." He shuffled up, grateful to be out of it. "My heart's still going fifty to the dozen."

"I don't need to ask what it was about. You were calling Wren's name."

He sighed sadly and edged up to the log a little further, using it as a backrest as the pair stared into the flames. Meg had woken up briefly, used to Jenny's own nightmares; she settled back down into a snoring sleep just as fast.

"I thought they might have made it back before dark." He had fallen into sleep, holding a vigil of the cavern's entrance. Every time he'd heard a noise, he'd hoped it was them returning, but he had finally passed out due to exhaustion.

"They wouldn't take any risks with the light. There's no way they'd travel through a forest in the dark. That would be suicidal."

"The whole thing's suicidal."

Jenny reached out once again and took his arm. "They'll be back tomorrow."

"You don't know that. You can't know that."

"No, I can't, I suppose. But I've got a feeling."

George felt irritable. He hadn't had enough sleep. His bones were aching and tired. He was scared for Mila and his granddaughters, and all he wanted was to be left alone with his thoughts, but he knew Jenny was hurting too. The people out there risking their lives were her family. She'd known them longer than anyone, and he'd caught sight of her looking towards the entrance like a loyal dog waiting for its owner every time there'd been a sound too. He placed his free hand over hers. "Well, let's hope your feeling's right."

*

"Jesus. This is a little different to the school I went to," Mya said as they drove up the winding drive to the grandiose-looking main building. The sports fields surrounding it were very overgrown, and one of the rugby posts had toppled, probably as a result of one of the previous winter's storms. But it wasn't difficult to imagine what the place had been like in its prime.

"And mine," Della said.

A large corrugated steel vehicle shed stood tall at one end of the gravelled yard, and even though they now had their transport into Glasgow, Mya was still keen to take a look.

She brought the truck to a stop and checked her rearview mirror to make sure Andy and Emma did the same. "Come on, Muppet," Mya said, opening the door and climbing out. Her faithful mongrel sprang from the passenger footwell onto the driver's seat and down onto the ground. Mya had loaded the two remaining shells in the shotgun before their journey began. She had expected to run into plenty of infected on the way, but they had only happened across a small handful, which she had taken out using the reinforced grille guard at the front of the truck.

She scoured the wide-open yard and car park, looking for any signs of danger. They'd killed their lights straight after the turn for the school to minimise the chance of being discovered by hungry RAMs, and their luck seemed to be holding.

"What now?" Emma asked as she, Sammy, Jules and Wren walked up to her.

"We do a sweep of the building, make sure there are no surprises lurking in there for us. Then we try to get a little shuteye before morning."

"Then what?"

"Then I'll head back to the cavern and get the others."

"By yourself?"

Mya turned to Della and Clay, who had just joined them. "Actually, I think I'm going to need a little help finding it."

"You don't have to worry about that," Della replied. "We've been here a few times before, and I'm sure our people will be missing us by now." Clay laughed, and the others smiled politely, acknowledging the depths of the problems they had back at the cavern.

"We'll come too," Wren said, gesturing towards Wolf.

"I'm not going to turn you down."

"Right then," Jules said. "Let's check this place out."

*

Clouds hung over the hills in the east, but the moon made the sea sparkle. Raj stood at the wheel and breathed in the cool fresh air. Normally, he loved this, but all he could think about was his friends on land. Despite Mike's bluster about them all getting down to Glasgow safely, he knew that any journey was dangerous these days, no matter how well-planned.

"On a night like this, it's hard to believe the world's come to an end, isn't it?" Beck said, seemingly appearing out of nowhere.

"The sea and the sky are always constants. It is what happens on land that causes the problems."

"I suppose." The two men stood side by side for a moment. It was the middle of the night, or very early morning, depending on which way one looked at things.

"Could you not sleep?"

"I don't know quite what time it is, but when I was

at Number Ten, I started surviving on about four hours a night, and it's a habit I never kicked."

"With the worries of the world on your shoulders, it must have been hard to find restful moments."

"I had a lot of help from some of the finest distilleries in Scotland."

Raj laughed. "As I understand it, alcohol is in plentiful supply down in Glasgow."

"Why do you think I was so eager to go?"

Raj laughed again. They stood in silence for a while longer before Beck spoke again. "What's your take on it all, Raj?"

"I'm sorry, Prime Minister. My take on what?"

"On what we're doing, where we're going, what's going to happen when we get there. Do you think this is going to be a permanent move? Do you think this is where we'll live out our days?"

"I am just a vet who is more of a sailor these days. What I think is of little consequence."

"On the contrary. You don't talk much, but you take everything in. You and Talikha have sage-like status among the people of Safe Haven, and from what I've seen, it's completely justified."

"I'm not sure about that."

"We'll agree to disagree. But I'd still be interested to hear your take."

Raj thought for a moment. "Mike and Mya are excellent judges of character. They believe this Griz is a good man, and I have no doubt that they are correct. He wants to help, but he also sees the potential in having people like Mike, Mya, Darren, Wren, Robyn and Mila in the community."

"Yeah. I think he's going to be disappointed when he finds out we're not all like that."

Raj smiled. "Maybe. But we have plenty of people who can make a substantive contribution to their society, whatever that is."

"So, that's it. You think we're going to move down there, be absorbed and live happily ever after?"

"I think there is that choice."

"Choice?"

"For those who want to."

"You've lost me. Wouldn't everybody want that?"

Raj cast his eyes forward, losing himself in the moonlit water for a moment. "I have known Mike for a long time."

"That's right. You met him down in Leeds, didn't you?"

"Not far from Leeds, yes. He is…."

"He's what?"

"I am trying to find the words to do him justice. He is an unstoppable force."

Beck shrugged. "No argument here. But what's this got to do with us settling down in Glasgow?"

"He will not rest until he holds Olsen's heart in his fist or he is dead. Those are the only two choices for him."

Beck laughed uncomfortably. "Surely all that stuff he came out with was just bravado. I mean when we were in Safe Haven, and we had something resembling a fighting force, that was one thing. But now we're just refugees. It's a miracle we're still standing at all."

"Mike does not forgive or forget. Olsen took Lucy and Jake from him. There is no happily ever after for Mike, only revenge."

"But that's insane. That's completely insane."

"It is Mike."

15

Mike's eyes flickered open. He couldn't move his right arm for some reason, but with his left hand, he pulled himself up a little, and everything came flooding back to him. They were in a tree. They'd each settled into a nook to last out the night, and now it was time to be on their way again.

"People will begin to talk about you two," Mila said, smiling, and he looked down to see that she and Keely were already on the ground. He turned to his right to find Robyn nestled into him.

"It's time to get up," he said quietly.

A low-pitched moan left her lips before she finally opened her eyes. They widened when they saw Mike's face in such close proximity to hers. "I suppose I should be grateful that we're both fully clothed, this time, at least."

"And suddenly I'm devastated."

"I hate to break you two lovebirds up, but I think we

should be going, yes?"

"I would literally kill for a coffee," Robyn said grumpily as she edged out onto a sturdy bough. She passed her bow and quiver down to Mila then dropped down herself.

Mike remained in the tree for a moment longer before jumping down to the ground to join them. "I'm guessing you know how to get back to the cavern from here," he said to Keely.

She looked around. She'd never been this far into the forest on this side. "Err … I'll feel better when I see the road."

"The road is this way," Mila said, pointing.

"Let's get going then." They had spoken briefly about their journey to Glasgow and the events leading up to Keely's rescue the night before, but now she wanted to learn more. "You said that Della and Clay were in the other group?"

"Yeah," Robyn replied as they all walked along, staying mindful of their surroundings and keeping their voices low.

"Who else?"

"What?"

"Who else from the cavern?"

"Err… nobody."

"What do you mean?"

"I mean that nobody else from the cavern came with us. The rest of the group was totally made up of our people."

Keely carried on walking with her eyes glued to the ground. A small rasping sound left her mouth, and Robyn looked across to see that she was crying. "I'm sorry. There was probably a better way I could have put that, but I'm not great with … y'know."

"Talking?" Mike asked. Robyn raised her middle finger, and Mike smiled. "For what it's worth, Keely," he continued, "it wasn't about you."

She let out a huff of a laugh through her tears. "Well, it certainly feels like it was about me."

"They were scared. You could see it in their eyes. Plus, that Owen bloke was a right twat. He was riling people up against Della and Clay. He seemed to be on some kind of power trip."

"He's always been that way." She wiped her eyes.

"Yeah, well. I think he saw it as an opportunity to stir some more trouble. And in fairness to the guy, he did pretty well."

Keely sniffed again. "Well, thank you for coming. Thank you for saving me."

"We were just returning the favour. I'm sorry we weren't in time to save your friend."

Her mind suddenly flashed back to Rupert's corpse, and fresh tears welled before she wiped those away too. "Do…." She stopped herself before she'd even begun. They'd briefly told her the night before about where they were going and why, but everything had been so bewildering, and she hadn't really taken it all in, but now she was thinking clearly once more.

"Do what?" Mike asked.

"Do you think I could join you? Do you think I could come with you to Glasgow?"

"Everybody in our community has to pull their weight in one way or another. And we'll be newcomers down there. We'll have to prove ourselves to them. It's not going to be a walk in the park."

"I'll do whatever it takes. I promise you. I never really fitted in back at the cavern, and despite what you say, I think the fact that so few people came out looking for Rupert and me proves it. I'll work my socks off, I'll fight, I'll cook; I'll do whatever anyone needs me to do, but I'd like to go with you."

"If it wasn't for you, I don't think any of us would have got out of that kitchen," Mike said appreciatively, remembering her actions the previous night.

"Yeah. The flip side of that is that if it wasn't for me, none of you would have been in that kitchen in the first place."

"Well, there is that, I suppose," Mike replied, smiling. He shrugged. "I don't make the decisions, but I don't see an issue with you coming along."

"Wow!" Robyn said. "Nice way to make someone feel welcome, Mike. I don't see an issue with you coming along. I'm going all warm and gooey inside." She turned to Keely. "Of course you can come along."

Keely laughed a little. "Thank you."

*

"The sun came up a while back. It's time for you all to clear out of here now," Owen said.

Not everyone was awake when he and his small posse had walked over. But he had made sure they heard his voice. "But not everyone's eaten yet," Jenny protested.

"Yeah, well. That's not my problem. We let you sleep here for the night, which was more than we had to do. Now I want you all gone, as per our agreement."

"Do we really need to do this?" asked the woman who'd told Jenny about the ridge the previous day.

"Yes, we do. We've been more than generous, more than fair. We lost two of our people thanks to them."

"You can't blame them for that."

"Oh, I agree. It wasn't just them. It was our glorious leader as well."

The other woman shook her head and looked at Jenny. "I'm sorry. I'll let the others know where you're heading."

"Thank you," Jenny replied weakly. She turned to the rest of her people. "Gather your things. We need to get out of here."

*

Crack, kick, crack. They hadn't been in the forest more than five minutes before the first two creatures attacked. Wolf and Muppet had both sounded the alarm moments before, and it was Mya who had dealt with the infected attackers swiftly and brutally.

The journey to the sprawling forest had not been a long one, and they had not discovered a single RAM in the surrounding countryside. Unlike the previous day, the sun was shining brightly, and there was not a single cloud in the sky.

"Y'know," Wren said, "you'd be welcome to come with us down to Glasgow."

Clay smiled. "Emma invited us yesterday."

"I know. But I'm just reminding you. What you did going after your friends was no small thing. You're different to the others."

"They need us."

"Oh, give it up, Clay," Della snapped. "They don't need us. They like having us around so they don't have to think. They like having their decisions made for them right up to the point where it causes them an inconvenience, and then you see exactly how much they value us."

"That's not fair. I did kind of pressure them into heading out when we heard the gunfire."

"Pressure them? Anyone with a decent bone in their body should have been falling over themselves to get out there. There are so few living left that we should all see it as our duty to help others when we can."

"It's not as simple as that."

"They make sure it's not, but it should be."

"What would you have me do, Della?"

There was a pause before she spoke again. "We should go with them."

"What?"

"We'll never be given an opportunity like this again. We should go with them to Glasgow. We should leave Owen to be the king of the forest people, and we should go."

"We were the ones who came up with this. We were the ones who sourced everything, who planned everything.

We were the ones—"

"And where the hell has it gotten us? Oh, sure, for the first couple of months, everyone was so grateful to be alive that we were living in a constant state of euphoria, but day by day, week by week, month by month, since then, things have been getting steadily worse and worse."

"That's ... that's not true. People aren't going hungry. People didn't go cold in the winter. The forest gives us shelter and a lot of foraging opportunities, and the remoteness means that we managed to avoid the infected in the main."

On cue, growls began in the back of Wolf's and Muppet's throats, but they were only fleeting as a bolt whistled through the trees, laying the advancing creature to rest. "Yeah. And that fire yesterday brought how many to the area? In the space of twenty-four hours, everything has changed."

"You're exaggerating."

"No, I'm not, Clay. It might be months – years even – before those things drift out of the forest. Hell, we might never get rid of them. The forest could become their new playground."

"She's right," Wren said.

"Look—" Clay began.

"No, you look," Della replied. "It's hard to step away from something you put so much time and effort into. Hell, I lost just as much sweat as you. I cried just as many tears. But at the end of the day, it's a glorified cave, Clay. It served its purpose. It got us through the outbreak in one piece. But now there's an opportunity for us to move on, to live with others, to thrive rather than just exist."

"The whole reason we wanted to get out of the cities was because they would be so dangerous. If the infected were going to be anywhere, it was there. Have you heard the words coming out of your mouth, Della? You're talking about us heading to the biggest city in Scotland."

"By the sound of it, the people there have found a

way to survive."

"We found a way to survive."

"Okay, I'll put this another way. I want to go, Clay. I want to get out of that damn cave. I want to live above ground. I want to see the sun rise and set. I want to live a different life to the one I'm living because all this," she said, gesturing around her, "was just a catalyst. If it hadn't been the lorry crash yesterday, something else would have been what caused Owen and his little band of merry men and women to kick off."

"I'll handle Owen when we get back."

"No."

"Look, I don't think this is the right time to be making decisions regarding our entire future, do you?"

"Oh no? Then when? When Wren and Mya and the others have left us and we've got no way out? Will that be the right time, Clay? Will you be happy to talk about our future then? Our future, not yours, not mine, ours."

"I did this for you, for us."

"I know." Some of the anger left her, and she reached out, taking his hand. She had meant every word she had said, and each of them had taken a toll on Clay as he looked at her with sad eyes. "I know," she said again. "But now it's time we moved on."

"And what about the others? Do we just leave them all behind?"

"You're not responsible for everyone, Clay."

"Anybody who wants to come with us can come with us," Wren said. "They'll all have to pull their weight and play their part, but they'll be welcome."

They all walked along in silence for a while before Clay broke it once more. "I remember the first time we came to this place," he said, and a smile appeared on his face. Funnily enough, we were heading to the Skye Outward Bounds Centre, and I took a wrong turn. Do you remember?"

The irritation and anger were gone from Della's face

now as her husband recalled happier days. "Of course I do. But I think it was more than one wrong turn you took."

"True enough. Anyway, it got late, and we decided to set up our tent in the forest. A month later, we came back here to explore the place properly—the river, the caves, the nearby mountain tracks. It was like some kind of paradise for people like us."

"Things change, Clay. Nothing can go back to the way it was, and this place is swimming with infected now. We need to get out of here."

Clay glanced around at the trees as they continued to walk and then looked across at his wife. A sad expression formed on his face. "It was nice while it lasted, though, wasn't it?"

*

"You found anything good?" Emma asked as she walked into the kitchen.

"Nah," Jules replied. "I'm guessing Della and her crew picked this place clean. There's plenty of cutlery and pots and pans. Andy, Rob and Jon are checking out the rest of the floor. "Where's Sammy?"

"She's on watch with Kat and Ephraim."

"How are you feelin'?"

"Tired."

"You know that's not what I meant."

Emma lifted herself onto one of the kitchen countertops, and Jules did the same on the opposite side of the aisle. "I'll be better when I know Mike and the others are okay."

"They will be okay, y'know."

A bitter smile flitted onto Emma's face before she sighed. "I know you're probably right. It's just…."

"I get it. Don't worry, I get it. But it was true what Mya said last night. We did provide them with a pretty good distraction, and you chucking that grenade was genius."

"Well, let's just hope it did some good."

"I'm going to check all the private rooms out. Do you

fancy coming with me?"

"What are you hoping to find in those?"

Jules shrugged. "You never know. We might happen across a secret stash of chocolate or sweets. These over-privileged little fuckers will always have been getting care packages from their parents. In the rush to get out of here, they might have left some behind."

Emma sniggered. "How hopeful are you?"

"I'm always hopeful, me. That's my middle name."

"Are you so desperate for a chocolate bar that you'd go searching through all the rooms?"

"Too right. I would literally kill my own brothers to get my hands on a Snickers or a Bounty."

Emma smiled. "M&M's."

"Oh God, yes."

"Maltesers."

"Oh, Jesus. Stop it. There was nothing I used to love more than shoving a handful of Maltesers into my mouth and just letting them all melt. It was heaven."

"Terry's Chocolate Orange."

Jules slid down off the counter. "That's it. I'm definitely going now."

"I'll come with you."

*

"They said it was about half a mile to the east. It's quite a wide formation, so if we head in that general direction, hopefully we'll find it," Jenny said, holding on to her spear unconvincingly. She kept looking down at Meg, who was more alert than ever, sensing the heightened tension in the air.

"Well, this is definitely east … ish," Liz said, walking by Jenny's side. A couple of the nurses were just behind her. They were all brandishing the same type of homemade spear, and they all felt woefully unprepared.

Jenny glanced over her shoulder, and her heart sank a little more. There was not one person she could label a fighter. They all carried weapons, but if an attack came, it would end badly. George had been in a world of his own ever since Robyn, Wren, and Mila left. Jack and James were doing their best to try to keep his spirits up, but even they were struggling given their current predicament. Ruby looked like she hadn't slept in a week. Dark circles hung beneath her eyes, and she had to keep one hand on Tommy's back as if she was almost forcing him forward.

"I don't think I've ever needed a drink so badly in my life," she said, turning back round to their direction of travel.

"Err … we're barely past dawn."

"And your point is?"

Liz shrugged. "No point. Just making an observation."

"I'm hoping that—" Jenny stopped, and her blood turned cold as Meg began to growl. "Oh, God!" She waved her arm, causing all the others to come to an abrupt halt too. The forest fell silent other than Meg's sound, and fear settled over them all like an icy shroud.

"Where are they? Where are they?" Liz whispered, her eyes darting all around.

Jenny had no idea. She was so far out of her comfort zone she may as well have been on Mars. She placed her feet apart and held the spear out in front of her as she'd seen others do in training. She scoured the forest, looking for any sign of movement but seeing only trees. *Please, God.*

Then she saw it. A single creature, wide and awkward, half running, half waddling towards them. Suddenly, it was not just Meg's growling they could all hear as the chilling sound of the beast rose into the morning air too. Jenny took a couple of strides forward. She was not the youngest or the fittest, but it was up to her to take the lead. She looked down to see her hands shaking, and then she felt something and turned to see Liz standing next to her once more. She heard movement on the other side and saw Jack, James and George all standing there too. For the moment, George was leaning on his spear for support, but despite this, some of the fear and apprehension left her as the five of them stood in a line.

Meg broke into a run towards the beast, and a part of Jenny wanted to stop her, but another part knew that she was probably their best defence. As old as she was, Meg was a scrapper when it came to protecting her pack. She leapt at the advancing creature, knocking it off balance. It bounced against a tree trunk and ricocheted onto the ground.

George started to limp forward, but the others ran to where the beast desperately scrambled to get back to its feet. Jenny was the first to strike. Her spear glanced the side of its head, opening a dark red rut but doing little to stop it. Jack was next. He lunged, harpooning the monster's shoulder as it rose to its knees. It continued to rise, unaffected by the wound that would have had any living being in agony. James swung his spear like a bat, cracking it on the side of the head and stunning it momentarily. Then it was Liz's turn. She ran at the beast, extending her weapon out fully. No one was more surprised than her when the point disappeared into the creature's skull.

It remained upright for just seconds then collapsed backwards, leaving its gory calling card at the end of her spear. Meg was ready for round two and looked bemused to find the fight already over.

"Jesus," Liz hissed as she looked at the bloody point and realised what she'd done.

"You did it," Jenny said excitedly, placing a hand on the other woman's shoulder.

"As much as I'd like to take credit, this was most definitely a team effort. It's done. That's all that matters."

"I suppose you're right."

"Let's hope we don't run into any more before we get to that ridge," George said, propping himself up once again as his ankle continued to pain him.

"We killed one," Jenny replied confidently. "We can kill others if they come for us."

"Given a choice, I'd prefer we didn't have to."

The reality of the situation finally caught up with her, and as empowered as she felt, even though she hadn't been the one to make the kill, she nodded. "Yeah. I suppose you're right."

16

Mike and the others had seen a couple of roaming packs but managed to avoid them rather than confront them. When they had crossed the road, there had been no sign of the tower of smoke, so they could only assume that the fire was out.

It was a double-edged sword. This meant no more infected would be lured to the area, but at the same time, the ones that were in the locale would begin to drift into the forest.

"It's not far now," Keely said as they entered a clearing.

They carried on for a few more minutes, and then there was the cave entrance. "How far's the school from here?" Mike asked.

Keely had heard about the plan to get to the school second hand from her current companions. She'd only been there a couple of times, but she was pretty certain she could remember the route. "About two miles or something. I think."

"You don't sound confident."

"No. It'll be okay."

"We don't need to worry. Della and Clay will escort us, yes?"

Keely looked a little embarrassed. "I'm not sure about that. When I tell them that I'm going with you, I think it'll put Clay's nose well out of joint. He takes everything that happens here very personally."

"Yeah, well, after the barney that he had with Owen, I think he'll understand," Robyn replied.

"Oh well. Here goes nothing." Keely was the first to enter the cave. She was greeted warmly by the two guards as they opened the thick wooden doors. They both asked where Rupert was and were both equally saddened to hear he would not be returning. In the subdued light, it was hard to judge what the expressions on their faces meant when they turned to the others. "Are Della and Clay back yet?"

"Err … not yet," one of the guards replied.

Mike and the others flicked on their torches, and the quartet continued down the tunnel as a whispered and frantic conversation ensued behind them.

"Am I imagining things, or were they totally not happy to see us?" Robyn said.

"They're probably just surprised that we made it back in one piece," Keely replied.

On reaching the cavern, the lack of Safe Haven residents was blindingly obvious, and despite the muted celebrations to see Keely back in one piece, albeit minus Rupert, the tension was palpable in the air.

"Where are our people?" Mike asked loudly, not to anyone in particular at first, but then he spotted Owen and marched towards him. "Where are our people?" he asked again.

"They left," Owen replied, glancing behind him to make sure he had friendly faces there.

"Left?" Robyn and Mila joined him.

"Yeah. They set off at first light."

"They just left?" Mike persisted.

"Yeah."

"Did my sister and Mya come back to get them?"

"No."

Mike took half a step back so he could see Owen's face properly in the fire and lantern light. "So, they just set off of their own accord into the forest."

Owen glimpsed behind once more to see if his number of supporters had swelled. Sadly for him, it was as if an invisible force field had created a circle around him but for the four sycophants within an arm's stretch. Hardly anyone had been comfortable in the cold light of day when the refugees had been turned out, but in the absence of anyone to stand up to Owen, they had gone along with it anyway. Now, though, the weight of what they had been a party to lay heavy on them. They would have to live with the guilt of their inaction, but they were more than happy for Owen to answer for it.

"We let them sleep here, and they went first thing."

Mike's eyes narrowed. "Went or were made to go?"

"W-we don't owe you people anything. We put ourselves at risk coming out to help you, and by the look of it, we've lost one of our own because of it."

"Yeah, well, considering none of you were willing to go look for him, it doesn't sound like you were too broken up about it."

"Y-you have no right to say that."

Mike reached out, grabbing Owen by the scruff of his shirt. One of the figures behind raised his bow, and Mike glared at him. "You point that thing at me, you'd better fucking use it. Otherwise, I'll shove that arrow so far up your arse it'll catch every time you brush your teeth." The other man stood there for a few seconds before lowering it once more. Mike turned back to Owen. "Where did they go?" he growled, sending a shockwave through the entire cavern.

Owen struggled, placing his hands around Mike's wrists in the hope he could shake himself free, but to no avail.

"The ridge," someone called out.

"What?" Robyn replied.

"I told them to head towards the ridge. There's a cave there where they could stay until you came back."

"Where is it?"

"To the east of here. About half a mile."

"I know the place," Keely said, turning to the others. "I'm going with them to Glasgow."

Gasps and sounds of surprise erupted from all over the cavern. "No, Keely. Think about this. You're one of us," said the woman who had spoken before.

Keely went across to her tent. "Is that why you all came out looking for me?" She turned to Robyn. "I'll be ready in a minute."

Mike maintained his grip on Owen despite the fresh information. "We're going to that ridge, and if I find a single hair out of place on any of their heads, I'm going to come back here and fucking gut you, you miserable little piece of shit." He finally released his grasp, and Owen staggered back.

"Wh-who do you think you are?" he asked, energised a little by his newfound freedom. "You can't come in here and—" The punch seemed to come out of nowhere, completely blindsiding Owen. He stumbled back, falling onto the ground, and Mike strode across to him, unleashing kick after kick in his ribs. Owen curled into a ball, crying out in pain while his loyal band of followers shrunk back, horrified and terrified by the explosive outburst. Everyone in the cave watched open-mouthed until a loud crack, signalling that at least one of Owen's ribs had broken, made Mike stop.

"You've bro-ken my ri-bs. You've broken my ribs," he cried like an infant.

Mike looked down at him for a moment, spitting and

whispering "Fucker" under his breath before turning to his friends. "Come on. Let's go find our people."

By the time they reached the entrance to the tunnel, Keely had joined them with the rucksack on her back.

"Err … are you okay?" Robyn asked as they retraced their torchlit steps.

"Fine. Why do you ask?" Mike replied with a bitter smile.

"Maybe 'cause you just half-killed somebody back there."

Mike shrugged. "Yeah, I figured if I killed him, I wouldn't be able to come back and fulfil my promise if any of our people were hurt."

"I say this with all due love and respect, but you're a bit of a frikkin' psycho."

"He got less than he deserved. He sent wounded and scared people out into a forest swimming with infected. Your grandad is out there."

"Yeah, but—"

"Like I said. It's less than he deserved."

*

"How far do you think we've come?" Liz asked as they continued their trek through the forest.

"I really don't know," Jenny replied. "Hell, I don't even know if we're heading in the right direction."

"No, I'm pretty sure we're okay as far as direction goes. I tend to be good with that sort of thing. My dad used to take the family out hiking every weekend."

"If that's the case, shouldn't you know how far we've come then?"

Liz laughed. "You've got me there. I lose track in forests for some reason."

"I'd say we've been walking for about a third of a mile or so," Jack chimed in.

"It feels further than that," Jenny replied.

"That's probably to do with the fact that some people think this is more of a death march than a walk to freedom."

Jenny and Liz looked behind at the other faces. It was true. Worry and fear were painted on all of them. Eyes darted suspiciously, looking for signs of the infected. They all gripped their weapons tightly, but they had already proved that without the likes of Wren, Mya, Mike and the others being there to fight with them, their resolve was non-existent.

"Oh no," Jenny cried as she saw Meg stop dead. The mongrel started growling loudly, and an air of dread settled over them all.

Liz took a deep breath and sidled up to Jenny once more, extending her spear out in front of her. Jack, James and George did the same. The two nurses who had been walking just behind Liz joined them.

"Get ready," Jack said, looking back over his shoulder, and the others reluctantly brought their weapons up too.

This time, three creatures burst out of the trees at a sprint.

"Oh, good grief," Jenny muttered under her breath.

Liz said nothing but was filled with the same sense of hopelessness. A sudden bloodcurdling scream rose from behind them, and they all turned to see two more infected charging from the right.

"Shit!" Jack cried, pivoting, trying to encourage a few others to do the same.

"This is it," Jenny whispered. "It's all over."

*

Mike and the others all launched into sprints. The scream was loud enough for them to hear, but it was some distance away. Each of them feared that by the time they reached the source, it would be too late.

"Keep your eyes peeled. That scream'll probably attract more infected," he said, leaping over a half-buried tree root.

"Three o'clock," Mila cried, and Robyn drew an arrow, nocked it, skidded to a stop and fired. She knew the second the missile began its journey that it was a kill shot, and she started running again. "Eleven o'clock," Mila shouted.

Mike was three metres in front of them and obscuring Robyn's aim. "Got it," he said, speeding up further and lunging at the creature as it got near. He parried its outstretched hands then whipped his blade around, slicing into the side of its skull. He withdrew his machete before the beast had even fallen, and he was on his way again.

*

Jenny could feel her heart racing as the three creatures charged towards her and the others. She'd been in a lot of close situations before today, but there had always been Shaw, Mike or one of the others with her. This time, she was close to their best hope, and the responsibility made her feel sick to her stomach.

She edged forward a little more, her breath shivering, giving away the emotional turmoil she was experiencing as the last few seconds of her life played out. Meg bolted, but as grateful as she was, Jenny knew that this time it would be in vain.

Bye-bye, beautiful girl. I hope someone finds you when this is over, and you get to spend your last days down in Glasgow.

Tears rolled down her cheeks, but she remained wide-eyed. She would defend her people until the last breath left her lungs, but that didn't stop it from hurting.

Meg pounced on the creature leading the charge, and the beast toppled, knocking the other two off-kilter a little before crashing to the ground. *My girl. My beautiful girl. Bye, precious.*

The stumble was quickly forgotten as the remaining two beasts tore towards them. Jenny took a deep breath. *I wonder if Lucy, Hughes, Beth, Barnes and all the others will be waiting on the other side.* She hoped so. *I was never good at being alone.*

*

Mike dived to his right, kicking out hard. The RAM

catapulted backwards, and he finished it off with an unceremonious hack before it had the chance to scramble back up. *How many of these things actually heard that scream?*

Ever since they had set off towards the panicked sound, they had found more infected than during their entire journey from the priory.

"I've got a really bad feeling about this," Robyn said, releasing her bowstring once more. Her target collapsed to the ground, and without missing a step, she swooped down, plucking the arrow from its head. *Dammit.* The shaft had snapped, and she dropped it, instead grabbing a fresh one from her quiver, ready for their next would-be assailant.

"We cannot think like that," Mila replied. "We can only believe there is time, or what is the point?"

Like so much that came out of her friend's mouth, it was true. Maybe their people were okay. Maybe it was just one they'd seen, or maybe something else had caused the scream.

Another creature approached from their right, and this time it was Keely who stopped and fired. She had felt more than entitled to take one of the spare bows and quivers from the cavern's supplies, and now everyone was glad she had. The arrow lodged in the beast's neck, and it stumbled a little before regaining its balance and making a beeline towards her. "Oh, shit!" She fumbled in her quiver for another, praying she'd have enough time, but Mila ran out in front of her, swishing one of her blades around high and fast. It sliced through the monster's neck as if it was cutting through butter, and the beast's head spun through the air while its body flopped onto the ground. Without taking a breath, Mila began to charge once more.

*

A gasp caught in Jenny's throat as one of the two remaining monsters homed in on her. She could feel Liz standing by her, shoulder to shoulder, both their weapons extended in front of them, but there was an inevitability about this day. It was as though she had been waiting for it, expecting it, ever since they were forced out of their home.

For all their brave words and plans about starting a new life down in Glasgow, Jenny somehow knew that she wouldn't get to see them come to fruition.

The growls, the pallid skin, the ghoulish, grey eyes and wild dancing pupils. The yellow teeth and near black gums. The reaching hands with overgrown claw-like nails. She'd seen them all before, becoming numb to them almost. It was a horror she had lived with for the longest time. But going alone into whatever came next was what truly scared her, petrified her in fact. A small whimper left her mouth as the beast crashed against the point of her spear.

The creature had leapt higher than either she or Liz had anticipated, and the weapons had smashed against its chest, somehow protected by the thick leather jerkin it wore. It rebounded back a full metre and, without hesitation, dived towards them once more. This time, its arms knocked both spears out of the way, and its body twisted a little, barging into Liz and making her fall.

Jenny dropped her weapon, reflexively reaching up and grabbing on to the beast's wrists. It lunged head first, its jaws snapping just centimetres from Jenny's face. She recoiled, but the monster continued to push. *It's like some unrelenting machine.* Out of the corner of her eye, she could see her friends doing their best to fend off the other creature that had attacked, taking all of them by surprise with its strength and viciousness.

The beast's gnashing teeth neared her once more, despite Jenny using every ounce of strength to fend it off. *It's no good. It's no good.*

Its eyes locked with hers. It was the thing she'd been dreading. She'd hoped she could have a different image in her mind to cross over to the other side with. Meg or Lucy or a field of daffodils or … anything. Something good, something pure. Not this.

The creature lunged again. "Aagghh!" She'd wanted to stay strong and silent. She'd wanted to remain dignified, not letting on to others that this was the single most terrifying thing that had ever happened to her. She wanted to be remembered for fighting bravely, but now that was gone too.

She fell back like a cut tree, the vile-smelling ghoul falling with her. Finally, she closed her tear-filled eyes, and as her body hit the ground, an image of Meg flashed into her mind. *Thank you. Thank you for this.*

17

Jenny waited … and waited. She waited for the inevitable bite to rip flesh from her neck or her face. She'd seen it happen plenty of times before, and now it was her turn. She waited a little more then opened her eyes.

The creature was slumped over her, not moving, and she raised her head a little. Everything around her was blurred and out of focus. Even the shouts and screams sounded distant, like a television playing at low volume in another room.

Is it stunned? What the hell's happening? She shuffled a little, trying to get away, but the beast's frame continued to pin her down. Then she saw it, and at the same moment, the blurred images around her all became clear.

A crossbow bolt protruded from the back of the monster's head. She turned to see the second creature on the ground as well. Jenny leaned up and stared just beyond the clearing to see Wren with her bow ready for any other beasts to emerge.

With newfound zeal, Jenny pushed at the ground, heaving herself up and turning to where the other pair of creatures had emerged. One of them was scrambling back to its feet. It had an arrow in its jaw and was starting its charge towards the convoy once more. Then, in less than a heartbeat, it was down again as a bolt disappeared into its temple.

A loud echoing crack made Jenny turn once more to see Mya standing over the body of the beast Meg had attacked. She raised her crowbar again, her head shooting from side to side, searching for any other creatures, but for the moment, there were none.

"Movement!" Wren called out, and the short time-out was over. Jenny followed the young woman's eyes as they travelled beyond her and the rest of the convoy to the path they had just walked. She twisted, fearful of what she might see next, but her heart lifted as Mike, Mila, Robyn, and Keely stormed into the clearing.

*

Robyn lowered her bow, and a childlike grin of happiness painted her face as she ran towards her sister. The two embraced tightly, and Wolf pressed against them both before it was Mila's turn to get squeezed by Wren.

"Are you okay?" Robyn asked.

"Just about. You?" Wren replied.

"I am now."

The trio searched out George in the crowd of faces that stared towards them. He was in a state of shock; that much was clear, but as understanding dawned, he dropped his spear and opened his arms. The three young women ran towards the old man, hugging and squeezing him with all their love.

"Keely!" Della cried, running towards her friend. "Where's Rupert?" The other woman didn't need to respond. The look on her face said it all, and Della leaned in, kissing her on the head. "I'm so sorry."

Clay stared at the full rucksack on Keely's back.

"What's going on?" he asked.

"These people said I could go to Glasgow with them."

"We're going too," Della said, smiling and taking her friend's hand.

"You're going? But the cavern is yours."

"It's not ours. It's a place we found, and we thought we needed it, but after yesterday, we realised just how much we didn't."

"Owen?"

Della let out a bitter laugh. "And others. But how did you guess?"

"You don't need to be Sherlock Holmes."

"Anyway, we're going back for our stuff; then we're heading for the school. We've got the vehicles waiting to take us to Glasgow."

Keely's face lit up. "This is really happening, isn't it?"

"Yeah. It's happening."

"Look, I realise you guys have probably got a lot of catching up to do," Mya said, "but maybe you could do it when we're not in the middle of a forest swarming with infected."

"You make a fair point," Clay replied.

"I'll go back with you to get your stuff, and then we'll all be on our way."

"I'll come with you," Mike said.

"Err … do you think that's a good idea?" Robyn asked as she, Wren and Mila joined them.

"Why?" Mya asked.

"Well, he kind of beat the living crap out of that Owen guy and threatened to go back there and kill him if any of our people got hurt, so, y'know. If they see him, they might get a bit … arrowy."

Mya raised an eyebrow. "Okay, Mike can stay here."

He shrugged. "Whatever."

"Robyn, Mila, fancy a little walk?"

"Oh, sure, yeah. We've just been chilling this

morning, so it would be nice to get some exercise."

"Did anyone tell you that we found an unopened box of Pop-Tarts back at the school?"

"What, really?"

Mya chuckled to herself. "You're so easy."

"Just so you know, I don't have a problem shooting people in the back when it comes to Pop-Tarts," Robyn said, nocking an arrow ready for their journey.

"Duly noted."

*

The arrival of the survivors back at the school and the subsequent reunion that took place was a source of great joy and celebration. There was a hope that the worst of the journey was behind them, but they were all experienced enough not to count on it.

Mike, Robyn and Mila had pressed Emma for a secret meeting amidst all the preparation for the rest of the journey, where they had played her the radio broadcast. It was surprising, baffling and a little unnerving to her that all this time, another large community had been and still was in existence, or so the broadcast said. Emma had asked them all not to discuss it with anyone. Its contents were too overwhelming to be absorbed off the cuff. This was something that needed to be listened to properly and talked about in depth. This was something for Beck, Shaw and the entire council to be a part of, not something that should be played to anyone who wanted to listen in order for the rumour mill to start operating.

This was just one more thing in a long line of things for Emma to think about as the new leader of the Safe Haven refugees.

It was still on her mind when she stepped into the large vehicle shed.

George put his foot down on the accelerator, and the engine roared once more. "You want to take this to Glasgow too?" Emma asked.

He turned the key, rendering the minibus silent once

more. "This has been looked after. I managed to jump-start it, and it's got more than half a tank of fuel. I only needed to pump one of the tyres up. It would be a shame to leave her behind."

"Okay. I suppose, if anything happens to one of the other vehicles, it will give us a redundancy too." George smiled. "What's funny?"

"Nothing," he replied, shaking his head. "I'm just impressed with how quickly you've taken to your new role."

"No harm in planning ahead."

"True."

Emma could see George's mind was elsewhere. "Are you okay? I thought you'd be giddy with your girls being back safe and sound."

"I am."

"You don't exactly look it."

When he had seen them in the clearing, he couldn't have been happier, but he wondered for how long. How long would it be before these girls, who in his mind would always be immature, bickering sisters, were in harm's way once more?

They had grown into young women, but more than that, they had become people whom the entire community depended on. "I'm just wondering what lies ahead for us, that's all."

"What do you mean?"

"I mean this was meant to be the easy part. It was actually getting into Glasgow that was supposed to be the hard bit."

Emma shook her head. "We can only deal with what we know, not what might be. We haven't lost a single person since leaving Skye, and I'm going to do everything in my power to keep it that way."

"You're not a miracle worker."

"No, I'm not. None of us are. But I'm going to fight to make sure we get to where we're going safely."

George looked at her for a moment. He remembered

the first time he had met her back at the Home and Garden Depot in Inverness. She had been formidable back then, but now she had come into her own. He nodded, and a vague hint of a smile was back on his face.

"Have I said something funny?"

"No. It's just you, Jules, Wren and Robyn; you've all come such a long way from when I first knew you all. I think I'm the only one who hasn't changed."

Emma reached out and took George's hand. "We've changed out of necessity. The fact that you haven't tells me that you were the finished article to begin with."

George laughed. "That's a polite way to say I'm too old and stubborn."

Emma smiled. "I'm telling you that you're this community's rock. You always have been, and you always will be."

*

"Jesus! There are hundreds of them," Trish said as she, Beck, Shaw, Raj and Talikha surveyed the banks on either side of the Clyde.

"Holy fucking Jesus Christ!" Doug cried, coming from below deck.

"I thought you were keeping everyone entertained down there."

"Don't worry about that. Mel's got it covered. What the hell are we going to do? There are millions of the bastards."

"I think millions is a bit of a stretch."

"Oh, forgive me. I'm sure semantics is the absolute worst of our worries at the moment."

"Doug does raise a good point," Beck said finally. "There's no way we're going to be able to dock anywhere."

"Mike and Mya said they had a plan in place, so we're just going to have to trust them," Shaw replied.

"Well, what are we worrying about?" asked Doug. "I feel so much better now. Has anyone told the infected?" He cupped his hands around his mouth and called out to the monsters following them along the course of the river. "Mike and Mya have a plan. You can all fuck off now." He waited a moment then turned to the others. "No, that didn't work. What next?"

"Big help, Doug," Trish said. "Thanks so much for your contribution."

"We need another plan," he replied, turning to Raj. "We need to go back. We need another plan."

"Calm down, my friend," Raj said. "In all the time I have known Mike he has never let us down."

"Yeah," Shaw agreed, doing his best not to show his own concerns. "He wouldn't have just let us sail up here with no out. He said they'd spoken to this Griz guy and come up with something together."

"Oh, brilliant. What am I worried about then? Kamikaze Mike and some Neanderthal who goes by the wonderfully endearing moniker Griz have come up with an idea to get us through the city of a million corpses."

"That's not fair," Trish said.

"Yeah," Beck added. "At the last census, there were more like six hundred thousand, not including the outlying areas."

"Thank you, Andy. You always make me feel so much better."

*

Mike climbed down from the cab of the truck and looked up and down the street before opening the gates. Their journey to the outskirts of Glasgow from the school had been the most uncomplicated part of their travels thus far. Now they had reached the destination Griz had told them about. Mike slid the bolt across and opened up the large gate. It was constructed from the same material as the palisade fencing surrounding the giant depot.

He watched all four vehicles enter then took another look outside before securing the barrier behind them and sliding the bolt across once more. He climbed back into the truck and Mya drove around to the rear of the building, where the fencing gave way to red brick. She pulled on the handbrake by a vast loading dock and turned off the engine.

"Well, now we just wait," she said.

Mike surveyed the grounds from the passenger seat, and even Muppet had uncoiled from the footwell and was wagging his tail. "At least we're not visible to the outside from here."

"Yeah, but how long are we going to have to wait?"

"I guess we're about to find out, aren't we?"

*

"We've just spotted the convoy at the depot, Griz," Diamond said, popping her head around the corner of what was now an office but had once been a hotel room.

Griz shook his head then ran his fingers through his Mohican. "Course you fucking have. It never rains, but it fucking pours. That wee walloper was meant to get down here long before the fucking boat showed up, and what happens? Both of the bastards arrive at the same time." He shrugged. "Why the fuck should I have expected anything else?"

"Do you actually need me here for this conversation?"

He turned towards Diamond. "Yes, as a matter of fact, I do."

"And there I was, thinking my life couldn't get any better." She spoke with a French accent, but her English was clearer and more easily understood than Griz's most of the time.

"Y'know, there are some people here who actually treat me with a small modicum of respect."

"Yeah, well, they don't know you as well as me, do they?" Diamond was five-nine, thin, verging on skinny. She had a bob hairstyle, which was dyed pink, but not a bright pink, a kind of washed-out tinge. She wore thick black eyeliner and black lipstick. The end of the world had come and gone, but she held on to the punky Goth image she had cultivated in the time before, the same way others held on to photos or family heirlooms. It was her link to the past but with a little bit of now thrown into the bargain. The diamond stud she wore in her nose was a recent addition and reminded her that new things still lay ahead.

"How come the only fucking grief I get is from the women in my life?"

Diamond smiled. "Because we're predators. We can sniff out the weak prey, and we go after it."

"Oh, very fucking funny. I love you too."

"Don't pout."

Griz let out a long sigh. "Thank you for agreeing to help me with this."

"Do not mention it. I've been working for the past thirty-six hours straight so your new best friend and his people have somewhere to call their own, but who needs sleep anyway?"

"As long as you're not bitter. That's the main thing."

"You know me, Griz. I don't hold grudges."

The two friends exchanged a smile as Griz climbed to his feet. "So, what's happening?"

"Zofia has taken Saffy and the first team to the waterfront."

"Already?" Griz asked, suddenly concerned.

"These were your orders, weren't they?"

"Well, yeah, but I didn't realise they were heading out straight away."

"Wellington Street was completely clear, so they took advantage of the fact."

"Okay." Griz nodded. "That's good. So, what about the others?"

"Clara has got people on the rooftops with more drones. The horde is currently outside the university."

"Already?"

"Already, yes. Is this your new favourite word? Each time I say something, you say already as if you have been asleep, as if we haven't discussed this plan a hundred times."

"Okay, okay, I suppose that's my cue, isn't it?"

"I will be up there," she said, pointing to the roof. "Be careful."

"I didn't know you cared."

"That is the only transport we have."

"Very fucking funny."

*

More people had drifted onto the deck only to head back down when they had witnessed the horrors lining the banks. Raj had kept the yacht steady, staying in the middle of the river, but as the sound of multiple drones rose into the air, he understood the time was approaching to put all his faith in Mike and Mya's plan.

Suddenly, the infected began to disappear from the banks, one by one at first, then in swarms like flocks of starlings instantly changing direction.

"I really don't like this," Shaw said. "I don't like not being able to see what's beneath us."

"The water is deep here. We are fine, my friend."

"How the hell can you be so calm, Raj?"

Humphrey sat down by his master's side, tail wagging, tongue hanging out as if this was just another brilliant adventure. Raj smiled and gestured to the banks. "Because our friends know what they are doing."

Shaw looked from one bank to the other. It was true. Nearly all the infected that had been following them moments before were now gone. He let out a long breath. "Let's just hope it continues to work."

*

Many of the former Safe Haven residents had dismounted from their respective vehicles and were quietly talking among themselves. Tall red brick walls surrounded them, but the noise of thousands of growling infected somewhere in the distance told them that this was not somewhere to take risks.

"That's a vehicle," Mike said.

"What?" Emma replied. They were standing in a wide circle with Wren, Mya and the others.

"That's a truck. It's Griz." Before anyone could say a word, he was sprinting around the building in the direction of the gate. A few seconds later, he opened it up so Griz could pull the giant articulated lorry inside. The second the entrance was secured again, Griz jumped down. There was no sign of any infected following, although both men made sure before greeting each other.

"You made it then, you mad Yorkshire bastard," Griz said, breaking into a broad grin and hugging the other man as though they were long-lost brothers.

"Yeah," Mike replied, reciprocating the embrace. "Had a couple of hiccups along the way, but we got here."

"Aye, well," Griz said, releasing the younger man. "You can tell us all about it when we're safe. Right now, I've got all hands on deck. Your boat's just arrived as well."

"What?"

"Aye. What do they say about the best-laid plans and all that?"

"So, what are we going to do?"

"We've got the drones herding the infected away from the banks. By the time they reach the Riverside Museum, it should be all clear, and then we can get everyone unloaded. I suggest keeping your people here other than those other mad bastards you came with last time. On the off chance we do come under attack, we'll need to put up a fight while we get everybody off the boat."

"Okay," Mike said.

Griz looked at his new friend and smiled. "I'm really happy you're here. I think you and your people coming is going to be good for all of us."

"Me too, Griz. Me too."

18

The evacuation from the yacht, the return to the depot where all the Safe Haven refugees met up once more, and the subsequent journey to Griz's strange high-rise settlement ran perfectly to plan. The vast majority of infected had been lured away from the area by multiple drones, and the small handful that they had to face were dealt with quickly and efficiently by Mike, Wren, Robyn and the others.

They parked the vehicles up on Wellington Street and made the short trek to the hotel, where the sense of relief was evident as daylight was blocked out once more by the sturdy metal doors.

They made their way up to the large open-plan bar and restaurant, where hundreds of unfamiliar faces were waiting to greet them. It was all like a whirlwind. It was all a little surreal and overwhelming, but the levity and feeling of optimism couldn't be mistaken.

"Emma?" came a vaguely familiar voice from the sea of faces, and she turned to see Zofia. Their meeting down in Leeds had been brief, but her kindness had not been forgotten. The two hugged tightly until Zofia spotted Sammy standing by Wren's side and rushed towards the young girl, grasping her too.

*

Humphrey was in his element, and dozens of people seemed to be lining up to stroke him, the other dogs and even Daisy. Raj and Talikha held hands, a little overwhelmed by it all. Beck and Trish stood with their girls, and Darren, Doug and Mel lingered close by. It had been a long time since any of them had seen so many people all in one place.

"Right. Now all of yous, calm the fuck down," Griz said, putting his hands up and trying to bring back some order. He turned to the new arrivals. "We're having a wee shindig tonight so you can meet everyone and get to know your new neighbours. But right now, you probably want to get settled and recover from your journey." He looked towards some of the older people who seemed exhausted from the stairs they'd already had to climb and then walked across to Emma, Shaw, and the group gathered around them. "Um, look. The journey up to the top can be knackering. We've got a few rooms free on the floor below this if some of you would prefer those."

He was trying to be as diplomatic as possible, but it was obvious what he meant. Emma had a quiet word with Liz and Trish and left it to them and those who would struggle to climb who went where. Two of the nurses led a handful of the still out of breath refugees to the stairs that would lead down to their new homes.

"Right then," said a smiling woman in her mid-twenties. She was well-spoken, and a sweet-looking girl of six or seven held her hand tightly as she greeted Emma and the others. "We'd better show you to your place."

"This is my better half, Clara," Griz announced.

"What, seriously?" Mike replied.

"Aye. Why?"

Mike shrugged. "How soon after you got married

did she regain her sight?"

"Y'cheeky wee bastard," Griz replied.

"What have I told you?" Clara asked, glaring at her husband.

"I tell him this all the time also," Zofia said.

"Oh, for fuck's sake," Griz muttered.

"Sorry?" Clara asked.

"Apologies, dear. I forget myself sometimes." He looked at his daughter and smiled then turned to Mike. "I meant to say y'cheeky wee … scoundrel."

Several of the new arrivals who were in earshot burst out laughing. "You take that back," Mike replied.

"I won't."

Mike shook his head. "Then I suppose a scoundrel I am." He turned to the little girl. "Your father can say the most hurtful things sometimes." The little girl laughed. She'd spent more time with the new dogs than she had with the new people, but their arrival was exciting, and the mood was bordering on joyous.

"This is Chuchu," Griz said proudly.

"Chuchu?" Emma asked.

"Her name's actually Patchouli, but whenever anyone asked her what she was called when she was younger, she always used to reply Chuchu, and it kind of stuck."

"I love that," Emma said, smiling.

"Aye, well. I wanted to call her Jennifer, but nobody gives a flying … err … whistle what I think."

"A flying whistle?" Mike asked.

"Button it, Yorkie boy, otherwise you and me'll be having a square go when all the ladies have gone to bed tonight," he replied, smiling.

"Seriously. What century is your brain stuck in, Royston? The ladies will go to bed when they choose, and no one is having a square go, a round go or any shaped go for that matter. Now, shall we get on and show our new friends their accommodation or do you want to stand here procrastinating until Christmas?"

Griz's shoulders slumped. "You're absolutely right, dear. Lead the way."

Clara and Chuchu walked hand in hand to the staircase and the others followed. "Royston?" Mike asked with a laugh in his voice.

"Clara is the only person on the fucking planet who calls me that, and only when she's pissed off. If you even think about using that name, I'll rip your nads off, boy. Make no mistake."

"No worries, Roy. You can rely on me."

"Y'little bastard," he muttered under his voice as they entered the stairwell.

They made the climb slowly so George could keep up. When they emerged through the fire exit and onto the roof, they all shared the same wonderment Mike and the others had experienced when they'd first laid eyes on the rooftop gardens and the sprawling network of bridges between the buildings.

"Hi," Diamond said as she approached them.

"This is Diamond," Griz announced. "She's responsible for pretty much all of this."

"This is a slight exaggeration," she replied, smiling. "It was a team effort."

"Aye, well, it wasn't the team that designed the bridges and made sure they were safe to cross. Without those, we'd be living in one hotel instead of being spread out."

"This is impressive," Beck said.

Many people had fallen silent when they had seen Beck among the refugees. They'd been told he was with them, but few had believed the story. Even Griz felt a little uncomfortable as he spoke to him now. "We've broken ground on a new one for you."

"What?"

"Aye. It's a wee bit smaller, but there's more than enough room for you lot. We've secured all the lower windows and doors the same way we have with this building and the other hotels, and Diamond and her team have been working non-stop on the bridge."

The crowd started walking once more, travelling from rooftop to rooftop, getting the full guided tour. Sammy led Daisy in one hand while gripping on to Emma with her other. Happiness was ingrained on her face as Zofia stayed beside them. George, Jack and James walked with Wren, Robyn and Mila, all appreciating the planning that had gone into everything. They finally reached the last bridge that sloped down to a roof yet to be adorned by raised beds.

"We scrambled all this together pretty quickly," Clara said. "We've got the materials to help you build veg gardens like on all the other roofs, but the main thing was getting the bridge in place."

The bridge overshot the lower rooftop by a couple of metres. Some makeshift steps had been built for the higher end. "It is not perfect, but it is safe. We will do some more work on it in the coming days," Diamond announced, climbing onto the structure and jumping up and down. The deck of welded steel sheets showed little give, but the bridge swayed a small amount, as one would expect. Four reinforced steel girders had been planted into the floor at either end then welded and bolted to the cross beams of the rooftops. The same thick suspension wire used on the other bridges had been used on this one for the main cable, and small strips of it had been knitted through the meticulously drilled holes to act as the suspenders.

"This is impressive," George said admiringly.

"If I'd have had more time, I would have been able to finish it off better, but Griz surprised us with the news that you were coming to join us. It is very safe. We have had people using it all day."

George was the first of the Safe Haven refugees to climb on, and he nodded appreciatively as he felt the structure's solidity beneath his feet. "Impressive," he said again.

Diamond looped her arm through George's. "I am going to like having you here. Come, we will see the rest of your new home."

They crossed the bridge, and as George spotted the acetylene torch and other equipment they'd used to build it, his eyes lit up. "I'm going to enjoy being here."

Griz, Carla, Diamond and the others stayed with them all for the best part of an hour, explaining the routines for meals and the general lay of the land before they departed, leaving their new neighbours to get used to their home.

Knowing how anxious Mike was about Daisy's welfare, Griz had constructed an enclosure for her on the roof. At the moment, it was quite crude, but it was safe, and he had made sure carrot ends, cabbage leaves, and potato peels were waiting in a large bucket so the beloved goat had plenty to chow down on while the others were settling in.

The dogs were as excited as the rest of them, running up and down the hallways, in and out of the rooms and generally appearing and disappearing like they were canine magicians.

Diamond had advised that they leave the top floor vacant as the sound of people walking on the roof would travel down. In the end, they chose to keep the top two floors vacant and adopted the next two as their new home.

"Are you serious?" asked Sammy. "I can have a room of my own?"

"Well, yeah," Emma said. "It'll just be like having a room of your own in a house."

Sammy's eyes lit up and she turned to Wren. "Can I have the one next to yours?"

"Yeah. Course you can," Wren replied, smiling.

They were in a large double room at the end of one of the hallways. "Why don't we take this wing?" Mike said.

They walked outside into the corridor. A couple of lanterns burned, but there was no need as all the room doors were open and there was still plenty of daylight.

"I'll take one of the ones closest to the staircase if that's alright," George said.

"Course," Emma replied.

"I'll take the room opposite yours then," Jenny said as she and Meg walked down the hallway with George to their new living quarters.

One by one, the friends and family dispersed to choose their new accommodation. The rooms were virtually identical, so there wasn't a lot to decide other than who would be next to whom.

"This is it then. This is our new home," Emma said.

She and Mike had chosen rooms at the far end of the corridor next to each other. Sammy's room was next, then Wren's, as agreed.

"Yeah," Mike replied. For the first time since their journey had begun, the two siblings were alone, and they looked out of the window down onto the street. It was empty. Saffy and the others had done an excellent job herding the infected while everyone got settled. There was not a single creature in sight, but the low-pitched eerie drone of their distant growls was a constant reminder that they were far from safe.

"Everybody seems nice," Emma said.

"They are."

She turned to look at him. "So we're here."

Mike nodded. "For a while, at least."

"We won't be able to live rent free."

"I wouldn't expect to. I'll do whatever is needed."

"I don't mean that. Obviously, we'll all have to contribute."

"What do you mean then?"

"I mean we'll have to commit. By living here, whether we mean to or not, we're going to be putting down emotional roots. We'll grow to care for these people. Their trials and troubles will become ours."

Mike understood what his sister was intimating. "I

don't doubt it for a moment. We're going to get close to these people. Some of them will become good friends, and others will feel like family. It's bound to happen if we spend any length of time here."

"But?"

"But I haven't forgotten, and I won't forget what I promised."

"We're a world away from Safe Haven here. We're a world away from Olsen."

Mike placed his arm around Emma, and she rested her head on his shoulder. "We're Safe Haven, Em. You, me, Sammy, Wren, Robyn, Mila, Jen, Raj, Talikha, Shaw, all of us. We're it, and it's us. Olsen stole our property, that's all. It was a heist. We're going to get it back, and she's going to pay."

"You do realise how crazy that sounds. We've got fewer resources than we've ever had. We're refugees. We've turned up here with little more than the clothes on our backs and the rucksacks on our shoulders."

Mike held her a little tighter. "Yeah, but we made it here, didn't we? And that's something. From today, we start building something else. We start building a future, and we start forming a plan to get back what's ours."

There was a knock on the door, and the pair turned to see Mya and Muppet standing there. "I'm sorry to interrupt."

The two siblings broke their embrace and gestured for the other woman to enter the room. "You're not interrupting," Emma said. "We were just chatting."

Muppet paused in the doorway for a moment then disappeared back down the corridor. "In all the time I've known him, I've never seen him so giddy."

"He's probably reacting to the sense of relief that everyone's feeling."

"Yeah."

"Where did you end up?"

"We're the floor below near the stairs. Beck and his

girls have adjoining rooms. Mel's next to them on one side, Doug on the other, and Darren and I are the bread in that particular sandwich. Clay, Della and Keely are across the hall from us."

"And everyone's settling in okay?" Emma asked.

Mya shrugged. "Sure, I suppose."

"I'll go round and check on everybody before we head to the big party."

"It's a bit surreal, isn't it?"

"How do you mean?"

"I mean, Jesus, earlier on today, we were fighting for our lives in a forest, and tonight we're the guests of honour at a party."

"Yeah, I suppose it is a bit surreal now that you mention it."

"So, anyway," she said, closing the door a little and walking further into the room. "I was wondering if we had any thoughts on a return visit to the priory."

"What? We've only just got here."

"You want to head back sooner rather than later?" Mike asked.

"Yeah. Even if it's just for a reccy."

"What's the urgency?"

"If the priory was attacked and overrun by infected, the sooner we get up there and make the place secure the sooner we can lay claim to their weapons, supplies and whatever else they had."

"Yeah, but none of it's going anywhere, is it? It's not like anyone's going to beat us to claiming it," Emma said.

"Well, it's unlikely but not impossible. What concerns me, though, is if the inhabitants were turned, they drift into the forest, and we'll never see them again."

"Why does that matter? Surely that would be a good thing."

"A lot of them will be armed. If they disappear, so do the weapons, and so does the ammo they're carrying.

The whole point of trying to take the priory is as a stash and possible future base. It would make more sense if we've got something to stash there, wouldn't it?"

"She makes a good point," Mike said.

"Doesn't your brain ever switch off just for a minute?" Emma asked.

Mya smiled. "I just wouldn't want to waste the good work you did with that grenade."

"Look, can we just get our first night out of the way and then we'll figure something out?"

"Sure. I just wanted to raise the point, that's all."

"And I'm grateful. My head's mush at the moment. After a good night's sleep, I'll feel better, and I think the less people know about the priory the better. We don't want word getting out to our new hosts. I'm sure as far as they're concerned anything salvaged or scavenged goes into the communal pot."

"Mum's the word."

"Plus, of course, we're going to have to talk this over with Shaw at some stage, but the less stress he has at the moment the better."

The door suddenly burst open, and Humphrey bounded in, closely followed by Muppet. The Labrador's tail swished wildly, and he almost knocked Mike over as he jumped up, placing his paws on his pal's chest.

"Hello, boy," Mike said, the serious expression gone from his face in a heartbeat as he leaned forward, fussing Humphrey and getting a big sloppy lick right across his face.

"I am sorry," Talikha said, following him into the room. "He is more excitable than usual today."

"I didn't think there was a more excitable than usual for Humph," he replied, finally relenting and kneeling down with him.

"I think we should stay here with him this evening. It may be a little chaotic if we go to the party."

"There are other dogs here, so I think it's only right

that he gets to meet them."

"I know what I will be doing for the entire night then," Raj said, joining them.

"How do you like your new accommodation?" Emma asked.

"Hopefully, we will soon be trading with the islands once more."

"Yeah. It might be a little while before we've got anything to trade."

"Actually, I'm pretty certain Griz and the others would happily trade with the islands. I'll talk to him about it tonight," Mike said.

"Look," Emma began. "Can we just take a breath, please?"

Mike and Mya looked at each other guiltily. Neither wanted their agenda to overwhelm one of the surest allies they had for the cause, and on a personal level, Mike didn't want to see his sister stressed. "Sorry, Em."

"No biggie, but let's just settle in. Let's go meet everyone. Let's try to have a good time. Let's sleep, and let's look at everything with a fresh pair of eyes tomorrow."

"You're right. Of course you're right."

"Well, I'll get back downstairs and see how everyone's getting on," Mya said, tapping her leg for Muppet to follow.

"I promise you," Emma called after her, "we'll figure all this out tomorrow."

Mya smiled and nodded before disappearing into the corridor.

A procession of people visited Emma over the course of the next hour or so, saying what they needed or what it would be nice to have in the rooms, or how this could be improved or that could be improved. The final people to show up were Della, Clay and Keely. They had no requests, no demands and no suggestions. They just wanted to thank her for allowing them to join the community.

"You're about the first people to show up who

haven't added to my to-do list," she said, gesturing to the open notebook on her bedside table.

"I bet," Della replied, smiling. "We love it here. I can't remember the last time I actually slept on a proper bed; I mean one with springs."

"I don't know how you managed it. I mean there's roughing it and roughing it."

"It wasn't all bad. We still got to cycle and spelunk and climb and stuff, but there was a price to pay."

"Yeah. Comfort, warmth, luxury."

"Well, I have to say, this is pretty luxurious. We're making up for it now."

Emma looked around the room. It was well furnished and comfortable, but it wasn't somewhere she would ever be able to call home, not in the true sense of the word, not in the Safe Haven sense of the word. "Yeah," she said. "It's nice."

"Nice?"

"I'm just used to something a little different."

"Better than this?"

"Just different."

*

"I thought she was never going to go," Robyn said as Sammy finally left Wren's room.

"Don't be horrible. She's lovely is Sammy," Wren replied.

"She is. Totally, but I don't want her to hear this."

"Hear what? Is this that thing you said you really needed to talk to me about?"

Emma had asked them not to discuss the radio broadcast with anyone. Mike had not strictly stuck to the agreement. He had told Mya. Neither Robyn nor Mila had spoken about it to anyone else, but there was no way they were going to keep something like this from Wren.

"Yeah," Robyn replied.

"What is it? What's the big secret?"

Mila closed the door behind them and joined Wren

and Wolf on the bed while Robyn sat on the dressing table with her legs dangling over the side. She pulled the small transistor radio out of her pocket and clicked it on, making sure it wasn't so loud that anyone outside the room could hear.

"... community that's growing all the time. If you can make it to Edinburgh by road, we have ten safe sites positioned around the city with enough food and water to last until we get to you. We send out armed patrols once a week looking for survivors. We are the Edinburgh Castle community, and we want to help.

"This is the Edinburgh Castle community. If you're listening to this message, then you're still alive, and that's something. Congratulations. We have supplies and a working wind turbine. We have a community that's growing all—" Robyn clicked the radio off and looked at her sister, who just sat there gawping.

"Well?" the older sibling asked eventually.

"Play it again."

Robyn glanced towards the door and turned the radio on once more, allowing the message to run for two full cycles before turning it off.

"So, what do you think?"

"Err … I don't know, Bobbi. You've just sprung this on me. What am I supposed to think?"

"There are people alive in Edinburgh."

"Yeah. I kind of figured that out."

"So?"

"It's … surprising."

"Duh!"

"What do you want me to say?"

"For all we know, we could have family there."

"Yeah. And for all we know, we couldn't too. It could be some elaborate set-up. Hell, it could be Olsen."

"There's nothing to suggest it's anything like that."

"And there's nothing to suggest it isn't. You need to take this to Emma and the council."

"We did. She told us to sit on it until they can have a meeting."

"Well, there you go then. They'll talk it over and figure out what to do next."

"Blah, blah, blah. And you know what that means. Nothing. Nothing will get done."

"We don't know that."

"We do. They'll say we need to try to gather more information about it, but there is no gathering more information." She lifted the radio. "This is all the information right here."

"What are you suggesting then?"

"We go."

"What?"

"We go and figure out exactly what the situation is."

"That's crazy for so many reasons."

"Why? Why is it crazy?"

"Because it could be a trap."

"And how are we possibly going to find out if we don't go?"

Wren ran her hands through her hair. "Oh God." She turned to Mila. "What do you think?"

Mila shrugged. "I see arguments for both sides."

"So you agree; it could be a trap."

"Ja. It could be."

"See, thank you," Wren replied, turning to Robyn.

"But also it could be genuine, and making contact with these people would make us far more powerful. If it is another community, then allying with them, if not joining them, will mean that if Olsen comes, we will be far stronger."

"Okay, but what if it is a trap? What if it is Olsen?"

"Wren," Robyn said, taking back the reins of the conversation. "I'm not talking about just rolling up and saying, 'Hiya.' I'm talking about sussing the place out. I'm talking about checking out what's going on over there.

Then, if it looks okay, we can think about making contact."

"It's so dangerous, Bobbi. And it's not like we won't be missed here. I mean I don't know if you've noticed, but people are relying on us more and more every day. We're not just those girls with bows and swords anymore. We're pretty much the first line of defence or attack. What if something happened here?"

"They've got Mike, Mya, Shaw, Darren. They've got Della, Clay and Keely now, plus all Griz's people."

"Oh yeah, and their army of air rifles."

"Just a couple of days. That's all I'm talking about. None of the committee will be as interested in this as us, Sis. It's our home town. I mean what if Aunty Mary or Uncle Phil are there? What if our cousins are there? What if—"

"Okay, okay. You don't need to go through a full list of family members; I get the picture. But the thing is, Bobbi, there's an astronomically high chance that they're not. The likelihood of them having survived at all is negligible."

"Yeah, it is," Robyn admitted. "But it's not impossible, is it?"

"No."

"And, forgetting about our family and who might or might not be there. What about the fact that there's a big community over there who could become our allies?"

"Well, I'm sure Emma and Beck and Shaw will—"

"Do nothing but talk about it forever and review things once we're settled here."

"And maybe that's not a bad thing."

"And maybe something happens in that time. Maybe the Edinburgh people don't know about Olsen. Maybe us warning them about her could save them. Maybe the delay causes a community of people who could become our allies to get wiped out."

"That's a lot of maybes, Bobbi."

"Yeah, it is. There are a lot of maybes." She held the radio up once more. "But tell me honestly that you don't really want to know."

Wren stared at the small transistor radio for several seconds before turning to her sister once more. "Let me think about it."

"We all know what that means."

"Don't do that. Don't dismiss me like that."

Robyn suddenly looked guilty. "I'm sorry. That wasn't fair."

"I promise you, Bobbi, I will think about this."

Robyn nodded and, rather than putting the radio back in her pocket, pushed it down to the bottom of her rucksack. "Okay."

19

When the guests of honour finally arrived on the bar and restaurant floor, the music was already playing and the drinks were being poured.

"Mikey boy," Griz shouted out as he saw him from across the room. Mike, Emma and their entourage followed and one by one were picked off by people, shaking hands and welcoming them to the fold. Even after everything they'd been through, or perhaps because of everything they'd been through, it was impossible not to get caught up in the carnival atmosphere.

"This is something, Griz," Mike said as he received another bear hug from the big Scotsman.

"Ach, you're welcome, brother. It's the least we can do." He turned around to the group he was with, still with one arm wrapped around the younger man's shoulder. "Y'see this mad Yorkshire bastard. Fiercest fucking fighter I've ever seen in my life, bar no one." His words were a little bit slurred but still intelligible. "I tell ya. I've never seen anything like what he did in that tunnel." He suddenly noticed Mila, Robyn and Wren standing with him. "What they all did."

"What can I tell you, Griz? It was a team effort. That's how we run."

"Aye. Well, I'm glad you're here, Mike. I'm glad all of yous made it."

*

"Oh, my God," Doug said. "It's like something out of a nightmare."

"Actually," Trish replied, "It reminds me of the time we had the Australian cricket team at Number Ten."

"Exactly."

"Come on, Doug," Beck said, patting his friend on the back, "where's your spirit of adventure?"

"It's fucking you, isn't it?" The accent was Glaswegian, and whoever had spoken had obviously been drinking for some time already.

"Err … it was the last time I checked," Beck said.

The man lunged forward, and for a split second, Darren and Mya were both about to leap into action, but the PM put his hand up, and the drunken figure threw his arms around Beck. "Best fucking prime minister we ever had. I voted for you," he said, staggering back and pointing at Beck. "I fucking voted for you. You're a top, top man. Best fucking prime minister we ever had."

"Thank you. That's very kind of you to say."

"It's the truth. Can you imagine if we had that other bunch o' wallopers running things when all this shit broke loose? We wouldn't o' lasted five minutes." The man gestured around him. "We're all here today 'cause o' you. Everything you did with the food, the power, everything. And what you did with the fuel. Fuckin' genius. Mixing in all those fuckin' antique oxides and bicycles to make it last longer. Fuckin' genius."

Beck looked confused for a moment, then it dawned on him what the other man was talking about. "Antioxidants and biocides?"

"Aye. Fuckin' genius."

"Yes, well, it's quite interesting you see. By adding stabilisers and biocides during the refining process, the shelf life of petrol and diesel is multiplied by up to—"

"You're a top, top man." The drunk staggered once, twice. "Anyway, I'm going to go find ma bird and tell her that I met you." With that, he disappeared into the crowd.

Beck turned to Trish. "You're right. It's exactly like that time we had the Aussie team at Number Ten."

*

"I'm Clark. This is Thea," said a tall, thin man as he walked up to Ruth and Richard. He extended his hand, and both of them shook it in turn.

"I'm—"

"You need no introduction. Ruth and Richard," Thea said, taking each of their hands and shaking them too.

"You've got us at a disadvantage. How do you know us?" Richard asked.

"Nothing stays a secret here. You're the librarians, right?"

"Well, yes."

Thea was in her mid-thirties. She wore glasses, and her long curly hair was tied back. Even though their clothes were casual, they were smarter than the vast majority of the partygoers.

"We kind of are too. I mean we're not qualified or anything, but we've always been massive readers, and we've got four rooms downstairs that are full of books. We and a few others hold lessons for the children, and we're trying to organise a system for lending the books out that might result in us actually getting some of them back at some stage."

"Yes," Clark continued. "We were hoping maybe tomorrow you could come down and take a look at our set-up. Maybe give us some advice."

"Oh, good grief," Ruth said. "We'd be absolutely delighted to."

"Where are our manners?" Clark said. "You've just walked through the door and we're harassing you already. What can I get you to drink?"

"Well, what do you have?"

"We pretty much have everything you can imagine. There was a massive cash-and-carry booze warehouse around the corner that was unfeasibly well stocked when everything turned to hell. I don't think we've even scratched the surface with it yet."

"Well, if there's a nice red, I wouldn't say no," Ruth replied.

"Oh, God," Thea said. "You and I are going to get on so well." She took the older woman's hand. "There's this Argentinian Malbec that I have an unhealthy addiction to. Come on, we'll go get a couple of glasses."

"Forgive me if I don't take your hand," Clark said, smirking. "But I've always been more of a bitter man. You fancy a Tetley's?"

"I'm sure I could try one to find out what all the fuss is about."

"We're going to get on too. I like people with a dry sense of humour. Come on, while there's no line."

*

"These fuckin' pants are riding right up my arse," Jules said, grabbing the back of her jeans and shuffling them around a little.

"If memory serves, those were the words Diana spoke directly before Charles proposed," Ephraim replied with a smirk.

"I've got some fuckin' words for you, you sarky little jumbo-eared twat."

"Funny, I think those were Camilla's," he fired back, pushing his glasses a little further up his nose. Jules' brothers, Kat, and the others surrounding them all laughed.

"Fuck all of yous," Jules replied, breaking into a wide grin before adjusting her pants a little more. They all sat around a large table with drinks set out in front of them.

A few of the hotel's inhabitants had come to introduce themselves, but the former Safe Haven residents were easing their way into the evening. The music was playing loudly, and a section of floor on the other side of the bar had been designated a dance area. Coloured lights flashed away as numerous solar generators powered the proceedings.

"It's very nice of them to go to all this effort for us," Kat said, looking around at all the friendly faces.

"Yeah," Andy replied. "Mike and the others must have made a hell of an impression when they were down here."

"Ha," Ephraim scoffed. "When does Mike not make an impression? I suppose we should just be glad on this occasion it was a good one and we don't have another army of strangers wanting us dead."

"There'll be plenty of time for that when they get to know us properly," Jules said.

Ephraim took another drink from his bottle and smiled. "So many true words are spoken in jest."

*

George, Jack and James sat in a corner with three beers in front of them. They were at the far end of the restaurant, as far away from the music as possible. Wren, Wolf, Mila and Robyn had stayed with them briefly before making their excuses to mingle.

"Hell of a lot of tools they've got just from what I've seen already," Jack said.

"Aye," George replied. "That Diamond lass knows what she's talking about. From what I've gathered, she's behind all the big projects here."

"You're the make-it-happen men," said a young woman in dungarees standing close to their table. She had a bottle in her hand and had been half listening to their conversation.

"The what?" James asked.

"The make-it-happen men. Whenever anything

needed doing, fixing or building, you were the men who made it happen."

They all looked at one another and began to chuckle. "Well," George said, "we had a lot of helpers, but yes, I suppose we were."

"Well, I hope you weren't thinking about retiring any time soon. We've always got a tonne of things that need doing around here, and we're in desperate need of people who know one end of a screwdriver from the other."

"We've got quite a lot of tools with us, but just from what we've seen so far, it's nothing compared to what you've got."

"Have you seen the workshops yet?"

"Workshops?" George asked.

"Yeah, up on the top floor."

"No."

The woman smiled. "How do you fancy a little walk? Trust me, it will be worth it."

They didn't need asking twice. George grabbed his stick, and all three of them followed the young woman, immediately forgetting about their drinks and the party.

*

"So, brother, I was thinking we might strike while the iron's hot," Griz said as he and Mike stood at the bar taking in the bubbly atmosphere that had only intensified since the arrival of the newcomers.

Mike looked across to Sammy, who lurked on the edge of the dancefloor with Wren, Wolf, Robyn and Mila. Emma and Diamond were sitting at a table close by talking and laughing like long-lost friends. He couldn't help but smile. For the moment, they were not in harm's way. There was no Olsen to think about, no infected. This evening was about relaxing, enjoying themselves, and as turbulent as the last few days had been and as much as the pain of losing Lucy and Jake was ever present, he was determined to enjoy it too.

"How do you mean?" he finally replied, taking a sip

from his bottle.

"Well, y'know, there's expectation."

"Expectation?"

"I told them about you guys, about what you did, about how you live. We've pretty much stayed local since the early days. There's been enough for us, and we've eked out a way to survive here."

Mike looked around at all the laughing faces. "Judging by the music, the lights, the food and all the booze flowing, you've done more than just eked out a living."

Griz shrugged. "We're doing okay. The rooftop gardens help supplement what we eat, and we're looking at expanding to other roofs, even of buildings we don't live in. But a parachute would be nice."

"A parachute?"

"A parachute, a safety net, whichever way you see it. Something that means we can take a breath if something goes wrong."

"I don't think you give yourself the credit you deserve here, Griz. If you can hold mad parties, you—"

"We needed this," Clara said, and both men turned to discover her standing next to them.

"What do you mean?" Mike asked

"It's been hard. Yes, we've got plenty of booze. And our solar generators are allowing us to put on a little light show for the party, and yes, the drones are a great way of herding the infected, and yes, we've done okay, everything considered. But Griz, myself, and Diamond have a lot of sleepless nights. Last winter, we lost over a dozen people. If we'd had some basic medicines, we probably wouldn't. Our stores of vitamin and iron tablets are dangerously low. Yes, we're growing quite a bit of good, vitamin-rich food now, but it's not enough for everyone, and the tins and packets we have in our stores don't provide the most balanced diet. We're doing okay, but we could do so much better, and as angry as I was when I found out that Griz had gone into those tunnels with you, when I heard what you'd done and discovered that you'd found transport, it was like a weight had been lifted."

"I don't understand."

"Everything has been down to us. When we went up against Tuck, we didn't know what the hell we were doing. It was nothing short of a miracle that we came out on top in that fight. We lost people, a lot of people, and yes, he disappeared with his tail between his legs, but we've got no idea if he'll come back. When I heard about another group of survivors who were just that, they'd actually survived out there in the real world, not in some surreal, high-rise wonderland, I breathed a massive sigh of relief. I knew that the burden for everything wouldn't just fall on us. I know that sounds selfish, and I'm probably not doing everybody here justice because we have some real fighters, but in truth, we've been hanging on by a thread." She raised her glass. "So, yes, we needed this. We needed this celebration because it welcomes you, and it tells everyone else that we're not alone anymore."

Mike nodded, taking in every word she'd said. "Okay. I get it. We need a show of intent."

"There. Yes. Exactly," Griz said, glancing towards his wife then turning back to Mike. "I knew you'd get it."

"I get it, Griz. Have you got a wish list?"

"What do you mean?"

"You must have a few places in mind where you'd liked to have visited if you'd had transport."

"Well, aye."

"Good. I'll get the gang together first thing, we'll look through the options, and this time tomorrow night, you'll want to throw another party."

Griz laughed raucously, pulled his new friend towards him and kissed him on top of the head. "Ya, little dancer. Things are going to start getting better and better here for all of us."

"Humphrey, NO!" The shout cut through the music and conversations, and Mike immediately broke free from Griz's grasp. He'd been here before. He'd heard the same anguish and panic in Talikha's cry, and it could only mean one thing. He put down his bottle and set off at a run towards the tables where the buffet had been laid out. For the moment, he couldn't see his golden-coloured friend, but he could hear surprised gasps and stifled screams as a single-minded entity worked its way through the gathered crowd like a shark swimming towards heavily populated shallows.

Then he saw him break free from the wall of bodies, but unlike the occasion of the Christmas party, this time, Mike was too late. The crazed beast was on his hind legs munching through a plate of custard creams like Cookie Monster on acid. Before he could move on to anything else, Mike snagged his collar and managed to bring him under control, but the plate fell to the floor, and the remaining biscuits scattered.

The out-of-breath figures of Raj and Talikha stood there with the remains of the extendable lead that Humphrey had bitten through to break free. Suddenly, Wolf, Meg and Muppet appeared too, searching the floor, scavenging for the sweet snacks. Mya, Jenny and Wren caught up with them seconds later, but it was all over.

Griz, Clara and many of the gathered crowd were in hysterics, but Raj and Talikha were mortified. "I'm so sorry," Raj said. "I'm so, so sorry."

"Ach, it's nothing, brother. The food's there for all of us to eat," Griz said, wiping a tear from his eye and patting the other man heartily on the back.

"I thought he would be secure on this," Raj said apologetically, holding up what remained of the lead.

"Honestly. That was classic. It was worth a hundred plates of biscuits."

"You are too kind," Talikha replied, taking the broken lead from her husband in the hope that she could jerry-rig something.

"Where've you guys been, anyway?" Mike asked.

"Doing our rounds," Raj replied.

"Eh?"

"So far, I have seen a cat with an infected paw. Another who has gone blind in one eye and a pigeon with a broken wing."

"I told you we'd put you all to work here."

Raj smiled. "Yes. I dropped my bag off in our room and came straight down here, but I hoped our entrance would not be quite as dramatic."

"Like I said. No harm, brother," Griz replied. "Now come on, let's get our new resident vet something to drink."

*

"How are you doing, Jen?" Jules asked, having left her comfy little corner and walked over to join the line of onlookers revelling in the high-jinx of the canines.

"I'm alright, darling. Why do you ask?"

"It's just ever since the school, you've been pretty quiet."

Meg finally finished her search for any remaining morsels of food and went to join her mistress once more. Jenny smiled at her beloved dog and bent down to give her a stroke. "I'll be fine."

"Okay, you've just gone from 'I'm alright' to 'I'll be fine', so obviously you're not." The crowd began to disperse once more, and Jules took Jenny's hand. "Come on. Let's go get a drink."

They went to the bar, and each got a bottle of beer before heading to a vacant table by the window. Meg went with them and lay down by Jenny's side as the two friends relaxed back a little in their chairs. "I suppose I'm not the actress I thought I was."

"So, what's up?"

"When we were in the forest this morning. When we were attacked by the infected. I've never been so sure in my life that I was going to die." She sniffed loud enough for Jules to hear her, and a single tear rolled down her cheek before the younger woman reached across and took her hand.

"We've all been there, Jen. It's scary as hell. It's more than that. It's traumatic. What you're feeling now is perfectly normal. There'll be a part of you that doesn't believe you got away."

"Yes," Jenny replied, laughing sadly and wiping away the tear with her free hand.

"I remember when I was shot. I was convinced that was it. I remember coming around and looking into the fire back at Lucy's place. I remember wondering if it was all an illusion and if I'd actually died. Then I heard that Mike had given me blood, and I was pretty sure I'd gone to hell." Jenny laughed, squeezing Jules' hand a little tighter. "I hadn't though. I'd made it because of the people around me, just like you. I heard what happened to you this morning, and I heard what a close thing it was, but we look out for one another. We help one another. We always have, and we always will. I get how you're feeling, Jen, but that feeling will go. You made it through today, and we've all been given a chance to start again down here."

Jenny released her grip on Jules' hand and sunk back a little further into her chair, taking her bottle with her. "How come I always feel better after talking to you?"

"Probably because if you can see me still smiling with the three fuckin' brothers I've got, then you know there's hope for anyone."

Jenny laughed again and looked across to where Andy, Rob and John were sitting. "They're good boys, your brothers."

Jules took a swig of beer and glanced towards them too. "Yeah. Yeah, they are. My mam and dad would be proud if they saw what they'd become."

"It's because of you they've turned out like that."

Jules shrugged. "It's because of me, because of you, because of Mike, because of Shaw, because of all of us. We're a family, Jen. We always will be. Doesn't matter where we're living and what's happening to us. We'll always be a family, and families watch out for one another."

*

By the time Wren and Wolf returned to the others, Sammy had joined a group of the younger hotel residents. The three young women remained on the periphery of the dance floor, watching people lose themselves for a little while at least.

Robyn had got them each a bottle of Becks, and they sipped them slowly, taking in the evening's proceedings. "You're right," Wren said suddenly, and Robyn and Mila turned towards her.

"Err … about what, exactly?" her sister replied.

"We should check it out." Then, in a lower voice, she continued, "We should check out the broadcast."

A thin smile cracked on Robyn's face. "Cool," she said, taking a sip of beer.

"On one condition."

"Okay, and what's that?"

"We let them have their meeting first, and we only head to Edinburgh if they're procrastinating."

"If you're trying to get me to agree to something I don't understand using big words, it's not going to work."

"Dummkopf," Mila replied. "This is my second language, and even I understand procrastinating."

"I'm very happy for you."

"It means putting something off, Bobbi. If they do what you think they'll do. If they table it, delay it, then we'll go. But if they agree to check it out, then we just have to be patient, okay?"

"This is fair, Robyn," Mila said as her friend pondered it for a moment.

"Okay, deal."

"What's a deal?" Mike said, walking up to them.

"Err…." Wren wasn't quite sure what to say.

"That if I get drunk tonight, nobody's going to prank me again," Robyn said, taking a drink.

Mike smiled. "Was waking up next to me really that

bad?"

"Totally."

"Thanks very much."

"So, have you just come over here to earwig on our girl talk, or did you have a reason?" Mila asked.

"Jesus," Mike said, putting his hands up. "I came over to say hi, that's all. I didn't realise I had to book an appointment."

"Hi then," Robyn said.

"Hi," Mike replied, taking a drink from his own bottle. "Anyway, I've been talking to Griz and—"

"And this is the reason you have come over, not to say hi at all," Mila interrupted.

"Am I really that transparent?"

"Yes."

Mike shrugged. "Fair enough. Griz would like us to go out on a scavenging mission tomorrow. I was hoping you three would be up for it."

"Okay, there are some things I can't unhear," Mya said. "But did you really just ask Wren, Robyn and Mila if they're up for it?"

The three girls laughed. "How come she doesn't get a dressing down for listening in on someone else's conversation but I do?" Mike asked.

"This is the girls' code," Mila replied.

"Totally," Mya said, smirking and high-fiving her German friend.

"Don't you have a politician to guard or something?" Mike asked.

"Agent Muppet and I have assessed the current situation and deemed there is no credible threat to the PM, his family, or their entourage. Plus, Darren and Mel are doing a pretty good job managing the situation from a PR standpoint."

"So, you're off duty?"

Mya grabbed the bottle out of Mike's hand and took a drink as her eyes sparkled mischievously.

"Technically. Why, what have you got in mind?"

"Nothing."

"Too bad."

Mike flushed red, and Mila and the others laughed.

"I'd come over here to ask if these three were willing to head out on a scavenging mission tomorrow. I was coming to see you next, but you've saved me a journey."

Mya shrugged. "What the hell, why not? It will show intent."

"Exactly. It will prove we're not freeloaders."

Mya finished off the rest of Mike's beer and handed the empty bottle back to him. "Go get me another, will you? I'm going to see Shaw."

Mike stood there with a bewildered expression on his face looking at the empty bottle before heading to the bar for another.

*

"Hey," Mya said, walking up to Shaw, who was standing in the vicinity of Vicky's table. She was holding an audience with Denise, Rory, Finlay and a handful of the hotel's longer-term residents.

"Hi," Shaw replied.

"This all seems pretty weird, doesn't it?"

Shaw laughed. "A couple of days ago, I was swimming naked in a loch, doubting that I'd ever see another living human being again. Yeah, you could say that this is pretty weird." Mya reached out, grabbing the bottle from Shaw's hand and taking a drink. "By all means, help yourself."

"Thanks," she said, smiling and handing it back to him. "Y'know, Shaw, I've been where you were."

"What, naked in the middle of a loch?"

"Not quite. I did wake up naked in the middle of an ice rink once, but that's not a topic for a casual conversation," she said with a smile.

"You strike me as someone who has lots of stories that aren't for casual consumption." He took a drink and then handed the bottle to Mya.

"We're going on a scavenging mission tomorrow."

"Okay."

"I think you should stay here."

"Hey, look. I realise you think I might have lost my edge, but—"

"People like you and me don't ever lose our edge. No, I'm going out, and as lovely as our new hosts seem, I haven't got a full handle on this place yet, and I'd like to know that there's someone on my wavelength back here."

"Emma's here."

"And Emma is impressive, and she's got this don't fuck with me thing going on, but she doesn't have the kind of experience we have."

"Experience or paranoia?"

Mya smiled and finished the bottle before placing it down on the table. "So you'll stay then?"

Shaw smiled. "Yeah. You just keep our people safe out there."

"You don't have to worry about that."

*

The night flew by, and it was not long before the last orders and the final song. The dance floor had spread out over the course of the night, and now it was ultimately anywhere that people wanted to sway their hips or move their feet.

The last song was a slow one, and Emma found herself in a corner with her arms looped around Diamond's neck. The taller woman reciprocated. They were a little drunk and couldn't stop smiling as they moved to the music. From early on in the evening, they had been glued to each other's side, exchanging histories, likes, dislikes, anecdotes, and generally hitting it off like you can only do with someone who you know is going to play a significant part in your future.

Emma had cared for Tabby, but it was never real love like she'd possessed for Sarah. But this.... There was chemistry. Both of them felt it, and as they gazed towards each other now, they couldn't help but beam.

"Would you like to come back to mine and maybe have a nightcap?" Diamond asked, speaking quietly into Emma's ear.

The warm air of her words made Emma's entire body tingle. "I'd love to, but it's our first night, and I want to be there in case Sammy freaks out."

Diamond pulled back a little. "You are a good sister."

Emma thought for a few seconds. Tonight was about relaxing, about having a good time, about forgetting all the crap that had gone before. She just wanted to enjoy herself, give herself to the moment, to the possibilities that lay ahead. "But we could take a bottle back to my room if you like. I mean, that way, I'd still be there if she woke up scared."

Diamond's eyes sparkled, and her mouth cracked into a wide smile. "This makes me happy. I do not want the night to end yet."

"No," Emma replied. "Me neither."

Gradually, the partygoers began to drift out. Everyone had enjoyed the evening, despite some of them originally having misgivings. Emma and Diamond walked hand in hand through the exit with a bottle of red wine and two plastic glasses. It had been a long time since either of them had been this happy. Although the threat of Olsen hung over their heads, although they were stuck in a city with hundreds of thousands of infected, although they had lost so much, and the future was uncertain, a small candle of hope burned in both their hearts, the likes of which they hadn't known for a long, long time.

20

Mike had enjoyed a couple of drinks but by the end of the night was still sober. He was tired, and he knew there was another challenging day ahead of them, and that was enough to make him go out like a light as soon as his head hit the pillow. A small handful kept the party going in their rooms for an hour or so after, but their muted celebrations did not make him stir.

The sound of thunder did wake him, however. It was louder than any he'd heard while living in Safe Haven, and he wondered for a moment if it was the echo of the city streets that made it so tumultuous. He lay with his eyes open for a moment, waiting to see a flash of lightning. His curtains were closed, but there was a slim gap on either side, and he was fairly certain the room would light up any second.

He heard muffled barks from across the hallway, and he smiled to himself. Humphrey and the other dogs would probably fanfare each time the thunder rumbled until the storm finally dissipated or drifted.

I'm not going to get much sleep until this is gone, he thought to himself as Meg started barking, too, and Wolf began to howl. He waited … and waited, but no flash came, and there was no more thunder. He wiped his eyes and shuffled his legs from under the covers, placing his feet on the floor. He looked towards the gap in the curtains once more and realised there was something other than the moon illuminating the night.

The dogs continued to bark and howl as he went across to the window, and it was only when he reached it that he realised the extra light was coming from below, not above. He looked across to the opposite building several floors down, and despite the warmth of the evening, a chill ran through him.

He fumbled with the latch as he levered open the window, and it was only then that he heard the unmistakable roar of flames. Pops, crackles and pings accompanied the sound, and he leant out as far as he could to see fire devouring their new home.

The thunder wasn't thunder. Maybe it was a gas tank or something. "FIRE!" he yawped at the top of his voice, turning on his torch and slipping his socks and boots on. "FIRE!" he yelled again, and now more panicked cries began to ring out. He flung on his jacket and his rucksack, and now he was holding on to all his earthly possessions as he had done hours before when they'd all arrived.

He burst out of his room, running next door to Emma's. She and Diamond were throwing on their clothes, but there was no embarrassment, only terror on their faces as the small lantern illuminated the horror apparent in Mike's eyes.

"Get Sammy," Emma said, and Mike turned to see Sammy already standing in the corridor with her torch on. Wren and Wolf came out of the room next door while Raj, Talikha and Humphrey burst out of the room opposite.

"We need to get everybody to the roof." He turned

back to look into Emma's room. "You clear this floor. I'll head downstairs and make sure they all know what's going on."

"Okay. Go. Go," Emma said, flinging on her T-shirt and slinging her rucksack over her shoulder.

Mike burst into the stairwell, and his heart sank a little further. The smoke was already thick, and there was an orange glow, which suggested the fire doors were open. *Which fucking idiot left the fire doors open?* Griz had told him how his people had worked relentlessly to get the place ready for them, but it took a special kind of stupid to do something like this.

He ran down the stairs two at a time exploding through the entrance and onto the floor below. Several people were already out in the hallway with their belongings. "How the hell did this happen?" Mya cried, running up to him.

"I don't know, but there's smoke in the stairwell, and I saw the orange glow. Do you think it's worth trying to close the fire doors down below?"

"If you can already see it, it's too late. We need to get everyone to the roof as quickly as we can and get across to the next building."

"Okay. Have you got everything covered down here?"

"Darren and Shaw are getting everybody sorted," she replied as more people appeared in the corridor with their possessions.

"Okay. I'll see you up top."

Mike heard coughing and spluttering as he re-entered the stairwell, and he panned the beam of his torch upwards to see figures heading to the top. *Everybody's moving. This is good. Everybody's moving.*

He heard the nervous barks of Humphrey, Wolf and Meg as they filed into the stairwell too. "Mike? Is that you?" Emma shouted, leaning over the safety railing as the door banged shut behind her.

"Yeah," he said, speeding up to join her.

"That's everybody out on this floor," she said before falling into a coughing fit.

The door from the level below creaked open, and the sound of feet charging up the steps rose to meet them. "Mya's getting everyone sorted down there," he said as the two siblings, along with Diamond, brought up the rear.

They continued following the others as torch beams danced around the stairwell. Finally, a few came to a standstill at the top. "Let's get that door open as soon as we can, shall we?" Emma called. "This place is filling with smoke, fast."

"I'm trying," Jules cried. "It's stuck."

"It can't be stuck. It's a fire escape."

"I'm telling you. It's fuckin' stuck."

Emma and Mike looked at each other with confused expressions before they, along with Diamond, weaved and pushed their way to the top. Sammy was with Wren and Wolf just a few steps down from the exit as they arrived to find Jules' assessment of the situation was accurate.

"Oh, fuck," Emma said then started coughing once more as others around her did the same.

Mike barged his way down to the landing below and elbowed the glass of the emergency case. A few seconds later, he was standing in front of the fire exit again. Screams sounded as the first axe strike echoed. Strike, strike, strike. With each powerful blow, more of the thick wood chipped away.

More and more people began to cough as the stairwell acted like a huge chimney making the smoke rise and rise until there was nowhere for it to go.

"We're all going to suffocate in here," Jules cried.

"What's the holdup?" Mya asked, having forced her way through the crowd and joined them at the top.

"The door's st—" Emma's words were cut short by a coughing fit, but it wasn't difficult for Mya to get the gist as the blade of the axe finally broke through. She shone her torch to see sweat already pouring down Mike's face.

She snatched the axe off him. "Take a breath." Smash, smash, smash. With each hit, a little more wood broke away. Until, finally, the section of the door around the panic bar snapped, and the substantial wooden barrier fell open.

People flooded onto the roof, greedily sucking in lungfuls of air while Mike and Mya hovered by the exit. Amidst all the other sounds, they had both heard the same thing—the jingle of chains as they fell to the ground. Their torches scoured the ground, but it was Muppet who was the first to discover it. They didn't say a word; they just looked at each other.

"MIKE!" Sammy's call had come from the roof's edge, and he and Mya ran across, but the cause of the concern was visible long before they reached it.

"Oh fuck," Mya hissed. "The bridge."

They leaned over to see the firelit street below. Dozens of infected had already gathered, and it was clear that hundreds more were on the way as the streets beyond their own moved like giant snakes.

"The boom we heard. It wasn't thunder or a gas canister exploding, it was the bloody bridge collapsing," Mike said, looking towards the door as the last of the hotel's residents made it to the top.

"What the hell are we going to do?" Emma asked.

"Don't worry," Diamond said. "Griz will be here soon. He will help."

"How the hell's he going to help from over there?"

"When we first set up a link to a new property, we erect ladders between the two sides. We secure them with rope and then—"

"And how the hell do we get the animals across?" Mya asked, looking down at Muppet fearfully.

Diamond didn't have an answer for that. She just shrugged apologetically as Sammy appeared through the crowd with Daisy. The family's beloved goat seemed skittish, not used to this many people and sensing the panic and fear in the air.

Children weren't the only ones crying, and when there was a whoosh and the sound of several more windows blowing out from below, another chorus of screams went up.

"What's the plan?" Beck asked, joining the others.

"Right now, sir, we're—" Before Mya could finish her thought, torch lights could be seen from the other rooftops, followed by cries of consternation. "I think we're about to find out."

It was nearly a minute before Griz and Clara appeared on the opposite roof. "Diamond," he shouted. "We'll be sending the ropes across in a second. Get ready to catch them."

"Okay, Griz," she shouted, putting her hand up to acknowledge understanding.

"Ropes?" Jenny asked, horrified. "We can't get across there on ropes," she said, crouching down and stroking Meg feverishly as if she was trying to extinguish a fire on the old dog's coat. "It's okay, girl. It's okay," she said quietly.

"Mike," Sammy said, pulling his coat sleeve.

"I know you're scared, Sammy, but I'm kind of busy right now."

"Mike."

"What is it, Sammy?"

"Wren, Robyn and Mila."

"What about them?"

"They've gone back in."

Suddenly, she had more than just Mike's attention as George, Jenny, Emma and all the others standing in earshot turned.

"What? Why?"

"She said she needed to find a way down for the animals. She said she wasn't going to leave them." Tears started to run down the young girl's face. "We're not going to have to leave Daisy, are we?"

Everything had happened so quickly that no one had thought through any aspect of their escape thus far. They were stuck on the roof of a burning building when, minutes before, they had been sleeping.

"Stay with Emma," Mike ordered, running towards the exit they'd only just escaped a short time before. Billowing smoke assaulted him as soon as he stepped inside. He panned the torch over the handrail and could see dancing beams a few floors below. "WREN! ROBYN! MILA!" he managed to shout before descending into a coughing fit. *Shit!*

He started to tear down the stairs in search of his friends.

*

"This is the worst nightmare I've ever had. I'm hoping someone wakes me up from it soon," Emma said as Mya came to stand by her side.

"Did you see the chain and padlock?"

"What?"

"What?" Shaw asked. He'd been further down in the stairwell and had exited with a swathe of others, so he had noticed little other than the ability to breathe once again.

"Someone padlocked and chained the door."

"And the acetylene lamp," Diamond said.

"What?" Mya replied.

"The acetylene lamp was on this roof earlier tonight. It is gone now. Someone deliberately brought down the bridge."

"Jesus. Who?" Shaw asked. "It's not like we've been here long enough to make enemies."

"Look, if we get off this roof, then we can find out, but knowing who did this to us isn't going to help right now," Mya said.

"She's right," Emma replied before backing up and gaining the attention of the frightened crowd. "Everybody listen. We need to try to remain calm. We're getting ladders across here, which will allow us to get to the other roof. If anybody needs medical attention, Liz and Trish are here. I suggest we try covering our mouths and noses to minimise the effect of the smoke."

*

Mike grabbed a T-shirt from his rucksack and wrapped it around his nose and mouth as he descended further. The smoke was getting thicker by the second, and he became increasingly worried that he'd be recovering bodies instead of persuading Wren and the others to head back up.

A single bark told him that his friends were nearer than he thought. "WREN!"

No reply came, but he could hear spluttering from multiple sources as he continued down the staircase. He finally reached them to see Robyn and Mila looking frightened and worried in equal measure. Tears were pouring down Wren's cheeks, and Wolf barked again, wide-eyed.

"We need to get back to the roof. We'll suffocate in here," Mike said before coughing violently.

"I'm not leaving him. I'm not leaving Wolf. I have to—" She fell into a coughing fit, too, before finally gathering herself for long enough to finish her sentence. "Find a way down."

Mike reached out grabbing hold of Wren's arm. "If you don't die from smoke inhalation, the fire will get you. We need—" It was Mike's turn to cough and splutter again. "We need to go back up to the roof."

"I'm not leaving him."

"We're not leaving anybody."

"Don't patronise me, Mike," she replied, crying more than ever as both Mila and Robyn started to cough.

"I'm not. I wouldn't. I'll figure it out. I'll figure out a way."

*

"Get ready," Diamond shouted, shining her torch over to the other side. "Get ready to catch the ropes."

There was a pregnant pause as others raised their torches towards the opposite rooftop, too, and then three looped ropes flew through the air.

Diamond, Mya and Darren lunged towards them, grabbing them tightly.

"Okay," Griz shouted. "Keep tight hold. We're slowly going to extend the ladders across."

It was only Diamond who knew what was going on, but as the base of three stainless steel ladders appeared over the safety railings and the rope became slacker, the others understood too. They each began to take up the slack.

*

Mike had a firm hold of Wren's hand as they all climbed the stairs once more. Robyn and Mila needed no persuasion. They were convinced it was a bad idea from the beginning, but there was no way they were going to let Wren go to her death alone.

Wolf matched them all step for step, checking to make sure no one was left behind. Deafening pops and bangs echoed up the staircase towards them as the fire took hold more by the second.

"I'm not leaving him," Wren sobbed once more, like a little girl.

Mike had seen her vulnerable a number of times in the past, but never like this. He squeezed her hand tighter. "I told you. We're not leaving anyone."

*

The echoing clang of the steel ladders bouncing against the reinforced safety rail chimed loudly enough to drown out the noise of the fire and the mass of creatures that had congregated below. The ladders were ten metres long, fully extended. The hooks wrapped around the security rail on the higher rooftop, but Diamond knew that Griz would have them tied by rope, too, to minimise the chance of movement or collapse.

"We need to secure these lines," she said, weaving the one in her hand around the vertical piers of the safety railing. Mya and Darren did the same with the ropes they had and then each of them shook their respective ladders. There was virtually no give, which was a good thing, but as they looked down, they all knew that it would be a miracle if they didn't lose people.

"This fire is spreading way too fast. It's going to be on us before we know it," Emma blurted as she joined the three of them at the makeshift bridges.

"Then we should not waste time."

"I'm sending the other ropes across now," Griz shouted.

"Other ropes?" Emma asked.

"Safety ropes for when we all have to climb across," explained Diamond.

Emma just stared at the ladders for a moment. *This is really happening. We're going to flee a burning building by crawling across to another one on a ladder with thousands of infected below just waiting for us to put a foot wrong.* "Jesus."

"If you believe in him, Emma, now would be a good time to call in a favour."

*

Robyn and Mila were the first to emerge from the emergency exit, coughing and spluttering. A few seconds later, Wolf, Wren and Mike came through in a similar state.

Mike finally let go of Wren and bent over, resting his hands on his knees while he tried to catch his breath. He looked across to the ladders as three more ropes shot through the air to be snagged by three more people.

"That's it?" he asked as Emma joined him.

"Yeah," she replied, placing a hand on her brother's back. "Are you okay?"

"I could have done without that, to be truthful." When he looked up at her, he could see fresh tears on her cheeks, even in the periphery of the torchlight.

"She was Gran's baby," Emma said.

"She still is."

"Sammy's going to be devastated."

"We're not leaving anybody on this rooftop."

"Mike. You need to be realistic. There's no way we're going to be able to get Daisy and the dogs across there."

They turned to see the three ladder bridges. Even with the ropes in place to secure them, they looked meagre. "We're not leaving anybody on this roof," he said again before heading over to the ladders.

"I suppose we just need to figure out who's going first," said Shaw as several more former Safe Haven citizens looked down to the streets below.

"That's easy," Mike said, grabbing one of the safety ropes that had been thrown across and tying it underneath his arms and around his chest.

"Okay, come on, Mike. I've got you, brother," Griz shouted.

All the air seemed to be sucked from the rooftop as everyone held their breath collectively. Mike climbed over the safety rail and placed his hands on the metal frame of the first ladder. He edged onto it fully and paused for a moment. He could feel the slight tension in the rope as Griz pulled, ready to take the weight if his friend slipped.

Mike looked through the rungs. Small amounts of burning debris had fallen to the ground illuminating the horror show below a little brighter. The fire had climbed at least two more floors since the last time he had looked, and he knew it wouldn't be long before the building was fully consumed. He took a breath and peeked over his shoulder towards his sisters before turning back and starting his climb.

One step, two steps. He could barely hear the clink of metal above the noise of growls and the fire. Three steps, four steps. He couldn't have gripped the ridged metal any tighter if he'd tried. Mike wasn't someone normally afraid of heights, but this wasn't exactly like the time he helped replace the shingles on a neighbour's roof. If he slipped, it wouldn't end with a trip to the hospital with broken bones. *There's no way some of them are going to be able to do this.*

Five, six steps. He felt the ladder begin to bend a little the nearer to the first extension he got, and butterflies began to flutter in his stomach. With each subsequent rung, the ladder arched a little more and now he could hear the fear and worry from the people on the rooftop behind him as they realised they would all have this journey to make too.

"You're doing great, Mikey, lad. Come on, keep going. You're doing great." Griz's words urged him on as he reached for the next rung and the next. The ladder continued to dip, and he expected it to give at any moment, but it held until, finally, he reached the third and final section of the extension. He shuffled up the last few rungs quicker than any previous ones, and as he felt hands grasp his jacket and belt and he set foot on the higher rooftop, he breathed a deep sigh of relief.

*

"I appreciate the fact that your brother wanted to show people how it was done, but it would have been nice to have him over here to try to get everyone else ready," Shaw said.

"Yeah," Emma replied. "Something tells me we haven't seen the last of him yet."

"What do you mean?"

"Let's just get three people ready, shall we?"

"That's going to be easier said than done. Jenny refuses to go without Meg. Wren's refusing to go without Wolf. Everybody's scared to death."

Emma looked around. Her focus had been on watching Mike, but now she understood what Shaw meant. Terror was etched on many of the faces, and despite the fiery peril that was spreading towards them, no one seemed eager to leave their respective positions.

The end of the rope Mike had worn flew back across, and Diamond caught it. She seemed to be the only one who wasn't overcome with fear. "Okay," Emma called out. "Who's next?"

*

"I thought you'd have been one of the last ones to leave that roof," Griz said, guiding the younger man away.

"I'm going back."

"You're doing what?"

"Daisy and the dogs. We can't leave them."

"Mikey boy, I appreciate the sentiment, pal, but that fire is spreading fast. We don't have the equipment or the time to try to erect hoists. I'm sorry, brother, but we just need to get as many people off that roof as we can as quickly as we can."

"Maybe there's another way."

Griz let out a long sigh. "I fucking knew you'd be trouble." Brief smiles flashed on both their faces. "Alright, I'm all ears. What do you need?"

*

"I need three more people to go," Emma said to Jules.

"And?"

"Mike's an anomaly. People have seen him do it, but if they saw—"

"A gommel like me, you mean?"

"I just meant someone like them. Someone they can relate to, and maybe Jon or Rob or Andy."

"Have I mentioned that I fuckin' hate heights?"

"We're running out of time, Jules."

"Ah, fuck it," she said. "Rob, John, we're next." Without another word, the three siblings walked up to the edge. They tied the waiting ropes around their bodies, and each took an audible breath before climbing over the safety rail and reaching out for the frame of their respective ladders. "See yous all on the other side," Jules said, trying to sound brave, but her voice quivered as the words left her lips.

*

Raj was not standing on the south side of the rooftop with the others. He was looking out to the east. That was the direction the sun would be rising in a couple of hours.

It was the direction from which the new day would start, but it was a day he wanted nothing to do with. Talikha stood by his side, and Humphrey sat, peacefully for once, in the middle. The two humans were sobbing quietly, doing everything they could to hide their sad sounds from each other and their beloved dog.

"Room for two more?" Jenny asked, the quake in her voice evident as she and Meg came to a stop beside them.

"You are always welcome to join us, my friend," Raj replied.

She reached out and grasped Talikha's hand. "It's as if they know. It's as if they know that this is it; that this is where it all ends. She's been glued to my side ever since we came up onto the rooftop."

The sound of breaking glass and combusting furniture travelled up towards them. With each pop and clank, frightened murmurs from the other side of the roof drifted in the smokeless air that remained.

"It will be like them going to sleep," Raj said.

"What do you mean?" asked Jenny.

"I can give them an injection. It will be like they are going to sleep with us by their sides. It will be like—" He broke down, and Humphrey whined, leaning into his master as if he was telling him it was alright. Whatever he had to do, it was alright. Raj fell to his knees and wrapped his arms around his beloved friend. He buried his head in his soft thick mane and cried like a child. Humphrey licked the side of Raj's head feverishly, trying to make it all better, trying to stop his suffering. *It's alright. It's alright. It's alright. I've had a good life. The best life.* The rational part of Raj knew that the words he was putting to his dog's actions were his own, but as the Labrador retriever continued to comfort him, he needed to hear them in his head at least. "I'm sorry, boy. I'm so sorry."

*

"Jesus, Mary, mother of Christ," Jules muttered to herself as she stared through the rungs of the ladder to the horde of creatures assembled below.

"Try not to look down, Jules," Rob said.

"Now how the fuck am I supposed to do that?"

"Just look up to where we're going, to the others."

She raised her head towards the rooftop on the other side. A long line of people eager to help were waiting. The man who had a hold of the safety rope knotted around her chest was willing her along, as was everyone. She threw a glance over her shoulder. Emma, Shaw, Mya and the others were willing her up and forward. The roar of the fire was becoming more evident by the moment, and she suddenly realised that every second she lingered on that ladder was reducing someone else's chance of escape. "Screw this." She gripped the next rung tightly and then the next and the next as her feet climbed too. Within a few seconds, she and her brothers were being hoisted to safety on the other side. She threw her arms around the man who held her line and kissed him roughly on the cheek. "Thank you."

He just nodded and flung the looped rope across to the other roof once more. Even though the ladder was ten metres fully extended, the gap was more like eight, given the gradient of the incline. Mya snatched the rope out of the air and gestured for Trish, Beck and the children to join her.

*

"Is this the corner for lost souls?" Wren asked, joining Jenny and the others.

"Come here, darling," Jenny said, embracing Wren tightly. The younger woman had done nothing to hide her tears and desperation, and she flung her arms around Jenny, almost as if pleading with her to make this horror end. "Raj says he can give them an injection. It will be just like they're going to sleep."

A scream sliced through the air as a small explosion reverberated from one of the floors below, causing the ladders to shift and rattle.

"Do you think he'll have enough left to put me to sleep too?"

"Don't say that, darling. Don't say that."

"I can't go on without him, Jenny. He's saved my life a thousand times. He's my best friend. He's my brother. He's my child. He knows me better than I know myself. I can't go on without him. I don't want to." She burst into tears once more, and the older woman held on to her a little tighter. She knew exactly what Wren was saying. She felt the same way about Meg. She had been the one constant in her life since they had met. She had made her feel good when times were bad. She had been her confidante, her priest, her everything.

"W-we'll get through. We'll get through together like we always do." She said the words because she was trying to make Wren feel better, but she didn't mean them. In truth, she didn't know how she'd get through this. She'd allowed herself to start feeling a little more optimistic, a little more hopeful. Earlier in the day, she had been convinced she was going to die. She had also been convinced that no experience could be as bad as that, but she was wrong. *It's so much easier to leave someone than for them to leave you.*

21

The tall, slim figure slipped through the open door of the fire escape and began to descend the stairs as more and more people were climbing to the roof to help. Some greeted him as he passed them. He nodded in return; after all, he was well-known in the community, even well-liked.

Being liked was something he never considered important until it started happening. Equally, being part of a community was alien to him, but he had adapted and fitted in. He had become a vital cog in the big wheel, and from having no hope and no future, he had begun to envisage longevity to his existence.

Putting down roots seemed to be a strange metaphor to use when you lived your life on the upper floors of a chain hotel in the middle of Glasgow, but that's what he'd been doing for the last few months. This place had become his home, and it felt more like a home than anywhere he had lived before.

Things were going well and getting better. He was enjoying life, yes, actually enjoying it, not just living it. And now, just like that, it was all over.

He'd seen an opportunity. It was a risk, but it should have worked. It had a better chance of working than all the other ideas he'd come up with that afternoon, but the second the three ladders were secured in place and that man, Griz's new best friend, placed his feet on safe ground, or a safe roof at least, he knew his hopes, dreams and his actual life in this place had come to an end. He had to get out, and that was exactly what he was doing. As much as he liked his life here, he knew it would be over if he stayed.

He'd managed to get through the day without being seen by many of the newcomers, or at least the ones who mattered. He'd stayed virtually invisible, taking guard duty on the ground floor and spending the afternoon in his room before being the nighttime roof sentry.

So close. It had almost worked. Almost but not quite. *Maybe if I'd used more accelerant. Maybe if I'd have started fires on more floors. Maybe….*

He'd drive himself crazy if he dwelled on what-ifs and maybes. *What's done is done.*

Having an almost photographic memory for faces was as much a bane as it was a boon. There were lots of faces he would have loved to forget, like the ones of those women who destroyed his chances of rising up the ranks of The Don's army. He would never ever forget their faces, and the chances were they wouldn't forget his. When he had glimpsed the sister of the one they called Mike, it was as if a sledgehammer had struck him in the chest. Then he had laid eyes on the two young women, Wren and Robyn, and he knew that if they caught sight of him, the game would be up too. He had seen them at that farm way back when the outbreak had just begun. He paused for a few more seconds as he remembered the hopes he'd had then. But now all his hope was gone.

Yes, setting fire to the newcomers' hotel was Gordon

Mckeith's last chance. If they'd all gone up in smoke with the building, then he could have carried on with his life. He'd have figured out a way to explain the destruction of the bridge. Maybe he would have smashed the back of his head against a wall and claimed to have been knocked out. Maybe he'd have said someone else had agreed to take over his shift and made them disappear. Lying wasn't hard for him. He had done it all his life. Violence wasn't hard either, but saying goodbye to all this. *This is fucking hard.*

His go-bag was ready should the worst come to the worst, and it was only when he reached the ground floor of their particular hotel block that the enormity of what he was doing caught up with him.

"Gordo, what the hell's happening up there?"

"Griz wants you on the roof, Chip."

"What? Why?"

"The other hotel's on fire. He asked me specifically to come down and relieve you of duty. He needs you."

The small lantern on the reception desk threw out enough light for Chip to see the tightly packed rucksack on his friend's shoulder. "What's with the bag?"

"It's bad up there. I wanted to make sure I had a few essentials in case the fire made it across here."

Chip's face suddenly drained of colour. "It's that bad?"

"Aye. You'd better hurry."

Chip nodded. "Okay," he replied, plucking a small torch from his pocket and disappearing into the stairwell.

Mckeith waited a couple of minutes before heading over to the door. He uncovered the small peephole and looked outside. He could make out enough of the street to see it was clear around the entrance, and he pulled each of the giant bolts across before unlocking the door. The latch would mean that once it closed behind him, the handle would need pulling to open it once again, and as simple as that task was for even a child, the logic of it evaded the infected.

There was a time when Mckeith would not have cared whether the door was left open or not. There was a time when he wouldn't have cared about anyone but himself, and that was still true to an extent. He weighed his welfare above that of all others. But he had grown to care for these people. He had shared laughs, tears and even a bed with some of them. His photo was on the darts championship wall of fame. A sad smile crept onto his face as he looked back to the small foyer one last time. Something as simple as a laptop computer and portable printer. Two things he believed he would never see or use again when he was with Fry and The Don were part of daily life now … or at least they were.

Where he would go from here he wasn't quite sure. What awaited him he had no idea. He opened the door and stepped out onto the street, and as the door closed behind him, he knew that all the plans he'd had for that life, a different kind of life to one he'd ever dreamed of when he was with Fry and The Don, were gone forever.

He looked up and down the road, and out here, it was easy to hear the ferocity of the blaze just a few streets away. He cast one final gaze towards the hotel that had been his home for so long, rolled his shoulders, making sure the rucksack was on safely and broke into a jog.

He'd heard the newcomers had arrived in a fleet of vehicles, and he only hoped that the keys were still with them. He waited at the corner of Wellington Street for a moment until a small pack of infected vanished from view, and then he stepped out. His eyes settled on a minibus. He'd driven similar ones plenty of times before, and he knew he'd be able to kit it out well enough inside for it to be his home on a temporary basis at least.

He climbed in and pulled down the visor. It was too dark for him to see the keys fall, but he heard them and felt them as they settled in his lap. He picked them up and fumbled them into the ignition then held his breath. The engine coughed for a moment before exploding into life, and he let out a long sigh of relief.

He would head towards the outskirts of the city and then north to the Highlands, to his future.

That fucking bridge. It all came back to that bridge and those women escaping. It was like something out of a movie that he had played over and over in his head. His return to Loch Uig should have been a triumphant one. Maybe The Don would even have given him a territory, maybe a town of his own to govern. Maybe, maybe, maybe. It was all maybes. Everything was maybes because the anchor had been drawn up and the ship had sailed long ago. On the day that should have been a new beginning, that bridge had signalled the end.

He put his foot down, speeding past the odd shambling beast as it made its way towards the noise and the glowing ash soaring ever higher into the night sky. He kept his foot down hard as he passed Waterloo Street and Cadogan Street then crunched down the clunky gears and applied the brake as he came up to the junction of Argyle Street. He took one last look in the mirror then left his life on Hope Street behind forever.

*

"Mike. I understand this is an emotional time, brother, but think about this."

"I have," he said, looking down at the two large, hefty bags Griz had presented him with. One was long and made from canvas. Up until two minutes earlier, it had housed a croquet set. The other was just a little shorter but wider and deeper. It had stains on the outside and had been used as a kit bag for an offshore worker. While not as aesthetically pleasing as the first, it was sturdier, made of thicker material, and it seemed like two tanks travelling in opposite directions would not be able to pull the stitching apart. Next to the two bags lay a variety of cargo straps. Mike scooped them up and placed them into his preferred bag, and then the two men headed back down the corridor.

"Brother, this could be the shortest fucking

permanent move in the history of fucking moving. I'm begging you again. Please think about this."

Mike stopped and angled his torch up a little so he could see the other man's face.

"I've thought about it, Griz. This is what's happening."

*

There wasn't a time in recent memory when Beck had craved a drink more. What he wouldn't give to have that warm amber fluid trickling down his throat, giving him the courage he so desperately needed now. Trish was on one ladder. His two girls were on the second, and he was on the third. The warnings from the other side were that the ladders were quite old and it strictly had to be one person at a time, but the girls were light, and they didn't want to leave each other or their parents. Suddenly, the first one came to a halt causing the two adults to stop as well.

"Come on, darling. You've got to keep climbing, just like we discussed," Trish said.

"I can't."

"Andy," Trish begged. She was not good with heights at the best of times, and this was not the best of times. She was trying her hardest to be strong for the two girls, but it was taking everything she had to be strong enough for herself.

"Is everything okay, sir?" Darren called out behind them.

Beck glanced back and nodded briefly before turning to his children. "Do you remember when Daddy made that big speech about the infection and what we were going to do to fight it?"

Tears were falling from both girls' cheeks now, down onto the infected below. "Yes," one of them said.

"Well, do you remember Mummy and I told you that I made that speech to stop people being scared and that you were both going to have to be brave and strong and show the rest of the country that you weren't scared at all, even though it would be difficult?"

"Yes," they both replied in unison.

"Well, this is exactly the same. You're going to have to be brave and strong now. You're going to have to carry on climbing because everybody down there is scared and they need to see how this isn't a big deal. They need to see that we can do it so they'll know that they can do it. Do you understand me?"

"But I'm scared, Daddy."

"I know you are, darling. Everybody's scared, but being brave isn't about having no fear. It's about doing the things that scare you despite the fact that they scare you."

The little girl turned back towards the ladder and reached up to the next rung then the next. Beck and Trish looked at each other. A line of lanterns had been set up on the opposite roof, and the fire below was burning brighter than ever. He could see the fear in her eyes. That scared him in itself. In all the time he'd known Trish, she had been unshakeable, the rock to which he always tethered in a storm, and he knew at that moment that he needed to be the one to give her strength. "We'll get through this. We'll get through this, and it will be just another story in a long, long book of stories," he said to her.

"I love you," Trish replied.

"I love you too. I always will. Now, come on."

*

The moment Trish pulled the rope from over her head Mike grabbed it, flung it over his own and headed back down the ladder. As he climbed off on the other side, he took the rope off once more and handed it to Emma. "Keep everybody moving. The fire looks like it's gone up two more floors since we first got to the roof."

"Where did you go? What are you doing with that bag?"

"Just keep everybody moving, Em," he said before going in search of Raj.

"Where the hell did you go?" Mya asked, grabbing

Mike as he broke through the crowd.

"Have you seen Raj?"

"I asked you a question."

It was clear that she'd been fighting back tears. He looked down to see Muppet by her side. The normally stoic dog was unusually skittish. "Come with me," he said, grabbing her wrist.

"What the hell? Where are we going? What are you doing?"

They reached Raj, Talikha, Jenny and Wren. Humphrey, Wolf and Meg gave barely perceptible wags of their tails as the others joined them. Mike looked across to the crowd to see Sammy on the outskirts looking forlorn. She was stroking Daisy as if it was her last goodbye.

Another whoosh from below reminded them all that it wouldn't be long before the fire reached them. Over the noises of the blaze, he could hear the sobs as they came to terms with what was about to happen.

"Raj."

His friend turned, and when he spoke, he could hear the familiar tremble in his voice of someone who was suffering, someone who was hurting on a cellular level, as one of the hardest things he'd ever have to do loomed ever closer. "Yes, Mike."

"I need you to put Daisy and the dogs to sleep."

Raj nodded. "I know, my friend. We were just spending a few moments … more with them." The last words caught in his throat, and audible cries rose from Wren and Jenny as they simultaneously fell to their knees to hold their loved ones a final time.

"No. I don't mean euthanise them. I mean put them out, knock them out. I'm going to get them off the roof."

"What?"

"What?" Mya echoed.

He pulled the large, sturdy bag from his shoulders and dropped it on the ground. It was the first time any of them had even noticed it given everything else that was happening. "I'm going to take them across one at a time on my back. After everyone else is over there, I'm going to place two of the ladders together to spread the weight; then I'm going to get them to the other rooftop."

"In that bag?"

"Yeah." He unzipped it, revealing the cargo straps. "I'll need someone to help me load up."

"Do you really think this will work?" Wren asked, standing once more, wiping her tears away as a tiny flame of hope rekindled inside her.

"It is very dangerous, Mike. Getting over there is hard enough without having another thirty or forty kilos on your back," Raj said.

"We're not leaving anybody behind."

*

"He's not going to go. I can't get him to do anything right now," Ruby said with one arm around her brother. Emma had kept the line moving, and so far, there had been a couple of nervous pauses out in the middle but no serious mishaps.

"We're going to have to do something, Ruby. This fire's spreading fast and it won't be too long until it's up here."

"Don't you think I know that?"

"Hey, Tommy," Richard said, walking up to the teenager. "I was looking for you earlier." Tommy just stared ahead. His eyes were not cast to the other rooftop but to the windows below. The reflection of the fire raged in them, but there was no fear on Tommy's face, no emotion of any kind. Inside, it was anyone's guess what was going on, but he had been unreachable since the crash, and if they made it out of this, it would no doubt add another layer of impenetrability. "They've got a library here." He paused for a moment. "Four full rooms of books from floor to ceiling. They've asked Ruth and me if we can help with the organisation. It would make it a lot easier for us if you helped too."

Nothing.

"Did you hear that, Tommy? A library," Ruby said, hoping it might trigger some kind of reaction.

Nothing.

"And y'know what, Tommy. At the party tonight, I saw some homemade cookies and cakes and all sorts." Richard was trying his hardest to think back to Mary Stolt's little packages for Tommy. He was trying to remember what had gained the biggest reaction. "I bet you anything they could make some stollen. What do you reckon? Should we ask them to make some stollen?"

A blink. Was that something or was it just a reaction to the rising smoke and ash?

*

"I am going to go across next," Diamond said over the rising noise.

"Oh, okay," Emma replied. As Mike had asked, she and Shaw had kept the lines moving. "I—"

Diamond reached out and touched Emma's face gently. "I am going to head over to the water tower and turn off the supplies to all but this building," she said, gesturing to the opposite hotel where Griz and the others were assembled. "I think maybe I can connect a fire hose. It might be useful. It might give us more time."

Emma looked beyond the neighbouring building and the next to the taller water tower, which had been shown to them earlier in the day. She had been told how Diamond designed and built it using above-ground swimming pools. At the time, she had thought it had been ingenious, but she never thought it might save some of their lives. "Be careful," she said eventually.

"I will." Diamond leaned in and kissed her on the cheek as if it was the most natural thing in the world. A looped rope sailed through the air, and she reached up, grabbing it before placing it over her shoulders and securing it under her arms. "Keep people moving," she said as she climbed over the safety rail and onto the ladder. "Every second counts."

*

"We could take it in turns," Mya said. "You could take one then I could take the next. It would be less of a strain that way."

"I'll be fine," Mike replied as they followed Raj and the others back to the crowd gathered around the ladders.

"Y'know, you are the most stubborn bastard I've ever met in my life."

"Look. I get how crazy this is. If it goes to hell, then it will be bad enough that I've taken an innocent animal down with me. I don't want to be responsible for getting you killed too."

"I'm not a fucking wallflower, y'know?"

Mike smiled. "I'll make you a promise. If I feel like I'm struggling, we'll swap."

"Okay. Deal."

*

"Come on," Darren said. He had taken the middle ladder. Mel was to his left and Doug to his right. He could comfortably have reached the other side half a dozen times by now, but the other two were almost rigid with fear.

"I can't," Mel said, closing her eyes. "I'm going to have to go back."

"Don't be so bloody ridiculous. If you want to get yourself killed, then that's a sure-fire way of doing it."

"I-I can't go on, Darren."

"Mel. Mel." It was Doug's voice. The usual condescending tone was absent. "Look at me, Mel." She raised her eyes beyond Darren towards Beck's special advisor. There had been times in her life when she had hated him with a passion, but, like her, all he ever wanted was to protect Beck, and now he was trying to help her. "Come on. We'll do this one rung at a time."

"I'm sorry. I can't." She looked down, well aware of the fact that it was the worst possible thing she could do. Fire lashed out from the lower windows, and flickering wisps of ash floated on the air like fairies. Below, far below, she could see the moving throng of bodies just waiting for one of them to fall.

"Listen to me, Mel. Andy needs us. He needs both of us. He always has and always will. I don't believe this is it. I don't believe we're going to end our days living on the upper floor of a hotel in the middle of Glasgow. You know it too. A new society will slowly build, and there's only one man who can hold that together, but he'll never be able to do it without us. I know you're scared. I am too. But you're not doing this for you. You need to get across there for him." Doug had drunk more than most that evening, and although he had been used to it when he'd been entertaining foreign dignitaries or journalists, he'd fallen out of practice. When he'd left the party, he was slurring his words and struggled to walk in a straight line. Now, though, he was stone-cold sober.

Mel brought her head up once more and looked in the direction of the roof where Beck and Trish both stood side by side, beckoning her across. She squeezed her eyes shut tight for one second, two, three, then took a breath and reached out for the next rung. "Okay, Doug. Okay."

*

"Wren's told us what you're going to do," Robyn said as she and Mila walked up to Mike. He had been trying to take a minute to gather himself mentally for the task ahead, but he knew his moment of inner peace was over.

"And?"

"Thank you."

"You don't need to thank me. Daisy and the dogs are as much a part of our family and the community as anyone. Daisy makes it feel like there's still a little part of my gran alive. And forget about the emotional aspect of the whole thing for a second. How many times have those dogs saved us? I don't mean figuratively; I mean literally. If it wasn't for Wolf and Muppet down in that tunnel, none of us would be here right now. And that's just one out of like a thousand times."

"You're right. But thank you anyway. Nobody else came up with this idea. I've never seen my sister so broken."

Mike glanced across to Wren, who was kneeling next to Wolf. Anxiety still painted her face, but the tears had dried for the moment. "Listen to me, both of you. If, for any reason, I don't make it—"

"Shush! You do not talk like this. It does no one good to fill your head with negative thoughts," Mila said.

"Yeah, whatever, look. Somebody did this to us. Somebody tried to kill us all. We were never meant to be up here on this rooftop. We need to find out who and deal with them."

"I don't know if you've noticed, Mike, but not many people listen to me and Mila."

"I don't give a damn who listens to you. You can do this yourselves. You two are our best fighters. You're the ones we've come to rely on to get us out of trouble. If I don't make it through this, you need to take more of a lead. Em will be grateful to have you by her side. And the first thing you need to do is find the bastard who did this and fucking crucify him."

"What makes you so sure it's a he?"

"You make a good point. Crucify them then."

"You're going to make it, Mike," Robyn said.

"Yeah. Course I will. But … on the off chance something goes wrong."

Robyn turned to look at her sister and Sammy, who was crouched down beside her with Daisy. "What about Mya? I'm pretty certain she'd happily rip the bastard who did this to shreds."

"Mya's going to be over here with me. That's why I'm talking to the pair of you. Shaw's got a long way to go before he's back to normal. Our people will need you more than ever."

Mila reached out and grabbed Mike's arm. "We will do whatever we have to do to keep them safe. We will find the person who did this, and I will look into their eyes as I drive my sword through their heart."

"Yeah," Robyn added. "What she said. But, y'know, with arrows. You're going to make it though."

"Yeah." He looked across to the ladders as another three people started the climb. "Yeah. Course I will."

22

Emma felt a presence by her side and didn't need to turn to know who it was. She carried on watching as George, Jack and James reached the opposite roof. Their three ropes fired back across the deadly chasm between the two buildings, and then she caught sight of Diamond on the other side, unreeling a giant firehose.

"She said she was going to divert the water supply. It might buy us a bit more time."

"She's a smart lady. I like her."

"Y'know, it would have been nice if I didn't have to find out what you were doing from Sammy. It would have been nice if you told me."

"Sorry. You seemed busy."

"Don't bullshit me, Mike." The pair of them turned to see Raj, Talikha and Mya with Wren, Jenny and their little sister. The animals were all anxious, but soon they would be asleep and blissfully unaware of everything that was going on.

"Mya's staying across here with me."

"So she's got a death wish too?"

"I don't have a death wish. I told you we weren't going to lose anybody else, and I meant it."

"There are some things that aren't in your control, Mike. Have you felt the roof lately?" she asked, bending down and placing her hand on the surface. "It's hot, Mike. It won't be long until the fire's reached us and this whole thing will collapse. I'd try to talk you out of this, but I know better by now."

"I love you, Em." She turned and breathed out a sorrowful breath, throwing her arms around her brother and squeezing him tightly.

"I love you too."

*

"You only get stollen at Christmastime. You can't get stollen through the year, only at Christmas."

When Ruth had come across to join Richard and Ruby, she had been convinced it was a lost cause trying to get Tommy to engage at all, let alone move. But now his brain seemed to click back into gear once more.

"Well, I bet I could speak to Griz and ask him if they could make some, especially for you," Richard said. "How would you like that? Not Christmas stollen, but Tommy stollen."

"Ha. Tommy stollen. Ha. Richard made a joke. Tommy stollen."

"That's right, Tommy. You can have all the stollen and all the books you want, but first, you're going to have to climb that ladder with me."

There was a small explosion from somewhere below, and multiple screams sliced through the ever-warmer night air, but Tommy didn't seem to hear them. "Tommy stollen." Suddenly, he charged towards the middle ladder, almost leaping over the safety rail; his hands gripped the frame tightly.

"Tommy, NO! You need the safety rope," Ruby

shouted as she ran to the edge. It was too late. He was already a third of the way across by the time she looped a rope over herself and climbed out onto one of the waiting ladders. "Oh, God, Tommy. Oh, God."

She couldn't move. As much as she wanted to go after him, she was transfixed. One wrong foot and that would be it. He would fall to an unthinkable death. She watched and watched, and it was only when she felt a hand on her arm and turned to see Richard's smiling face that she understood she hadn't dreamt it. Her brother had made it to the other side and was safe.

"Come on," Richard said. "I suppose it's our turn now."

*

"I'm staying too," Raj said as Wren, Sammy and Jenny placed the looped ropes around themselves and cast fear-filled looks back to the anaesthetised animals.

"No," Talikha cried. "You must come with me."

He reached out, grabbing her hands. "I will be along shortly, my sweet. I need to stay here to help."

"Raj, it's okay," Mya said. "I've got this. You go with—"

"Humphrey is my family. I will stay until he is off the roof."

"Then I will stay too," Talikha protested.

"No. You must go. You are needed on the other side. There is no finer veterinary nurse in all of Glasgow," he said, trying hard to smile.

Talikha grasped her husband firmly and squeezed. "You promise you will come back to me."

"I promise."

It was a few more minutes until the roof was clear of everyone but the animals, Mike, Raj and Mya. They untied one of the ladders as Griz did the same before shuffling it along the railing until it was next to the other. They bound it to the middle ladder before retying it to the railing.

"Okay, who's going first?" Mya asked.

"Daisy," Raj said.

"Why Daisy?"

"She is by far the lightest of the animals, and it will give Mike a chance to get used to having a weight on his back."

"Good thinking."

"Okay. Load me up," Mike said. He watched as Raj and Mya laid the unconscious goat in the large kitbag before zipping it up. Mike knelt down, and they carefully hoisted it onto his shoulders then used the cargo straps to secure it further.

"How does that feel?" Mya asked.

"Like I've got a goat strapped to my back."

"Good then. That's how it's meant to feel."

There was a booming clang from the stairwell, and they all turned. The sound continued for several seconds making the whole rooftop vibrate. "What was that?" Raj asked, panicked.

"My guess is that the staircase has just collapsed." Mya turned to Mike. "We haven't got long. Good luck."

Mike climbed over the rail and reached out, straddling the two ladders. They seemed solid bound together. He'd have preferred just to be climbing one, but spreading the weight was safer. No one knew how old the ladders were or what the maximum threshold was. Mike was powerfully built, and having a forty-kilogram dog on his back might well have proved too much for one ladder, so this was the only option.

All his muscles flexed as he climbed one rung at a time. The straps were bound tightly around him, meaning his precious cargo barely moved as he ascended. The noise of the creatures rose through the night air. It was a familiar but terrifying sound, and despite the heat of the fire, it made the blood in his veins run cold. He raised his head to the other side to see his sisters, Griz, Diamond and a host of other friendly faces willing him on.

He could feel the sweat rolling down his back. He

could feel it on his brow. He paused in the middle as a coughing fit struck him. He closed his eyes for a few seconds until it was over; then he continued.

Four, three, two, one. Suddenly hands reached out to grab him. They took off the rope for a moment while they removed the straps and the bag. Darren and Andy carried it one handle each over to where Talikha was waiting with Raj's vet bag. Less than a minute later, Mike was heading back down the ladder with the empty bag over his shoulders and the safety rope looped around his body.

"How was that?" Mya asked.

"Fine. It was fine," Mike said.

"Meg next," Mike said. Without further conversation, Mya and Raj removed the bag from Mike's back and carefully placed in Jenny's beloved companion.

Mike knelt once more as they manoeuvred the straps over his shoulders and secured it into place as they had done previously. There was a noticeable weight difference as Mike stood, and he staggered a little. "Are you okay?" Mya asked, reaching out to steady him.

"Yeah. The extra weight just took me a little off guard."

"We can swap. I can do this."

"I'm fine." This time, he was a little slower walking across to the edge, and as he made contact with the ladders, they seemed to judder more. He paused for a moment. *Shit. Wolf and Humph are a hell of a lot heavier than Meg. I hope these things hold.*

"Are you okay?" Emma called out from the other roof. He knew the safety rope around him was secured to the brick mount of an air conditioning duct, but at least three people were feeding the line back and forth too, and his sister was the first of them, with Griz standing right behind her.

"I'm fine." *Got to do this.* One rung, two rungs. He started to move more quickly as he adjusted to the weight. Four windows blew out, and a breath of fiery air belched beneath him as gasps and screams erupted from the other rooftop. He took a beat and glanced back. *It's reached the top floor. It's reached the top fucking floor.* He turned towards Mya and Raj. They couldn't see what he could see, but anguish painted their faces as the sounds around them became evermore terrifying.

One hand, one foot, one hand, one foot. It was the only way to do this. Eager claw-like hands grasped his jacket as he reached the other side.

"You're doing fine, brother. You're doing fine, boy," Griz said, helping him kneel down while the kit bag was carefully removed from his back. This time, it was Jules and Wren who took the strain and carried it across to where Talikha had set up her small field hospital. Jenny stood by her side like a fretful mother, and she was about to head across to thank Mike when he pulled the bag back on his shoulders, looped the rope over his head and climbed down once more.

The temperature on the roof was noticeably hotter than it had been when he was last on it just minutes before. He knelt, ready for the next load, and he could feel the heat on his knees. "Jesus. We'll be lucky if we've got more than a few minutes left on this roof."

It was Wolf's turn now. "Are you sure you're okay? Are you sure you don't need a rest?" Raj asked.

"If we get out of this, we can rest all we want," Mike replied, doing his best to disguise the burden of Wolf's extra mass.

"You don't need to do this by yourself. Let me take him."

"I'm fine," he replied, trudging back to the railings and climbing over. It creaked loudly under his weight this time, and as he touched it, he realised it was conducting heat from the floor below. "Shit."

"What is it?" Mya asked.

"Nothing. It's all good." *I'm going to run out of time. I'm going to run out of fucking time.*

Even the rungs of the ladder felt hot as he began to climb once more. He looked across to the other side, the burden on his back almost forgotten as the certainty of what was about to happen gripped his heart like a vice. More sweat than ever was pouring down his forehead and back. A loud metallic groan rose up behind him, and he stopped dead. The two ladders he was straddling weren't even anymore. One was lower than the other by about three centimetres. *Oh fuuuckkk!*

"Mike! MIKE!" Emma's cries were feverish as the groan came again.

Fuck! Fuck! Fuck! Fuck! FUCK!

The sound came to an abrupt halt. Mike tightened his grip around the rungs and held his breath. Everything happened in the blink of an eye, although he didn't blink once.

Simultaneous cries of desperation rose from in front and behind as the ladders began to drop. The wind rushed up to meet him as though he was on some hellish rollercoaster ride, yet still he held firm. Fear gripped him as the opposite wall sped towards him.

It sounded like a full skip of scrap metal being dropped from a height onto concrete. It felt like every bone in his body was being struck by a hammer. But still, he held on as the ladders crashed against the side of the hotel. Somehow, he didn't know quite how, but somehow, the hooks were still wrapped around the safety rail at this end, and the securing ropes were in place.

The sound continued to reverberate in his ears. The pain continued to travel up and down his body in a moving wave. He could feel the bag still on his back and was never more grateful for the cargo straps that Mya and Raj had used to secure it to him. The force of the impact would probably have ripped his shoulders out of their sockets otherwise. He looked across to see his two friends staring towards him, terrified, amazed he was still holding on, still in one piece. He could feel the safety rope stretch, and he looked up to see Griz and Emma pulling with all their strength.

"Are you okay? Are you okay, Mike?" The ringing in his ears had subsided, and he could hear his older sister's voice. He could also hear Sammy screaming at the top of hers. "Mike? Mike?"

"I'm okay," he shouted and reached up, taking hold of the next rung.

"He's okay. He's okay," Griz echoed and quiet murmurs of disbelief and surprise flitted around the rooftop.

"I've got you, Bruv. I've got you." He knew Emma would never let go of the rope, even if it meant both of them falling to their deaths. One step at a time, he continued to climb and be pulled until he reached the ledge. There he saw it wasn't just Griz and Emma playing tug of war with his bodyweight but a line of people including Jules, her brothers, Ephraim, Kat, Vicky, Della, Clay, Keely and more besides. He reached up as Jack's firm hand gripped his own. The pair exchanged smiles, but the smiles were only fleeting as another deafening metallic groan ripped through the air.

"The rail's about to give," someone shouted. No further explanation or context was needed. The rail on the other building had already collapsed; there was only one more to go. Jack pulled harder, and Mike hustled faster, heaving himself and his cargo onto the roof.

He knelt exhausted on the gravelly surface for a second as a cacophonous noise erupted behind him.

"The ladders," Griz said. "The fucking ladders."

The ladders had been secured to the barrier, so as it fell, so did they. The three safety ropes were still in place around the concrete foundations of the air conditioning ducts, although they were of little use now.

The horror of what the barrier disappearing meant was lost on no one, and even Wren, who was so grateful to have Wolf back with her, couldn't help staring towards the opposite roof in horror. "Can somebody help me get this bag off?" Mike asked as the sweat continued to pour from his forehead.

George and Rob unbuckled the straps and carried the precious cargo across to where the other unconscious animals lay. Talikha was not with them though. She was standing centimetres from the edge of the rooftop staring across at her husband in open-jawed disbelief. Tears streamed down her face as he gazed back at her.

"My love. My love," she whispered, not loud enough for anyone to hear, but as Mike watched her, he understood. Sweat was still rolling down his back, and he remained knelt down as firm hands gripped his shoulder for a job well done despite the despair that was unfolding around them for the four souls left trapped on the other rooftop.

There was another loud eruption and all eyes turned to see the far end of the roof collapse and flames lash up like fiery reaching hands.

*

Raj smiled. It was all he could do. It was the image he wanted to leave his wife with. He didn't want to show how terrified he was, how heartbroken he was. He didn't want to give her any impression of the horrifying, agonising, tortuous thoughts that were going through his mind. He glanced down at Humphrey and Muppet. *At least they're unconscious. They're not going to know about any of this. They're not going to experience anything.*

It was some small comfort to know that his best friend would not suffer. He would not feel the agony that Raj and Mya would feel. He turned back to Talikha and held his fist up to his chest. "I love you. I love you. I love you." He said the words over and over, and despite his best efforts, he started to cry. He would have liked the opportunity to hold her hand once more, to kiss her, to caress her cheek. He would have liked the opportunity to clutch her in his arms, to share one more intimate moment with her. "I love you," he said again, his eyes not leaving her for a second. *I love you.*

*

There was another roar as more of the rooftop behind them caved in. Mya had come face-to-face with death more times than she could count, but she never thought it would end like this. She never believed she would be so powerless, so helpless to do anything about it. She looked down at Muppet and gulped. *At least we'll die together. At least I'll die with my soulmate.*

It was a sad admission. She'd had friends and lovers, but nobody had affected her like Muppet. He had been a constant ever since entering her life. He had been the one to keep her going when the world had come to an end. He was the one who had made her smile on the days when there was nothing to smile about. He was the one who gave her strength when her body said no more.

"They won't wake up, will they? They won't feel anything?"

Raj shook his head. "They will not be aware of anything," he replied, despite his tears.

Mya started to cry too. "I'm scared. I'm scared of what's waiting for me. I'm scared that…." She couldn't continue. To admit it out loud made her sound like a witless child. *I'm scared that all the people I've killed will be there on the other side. I'm scared that I'm going to spend eternity with them. I'm scared that these flames won't be the last ones I'll see.*

"You are a good person, Mya. You have a good heart and a good soul."

"You don't know."

"Maybe not, but he does." He pointed to Muppet. Raj reached out and squeezed Mya's hand. "Whatever awaits us on the other side, we will face it together." He tried to force a smile. He tried to be brave despite what he was feeling. Eventually, he broke his grip and turned to look at Talikha one last time. He knew it wouldn't be long before the roof gave way, and her face was the last thing he wanted to see before the torturous end that awaited him.

23

Everyone was transfixed with the unfolding events on the other roof. It was gut-wrenching. It was more than that. It was the worst, most terrifying, most horrific thing any of them had ever witnessed, and they had witnessed plenty.

"Oh, Jesus," Emma cried, reaching out to grasp Sammy's hand as another section of the roof disappeared. Even people who hadn't met Raj or Mya were in tears. Watching them helpless and waiting to die was a torment like no other.

Emma felt someone next to her and turned to see Ephraim. His face was lit by the fire, and she could see rivers of tears running down his cheeks. Kat was by his side, and she was the same.

This is hell. This is hell. This is hell.

*

The fire continued to roar, but the ever so slight

breeze meant that, for the time being at least, there was little chance of the flames jumping over to the building they were on. Griz felt sick to his stomach. *I invited these poor bastards down here. I invited them to join us.*

Almost as if he'd spoken the words, Clara grabbed his hand in both of hers. Chuchu was downstairs with the other children. It was little comfort to them. Zofia and Amelia were next to them. They had been on standby, ready to help Trish, Liz and the nurses with any injured. Incredibly, there had been nothing more than the odd sprain, but the four left on the other roof were more than going to pay the price for the others getting off so lightly.

Someone grabbed Griz's arm, and he turned suddenly. "Keep the safety lines as tight as you can," Mike said.

"What?" Griz replied as Mike marched across the roof to the air conditioning duct. Griz remained a little perplexed as he watched the younger man disappear into the shadows briefly. He could just make out his silhouette as he looped one, two, three ropes over his head, and then, without missing a beat, he broke into a sprint.

"Remember what I said," he yelled. "Keep them tight."

*

The giant bag on his back acted as a windbreak, but he still managed to build up a good speed. By the time he launched, all his doubts about reaching the other side were gone. Thanks to the height difference between the two rooftops, he would probably overshoot by a good couple of metres.

Nobody understood what was happening at first. It looked like something had been catapulted across to the other side. It was only when people's eyes focused from Raj and Mya to the object moving like a bullet towards them that they realised it was Mike.

Emma and Sammy froze. Their tears even stopped flowing for a few seconds as they watched on in disbelief.

Mike landed heavily, rolling once, twice, three times. Without pause, he leapt to his feet as Raj and Mya ran over to him. He lifted the first and then the second safety rope from around himself, handing one each to his friends. He flicked the bag from his back.

"We're going to have to try to get both of them in here," Mike said.

"Mike. This is madness. This whole roof could collapse at any second," Raj said as he watched his friend run across to where the two dogs lay.

Mya looped the rope over her head and under her arms, understanding they now had a chance, albeit a slim one, of getting off the roof alive after all. "Come on, Raj," she ordered, pulling the other man.

Mike had already laid the bag out flat by the time they reached him. "Let's get Humph in first."

Another thunderous boom sounded behind them as more of the roof disappeared into the hungry fire.

*

Griz had been as shocked as everyone else when he'd seen Mike jump. He hadn't quite believed it until he'd watched him land on the other side, but, finally, the younger man's words made sense to him. "GRAB THE LINES. GRAB THE FUCKING LINES."

There was a sudden rush of bodies as each of the three safety lines were seized by dozens of willing helpers.

*

"There's no way we can zip it fully," Raj said.

Mike and Mya didn't care. They both understood that all of this was one giant longshot. They had to do their best. They had to do whatever they could. They each weaved a cargo strap underneath the giant kit bag, then another, securing the dogs tightly, despite the bag being half open.

"I'm going to need this in front of me rather than behind. I'm going to have to hold on to it, but I'll need both of you to help lift it over my shoulders."

They all turned as another tumultuous sound echoed.

They gawped in horror as more of the roof disappeared before their eyes, a few square metres at once. This time, it didn't stop. It just kept moving towards them.

"COME ON!" Mike screamed, doing his best to hoist the long carry strap over his shoulders. The bag was too heavy, even for him, but suddenly he felt Mya's shoulder pressed against his, and together they lifted the giant holdall, looping the strap over their necks. Each taking a handle and holding on to the giant bundle as if it was a suitcase of money that had burst open, they moved to the edge as quickly as the extra weight allowed them.

Raj looked back as the rooftop continued to disappear. "Run. RUN!"

They didn't jump. Mya and Mike couldn't. They stepped off and hoped. The second there was no longer anything solid beneath their feet the pair gripped the handles and the bag tighter than ever. There was a good possibility they would fall to their deaths. Their weight might be too much for either the people on the opposite roof or, indeed, the ropes themselves to hold. But hope cost nothing, and holding on to the dogs gave them a sense of purpose if nothing else.

As if they were a giant bob on a pendulum, they swung towards the opposite wall as the ropes took their weight for the moment at least.

"Brace yourself," Mya said through gritted teeth as smash; they crashed, feet first, into the wall. Both of them cried out in pain as the force of the impact travelled up through them as if they were a pair of tuning forks. They held on to the bag even tighter than before. Their shoulders, their muscles, their fingers, their fists, every part of them worked as hard as they could to make sure the bag stayed closed, stayed in one piece, stayed in their grasp.

The soles of their feet came to rest on the vertical wall, and their eyes followed the lines up to the rooftop, where several heads were already peeking over to see if the three of them had survived.

Raj was already being hoisted upwards, but it was as if Mike and Mya had been glued to the spot. They continued to watch as their friend reached the top and then disappeared over it.

"He's made it. Oh, thank God, he's made it," Mya cried, but still they did not move.

Suddenly, two more ropes dropped from above, and Griz leaned over the side. "Try to get those around you. The two you've got on are fraying like fuck, which is why we haven't tried to pull you up."

"Okay," Mike said, maintaining his grip on the bag with his right hand while sliding his arm around Mya with his left. "I've got you. You first."

It was an awkward manoeuvre, but she finally managed to shuffle the rope over her head, beneath the carry strap of the bag and under her arms. Then she reciprocated and held on to Mike while he did the same.

"Are you fucking done touching each other up down there?" Griz said, doing his best to make them crack a smile despite the dire situation.

"We're ready, Griz," Mike replied.

"Okay. Hold on the pair o' yous. This is probably going to be a bumpy fucking ride."

The inferno continued to blaze opposite, providing them with more than enough light to see what was going on. "We're really going to have to have a word with Raj about putting Humphrey on a diet if we get out of this alive," Mya said, smiling weakly.

The dried streaks were still visible on her face, and Mike stretched his fingers across to the other handle to brush against hers briefly. "We're going to be okay. The worst of it's over now. We're going to be okay, Mya."

The ropes hoisted them, and they climbed the wall a few centimetres at a time, dreading a sudden drop or the sound of a line snapping. Finally, they could see more than just the few heads peeking over the side. In a concerted effort grasping, grabbing hands reached out, gripping the bag, the ropes, their jackets, their belts, pulling them, dragging them onto the rooftop.

The bag was disentangled from the safety ropes and carefully carried over to where the other animals still lay unconscious. Before either of them had a chance to breathe, arms wrapped around them, lips pushed against the sides of their heads, words of love and thanks and admiration poured out in a virtually incoherent torrent.

It was overwhelming for Mike, Mya and Raj. All they needed was a moment to come to terms with what had happened, what they'd been through, but it remained elusive. Robyn, words, hugs. Mila, words, hugs. Wren, words, kisses, hugs. Jenny, kiss, kiss, kiss, squeeze, kiss, words, squeeze, kiss, kiss. Lines of people queued up to thank and congratulate them.

Eventually, the outpouring came to an end. Clara, Zofia and Amelia went about the task of organising accommodation for the little that was left of the night. Diamond and her team remained close to the edge of the rooftop, watching the fire with a hose at the ready. More of her people were distributed throughout the lower floors keeping a watch, too, making sure that there was no chance of the flames reaching them.

In the end, the former Safe Haven residents were given the top floor of the hotel Griz resided in. It would be noisy when people got to work on the roof, but considering the events of the night, everyone would be rising a little later.

By the time they all found rooms, the animals had started to come around. They were groggy but all well. Raj and Talikha checked on them regularly for an hour before they finally crashed on the double bed in their room with Humphrey lying in between them with his body and legs outstretched.

"That was something, brother." Griz spoke in a hushed tone as he made his way to the stairwell. "You're a mad, mad bastard, d'you know that?"

Mike shrugged. He'd left Sammy, Emma and Daisy sleeping in their newly allocated room, but he wanted to say a final thanks to his new friend before he turned in for the night.

"I really don't have the words to thank you for what you did, Griz."

"I don't have the words to tell you how fucking sorry I am about that whole thing."

"Tomorrow, we're going to have to find out what the hell happened. Somebody wanted us dead, Griz."

"Aye, well. I think I've got a lead on who that is."

Mike's tired eyes suddenly widened. "Who?"

"He skipped out on us in the middle of it all."

"Skipped out?"

"I got Saffy to send a drone up to check on a hunch. The fucker scarpered with the minibus."

"Who? Who was it?"

Griz put his hands up. "We'll talk about all of this tomorrow. I mean I can't be sure it was him, it just seems, well, fucking coincidental, doesn't it?"

"What was his name?"

Lanterns lit the small corridor, and Griz could see this was something the younger man wouldn't let go. He placed a hand on his friend's shoulder. "Mike. Brother. Please. I'll tell you everything tomorrow. Right now, I want to go hold my family and get a couple of hours' kip."

Mike stared at Griz for a moment then finally relented. There was nothing he wanted more than to get to the bottom of what had happened, of who had done this. But if he had gone, then it could wait. "Okay. Tomorrow."

"I promise. I'll tell you everything I know."

The pair shook hands and hugged before Mike watched Griz disappear into the stairwell. All was quiet as he headed back down the corridor. Mike was about to step back into his room when the door opposite opened. It was Mya's room, and he looked inside to see a small lantern by her bed and Muppet sprawled out fast asleep. Mike smiled.

"Looks like it's the floor for you tonight then."

"Yeah."

"Griz thinks he knows who did this."

"And?" Mya replied, the tiredness suddenly disappearing from her eyes too.

"He did a runner while it was all happening."

"And who was it?"

"He said he'd go through it all tomorrow."

Mya relaxed a little. "I suppose it's been a long day."

"Yeah. You can say that again. We'd better see if we can get some sleep." He turned to head into his room.

"Mike."

"Yeah," he replied, turning back.

"I never got the chance to thank you for what you did."

"You'd have done the same for me."

"Maybe. But you were the one who did it for me. Thank you." She stepped forward, pulling him towards her. Their lips met in a gentle lingering kiss until Mike remembered himself and pulled away.

"Lucy," he whispered. No other words needed saying. It was obvious by his guilt-wracked expression and the sadness behind his eyes that it was way too soon for him to even contemplate any kind of intimacy with someone else.

Mya placed her hand on his face and caressed his cheek. Her smile was warm, caring, and understanding. "I didn't want to make you feel uncomfortable."

Mike shook his head. "It's just…."

"Too soon."

"Yeah. I mean there are times when I think she's still going to walk around the corner." He smiled. "That's how monumentally fucked up I am about it. So, you see, I'm doing you a favour. I'm saving you from getting involved with some psycho who's hoping his dead wife might reappear at any moment."

"You're no psycho, Mike. Trust me; I've known

plenty." She removed her hand from his face and leaned in, pecking him on the cheek. "That's from Muppet. Thank you for what you did." She turned and disappeared back into her room.

Mike just stood there for a moment before heading into his own room. He'd been getting closer and closer to Mya. They were usually on the same wavelength. They had a similar sense of humour. They both worked tirelessly for what was best for the community. He really liked her. *Have I been sending out signals?*

He could still feel her lips against his, and another shudder of guilt ran through him. It was only a heartbeat since the love of his life had passed away. *No one will ever hold a candle to her.* He looked towards Mya's door. *It's been a confusing night. It was just a thing that happened. Two people so happy to be alive when, by all rights, they should be dead. Just a thing that occurred on the spur of the moment, and now it's over.* The next day, they'd wake up, and it would be like nothing had happened. They'd go back to what they did best, looking after the community, looking after their people, looking after their family.

He finally turned and stepped back into his room. Emma and Sammy were cuddled up together on one bed. Daisy was laid out on the other.

He smiled to himself. This was all that mattered. This was all that ever mattered. Family.

The End

A NOTE FROM THE AUTHOR

I really hope you enjoyed this book and would be very grateful if you took a minute to leave a review on Amazon and Goodreads.

If you would like to stay informed about what I'm doing, including current writing projects, and all the latest news and release information; these are the places to go:

Join the fan club on Facebook
https://www.facebook.com/groups/127693634504226

Like the Christopher Artinian author page
https://www.facebook.com/safehaventrilogy/

Buy exclusive and signed books and merchandise, subscribe to the newsletter and follow the blog:

https://www.christopherartinian.com/

Follow me on Twitter
https://twitter.com/Christo71635959

Follow me on Youtube:
https://www.youtube.com/channel/UCfJymx31Vvztt
B_Q-x5otYg

Follow me on Amazon
https://amzn.to/2I1llU6

Follow me on Goodreads
https://bit.ly/2P7iDzX

Other books by Christopher Artinian:

Safe Haven: Rise of the RAMs
Safe Haven: Realm of the Raiders
Safe Haven: Reap of the Righteous
Safe Haven: Ice
Safe Haven: Vengeance
Safe Haven: Is This the End of Everything?
Safe Haven: Neverland (Part 1)
Safe Haven: Neverland (Part 2)
Safe Haven: Doomsday
Safe Haven: Raining Blood (Part 1)
Safe Haven: Hope Street
Before Safe Haven: Lucy
Before Safe Haven: Alex

Before Safe Haven: Mike
Before Safe Haven: Jules
The End of Everything: Book 1
The End of Everything: Book 2
The End of Everything: Book 3
The End of Everything: Book 4
The End of Everything: Book 5
The End of Everything: Book 6
The End of Everything: Book 7
The End of Everything: Book 8
The End of Everything: Book 9
The End of Everything: Book 10
The End of Everything: Book 11
The End of Everything: Book 12
Relentless
Relentless 2
Relentless 3
The Burning Tree: Book 1 – Salvation
The Burning Tree: Book 2 – Rebirth
The Burning Tree: Book 3 – Infinity
The Burning Tree: Book 4 – Anarchy
The Burning Tree: Book 5 – Redemption
Night of the Demons

CHRISTOPHER ARTINIAN

Christopher Artinian was born and raised in Leeds, West Yorkshire. Wanting to escape life in a big city and concentrate more on working to live than living to work, he and his family moved to the Outer Hebrides in the north-west of Scotland in 2004, where he now works as a full-time author.

Chris is a huge music fan, a cinephile, an avid reader and a supporter of Yorkshire County Cricket Club. When he's not sitting in front of his laptop living out his next post-apocalyptic/dystopian/horror adventure, he will be passionately immersed in one of his other interests.

Printed in Great Britain
by Amazon